THE IRISH BLESSING

LISA CATHERINE PARTEE

To my husband, Carlos, and my two daughters, Vanessa and Erica. Thank you for your continuous support and belief in my project. You gave me the encouragement to continue when I needed it most.

To my beautiful grandchildren, Phillip, Sierra, and Cheyenne. Believe in your dreams and never give up. The result is worth the journey.

And a special thank-you to my amazing beta readers, whose valuable support helped move my project forward. Thank you, Christopher, Vanessa, and Ashley.

CHAPTER 1

TURKS AND CAICOS

THE WHITE SCRAP of paper next to my boot caught my attention, its color a stark contrast to the dark-blue-and-charcoal-patterned carpet. Reaching down from my chair, I picked it up and turned the document over in my hand. The boarding pass had my name on it, Alyssa Whalen, but I didn't recall dropping it. Then again, nothing was going right with this vacation so far. Besides challenging, it seemed different somehow. Call it premonition or gut feeling; there was something odd about it, as if a life-changing event were supposed to happen. Lost as to what that could be, I stuffed the paper into my pocket.

What should have been a boringly routine red-eye from San Diego with my childhood best friend, Melody Bradley, had transformed into the opposite, our latest debacle becoming the crown on top of a pile of hurdles. A mechanical failure on our plane had caused our connecting flight to Providenciales in Turks and Caicos to become delayed, increasing our layover in Miami from one hour to six. This incident was on top of multiple schedule changes, unwanted seat assignments, and an intoxicated and belligerent passenger.

Frustrated, I scanned the mix of passengers waiting at my departure gate, my chair shaking when a man in a business suit hastily settled into the seat at the end. I shifted my body, turning to focus my attention on the couple across from me. They appeared close to my age of thirty-two. The woman nestled her head on the man's shoulder, her hand on his thigh, while he wrapped his arm around her. Lonely, I missed those moments of comfort with the man I loved, my husband killed in a motorcycle accident three years ago. Although I still missed Alex terribly, I was finally ready to move forward and hoped to find someone to share my life with, a man I could love and who would love me in return.

With two hours to go before our flight, I was running out of things to do. I stood and stretched my legs. At five feet nine inches, I was taller than average for a woman. My husband, a man of tall stature, had appreciated my height and slender figure, along with my dark hair, green eyes, and the sprinkling of freckles across my nose and cheeks—his blond hair and blue eyes quite different from my appearance.

"Liz. Where are you going?" Mel sounded sleepy. She had her elbow dug into the armrest of her chair, her head precariously perched in her hand.

"I'll be back. I can't sit here any longer. I'm going to take another walk around the gates. Do you want anything?"

"Other than to be at our hotel in Providenciales? No. Speaking of our hotel, did they email you back?"

"I don't know. I didn't expect the hotel to respond. My email to them was only a courtesy notice that we'd be checking in five hours later than planned. It shouldn't matter to them, but I'll check to see if they sent me an email anyway." I pulled my phone from my purse and scanned my email. There was one from our hotel. I clicked on the message and began reading it. No, no, no. There was no reservation in my name. This person said I'd canceled, and they'd refunded my credit card. I could rebook, but the nightly rates listed in the email were expensive. I rubbed my forehead, having a tough time believing what I was reading.

"What happened now? You're not saying anything, and you look upset." Mel sat straight up, her hands gripping the arms of her chair. "A stupid systems error completely jacked up our flight. Don't tell me another ridiculous fiasco messed up our hotel reservation too."

"It looks like it did. The hotel says I canceled our reservation, which I didn't do. According to the email, we can rebook, but not at the discounted rate that we originally paid. I'm going to take a walk and cool off before I contact the hotel. We still have time to work it out since our flight doesn't leave for almost two hours."

"Well, you better do something. If you don't, I will, and the hotel won't like hearing from me."

"Don't worry. I'll take care of it as soon as I get back."

"Fine." Mel flopped backward in her chair, a scowl on her face.

I left the gate and hurried across the expanse of gleaming tile, beeping golf carts, and hordes of people rushing past me. I stopped at one of the coffee stands and ordered a hot tea, hoping it would help me relax and calm down. Retreating to the nearest wall, I leaned against it, taking my time to sip the steamy brew. Finished, I turned to look for a waste receptacle and noticed a man standing near me. He reminded me of Alex. It wasn't his physical appearance that was similar. It was more his stance and the confidence the man exuded as he stood there. Three years older than me, Alex had been young and in the prime of his life when he'd died. We had been together since I was sixteen, and he'd been the only man in my life. After thirteen years, we were still deeply in love with each other. Now that he was gone, I was convinced I'd never find a relationship like the one I'd lost.

The man walked to the gate across from me and took a seat in one of the chairs facing the floor-to-ceiling window. Tossing my empty cup into the trash, I strolled into the shop behind me. After walking around displays of neck pillows, chocolates, and T-shirts, I stood in front of a wall of books. I was scanning the titles when I caught movement next to me and looked up, gasping as I stared at the uppermost carton in a six-foot-tall stack of boxes. Appearing too heavy to be on the top, it was crushing the box below it, causing its corner to dip inward under the weight. The carton teetered on the edge of the box below it, ready to come down on top of me any second. I jumped out of the way, tripping over a man standing behind me as the box came crashing down. He caught me before I fell to the floor.

"Christ. Are you all right? That box almost landed on you." The stranger with an intriguing accent steadied me on my feet, concern in his voice as he looked me up and down.

After extracting myself from the man's arms, I motioned to the panic-stricken employee rushing toward me that I was all right. I turned to face my rescuer. His strikingly handsome appearance startled me, a warmth spreading across my cheeks. Shifting my attention back to the books, I attempted to hide my discomfort. "Thank you for helping me. I think the tricky little ghost that messed with my flight and hotel reservation must have given the box a good push off the top. Nothing like one more problem on top of all the others."

"I take it you've had a few snags?"

"I'd rather think of them as adventures. It's quite thrilling to have your meticulously laid-out plans explode spectacularly before your eyes."

The man appeared amused by my comments. He turned to face the wall of books. "Are you looking for a particular title?"

"I was trying to find a book titled *How to Pass the Time in the Miami Airport for Six Hours*, but I couldn't seem to find it. Of course, I could have used the book four hours ago."

"It sounds like you did have a problem with your flight." The man laughed and shook his head. "What happened to your hotel booking?"

"I found out I didn't have one."

The man cocked his head at me. He looked intrigued, as if he wanted to hear more.

"I emailed my hotel to let them know I'd be checking in five hours later than expected. They emailed me back, informing me there was no reservation in my name."

"Well, I hope your rebooked hotel is better than the

last one, or should I say the one that didn't exist?"

"I hope so. I'll find out after I book one."

"You don't have a room yet? Where are you going?"

"My girlfriend and I are traveling to Providenciales."

"Ahh, I might be able to help you out with that. The Island Palms Resort is a wonderful hotel. It's in an excellent location on Grace Bay, and the staff is supposed to be phenomenal. You might want to contact them and see what their availability and rates are at the moment."

"Since I've had nothing but bad luck so far, you aren't secretly recommending a fleabag hotel and sending me off to a horrible location off the beaten path, are you? That would finish off my day rather nicely."

"No, I'm not." The man put his hands in the air and chuckled. "I swear. It's a top-quality hotel, and I'd stay there."

"Thank you. I appreciate the recommendation. If you don't mind my asking, where are you from?"

"I guess my accent isn't as undetectable as I thought." The man ran his hand through his wavy chestnut hair, the ends curling around his ears. "I'm from Ireland. I came to the United States when I was twenty to attend college. I never went back home, so my accent isn't quite as strong as it used to be."

There was a loud commotion at the cash register near the entrance. I swung around to see a tall, stunningly beautiful blonde woman in a lavender blouse arguing with the young salesclerk. The woman scowled and gave the young girl an icy stare while the poor salesclerk shook her head vigorously as she wildly waved her arms. I winced as the woman shouted at the girl and threw a package down on the counter.

"Dammit." The man focused his attention on the two women, his body becoming tense.

"The rude blonde woman seems to be a handful." Floored, I shook my head at the woman's behavior. "I can't imagine what reason she'd have to treat the employee like that. She must be one of those self-centered people who think they're superior to everyone else. I certainly wouldn't want to deal with her."

"Yes. Anna can be a handful at times."

I turned toward the man, my face burning as I stood there wishing I had kept my mouth shut. "I'm so sorry. I didn't know she was with you. I shouldn't have been so rude."

The woman suddenly yelled and stormed out of the store while the salesclerk stood frozen at the counter, appearing ready to burst into tears.

"No apology necessary. Excuse me." The man hurried toward the exit. He called the woman's name and dodged between customers to catch her. Unsuccessful, he disappeared into the crowd of people filling the concourse.

I left the shop and walked over to a nearby group of chairs, the scent of the man's cologne still filling my nostrils. It was woody and earthy, with a hint of leather. The smell was sensual, the kind of fragrance that made a woman want to bury her face in the wearer's neck. I rubbed my forehead, mentally chastising myself. The headiness of the man's cologne wasn't something I wanted to dwell on, especially since I was very much alone. I had tried dating a few times, but so far, it hadn't worked out. I wanted someone who evoked the same level of love, friendship, security, and trust that I'd had with Alex, which at this point seemed impossible to find.

After retrieving my cell phone from the front pocket of my purse, I went to the travel website I used and looked up the hotel the gentleman had recommended. It looked well beyond satisfactory, and the rates were much better than my previous hotel was offering. Rather than spend my time arguing with the reservation clerk that had emailed me, I decided to rebook at this resort. I just hoped the man's recommendation was as good as he said.

Mel was drumming her fingers on the arm of her chair, an eager look on her face when I finally returned to the gate. "Liz. You've got to check out the guy sitting by the counter with his back to the windows. Dang, he's hot. He's the one in a green shirt and jeans. Oh, geez. He's grinning at you. What's up with that?"

I glanced toward the chairs, an expanse of windows behind them. An airplane was visible as it climbed in altitude, leaving Miami behind. Meeting the man's gaze, I quickly turned away. "I tripped into him at one of the stores. The lady next to him made a huge scene, yelling at the salesclerk. Have you heard the phrase open mouth, insert foot? Well, that's what I did when I commented on the woman without knowing she was with him."

"You didn't?"

"Oh, yes. I did. Talk about embarrassing." I shifted in my chair toward Mel, refusing to look at the man and giving him a view of my back instead. I neglected to mention how the man's handsome appearance had startled me when I'd pulled myself from his arms or how pleasing I'd found the scent of his cologne. Constantly harping on my single status after three years of being alone, Mel would have made a bigger deal out of my comments than was necessary, and I didn't want to discuss it.

"Umm. It's obvious you're trying to ignore the man. He must find it funny because now he's laughing. The woman with him hasn't even noticed. He might as well be invisible with the way she's buried her face in her cell phone the entire time they've been sitting there."

"I'm glad I could make his day. I wish someone would make ours." I shifted in my seat, keeping my back to the man. "I booked us in a two-bedroom suite at another hotel while walking around. The rates are better, and it looked nicer than our original resort. The gentleman you keep eyeing recommended it."

"He must be staying there since he recommended it and is flying to Providenciales. Oh, this is going to be a fun week." Mel leaned back in her chair, a mischievous grin lighting up her face.

Mel and I had taken several trips together, but this one seemed different. It had been nothing but drama from the start. We were flying to Turks and Caicos for a relaxing and much-needed vacation. I was an investment manager for a government agency, and Mel worked as a project manager in construction. This trip was supposed to be fun, but it was becoming the opposite. It was as if a gremlin waited to sabotage every move I made.

One of the ticket agents picked up a handheld microphone and announced, "This is the preboarding announcement for flight fifteen eleven to Providenciales.

We are now inviting those passengers with small children and any passengers requiring special assistance to begin boarding at this time. Please have your boarding pass and passport ready. Regular boarding will begin in a few minutes. Thank you."

I stood, pretending to focus my attention on the passengers walking up and down the concourse. Sensing the man in the green shirt was still watching me, I feigned disinterest, refusing to let on that he intrigued me.

There was another announcement. "At this time, we would like to invite our first-class passengers and Diamond Medallion members to board."

"That gorgeous-looking guy is boarding. Lucky dogs. They're flying first-class." Mel got up from her seat and stretched her petite frame. She pulled her long red hair away from her face.

Curious, I peeked at the couple over my shoulder. "Do you think the woman is a model? She's too perfect and doesn't seem fazed by the attention she's attracted."

"I don't know, but she sure has a lousy personality. Poor guy."

The ticket agent picked up the microphone again. "We would like to invite our Comfort Plus passengers to board at this time."

"That's us. Let's go." I picked up my carry-on bag and headed toward the ticket agent, with Mel following behind me. After walking down the ramp to the airplane, I squeezed down the aisle in business class, my carry-on bag in my hand.

The man in the green shirt watched me, the corners

of his mouth twitching.

I turned my head away, trying to ignore him.

"He's even cuter up close. Did you see his dimples?" Mel leaned toward me as we settled into our seats.

"Yes, I saw the dimples."

"Dang, Liz. How can you ignore such a gorgeous male specimen?"

"He's a man, not a lab rat. In case you've forgotten, he's also with a woman. I don't care how good-looking the man is. I'm not going to ogle him; it's disrespectful. The man was only paying attention to me because I rudely commented on his companion and embarrassed myself. So, can we drop it, please?"

"I still think there's no harm in looking."

I shook my head at her comment. Besides lacking decorum, Mel had a one-track mind that revolved around men and sex. I'd have been more offended by her behavior if we hadn't grown up together. Mel and her family had been my only source of comfort for several years following my mother's death.

WE WERE IN Providenciales in Turks and Caicos in less than two hours. Mel and I walked out of the airport terminal and looked for our driver. He was supposed to be waiting for us outside the exit. We scanned the crowd of people that stood behind the rope barricade in front of us, their faces searching the mass of exiting passengers.

"I don't see him. None of the signs the people are holding have your last name on it." Mel paced back and forth as she continued to scan the crowd. "It is your name we're looking for, right? You didn't book it in my name, did you?"

"I booked it in my name, but I don't see it on any of the signs." I looked around the area again. "We've had nothing but problems since we started this vacation. I swear. Somebody keeps messing with us. Our missing driver better not turn into another reservation issue. Speaking of issues, now is as good a time as any to set the ground rules for this vacation. There will be no attempts to pair me up and no putting me in the middle of an awkward situation this week. Last year, our vacation to Aruba was a disaster, with you constantly trying to play matchmaker. I prefer no replays. Got it?"

"Dang. You sound like a warden or something. Okay. I got it. But one of these days, you'll get tired of being lonely and lower your ridiculous expectations. I'm just trying to help you out."

"I don't need any help."

"Fine. Let's just find our driver. I want to get to our hotel and have a drink. You make me feel like I'm back in school with all these rules." Mel scanned the crowd. "There's our driver." She pointed towards a tall, dark-skinned man with long dreadlocks. Dressed in a dark suit, he held a sign with my last name displayed on it. Mel led the way toward the man.

"Hi. Is one of you Alyssa Whalen?"

"Yes. That's me," I said.

"Geez. After twenty-eight years, it still seems weird to hear that name." Mel pursed her lips as she stared at me. "It doesn't even fit your personality."

"You're not Alyssa Whalen?" The man appeared worried, wrinkles lining his forehead.

"No. I mean, yes. That's my legal name. I don't use it and go by Liz instead."

"That's cool. I'm Thomas. Liz suits you better, or at least it sounds better."

"Thanks. Mel here is responsible for my nickname. She started calling me Liz when we were little kids because she couldn't pronounce Alyssa."

"Hey, don't complain. I could have called you something weird."

"Ladies, if you don't mind, I'll take your bags, and you can follow me. I parked my car in the lot across from the terminal." Thomas led us down the sidewalk to the end of the building. We crossed the road, walking along the edge of a traffic circle until we were in the parking lot. He stopped at a black Cadillac Escalade. "Okay. Here we are. As soon as I load the bags, we'll be going." He walked to the rear of the vehicle and opened the tailgate. Realizing he'd left us standing next to the car, he darted back and opened our door.

The two of us settled in the back seat, and Mel giggled. "This guy is funny. He's like a cross between Bob Marley and the butler from that old television show. Oh, what was it called? *The Fresh Prince of Bel-Air*. That's the name of it. I like him, and he's cute too. I bet he'd be fun. You should go for it." Mel nudged my arm as she observed Thomas through the window.

"Cute or not, please don't start. May I remind you, I'm not here to find a playmate. It might be your style, but it's not mine."

Thomas opened his door and sat in the driver's seat, appearing distracted as he rifled through a stack of paperwork on the dashboard. Unable to find what he was searching for, he tossed the paperwork on the console next to him. He looked at us in the rearview mirror. "Where am I taking you?"

"We're going to the Island Palms Resort. You know where it is, right?" I expelled a deep breath. Our day was getting worse rather than better.

"Island Palms. That's right." Thomas pulled away from the parking lot and drove down the two-lane road. "It's about a ten-minute drive up the highway. It's a pleasant hotel. I know one of the bartenders there. His name's Kip." Thomas chuckled. "Be careful if he serves you. He can mix some strange concoctions, and they're strong too. In case you're looking for a place for dinner outside your hotel, I'd recommend a restaurant at the marina called Kiki's. Their bartenders are pretty cool, and they have the freshest seafood and one of the best chefs on the island."

"Thank you for the warning and recommendation. It's good to know," I said.

We turned off the highway onto a private tree-lined road. A minute later, we were parking under the attached portico next to the hotel lobby.

Mel's eyes darted along the hotel's exterior as we climbed out of the vehicle, a palette of reds, pinks, and yellows bursting from the flowerbeds. "Hmm. For a last-minute booking, we ended up at a classy place. I like it better than our original hotel. Now I'm glad they screwed up our reservation." She spun around and walked toward the area inside the curvature of the driveway. "Check out the fountain with the dolphins. That thing is huge."

"That's the largest fountain I've ever seen. The design is intriguing with the way the dolphins are leaping out of the jets of water." I turned toward Thomas, giving him a tip after he set our luggage on the driveway. Walking over to Mel, I scanned the colorful landscaping, sucking in my breath as a spray of water from the fountain hit me in the face. I wiped the liquid from my cheek, wondering what or who was going to target me next.

CHAPTER 2

SHANE

AFTER CHECKING INTO the hotel and getting situated in our room, Mel and I went downstairs to the poolside bar. With all the drama and hiccups to get here, all I wanted to do was unwind and get something to drink. Nestled between flowerbeds filled with tropical plants and palm trees, it had a relaxing appearance. A row of tables sat between the oval-shaped bar and the swimming pool, and a deck area with more tables and an open space for musicians and dancing was to the right. A social gathering spot, the place was busy, with a trio of bartenders scrambling behind the counter.

"How about the far side of the bar? There are two empty seats between those middle-aged ladies in the bright yellow and pink blouses and that auburn-haired woman in the red shirt." I pointed to the chairs, their backs to the swimming pool.

"Looks good to me," Mel said.

We maneuvered around several groups of people standing near the bar as we made our way to the other side and slipped into the empty barstools.

"Hello. I'm Caitlin." The auburn-haired woman sitting next to me turned to face us.

"It's nice to meet you. I'm Liz, and this is Mel."

Mel gave Caitlin a fleeting glance, her attention focused on two guys on the other side of the bar.

"Where are the two of you from?" Caitlin took a sip of her drink, the ice clinking against the empty glass as she set it down.

"We're from San Diego." I paused a moment. The woman's accent sounded familiar. "Are you from Ireland?"

"Yes, I am. My husband and I flew here yesterday from Dublin. I'm surprised you could identify my accent. Few people get it right."

"I normally wouldn't. I met someone from Ireland this morning, and your accent sounds like his, although yours is stronger."

"Ireland. Isn't that the land of leprechauns? I'd love to go there and find a hot, sexy-looking one." Mel giggled like she did when we were teenagers.

Caitlin reached across me and touched Mel's arm. "You know there's no such thing as a leprechaun." Her voice was low and full of concern.

I shook my head. Mel had such a one-track mind. "I'm sorry, Caitlin. You'll have to excuse Mel. Her comments can be a little colorful. She wasn't referencing a leprechaun."

As she thought about it, Caitlin's cheeks turned pink. "Oh, you are horrible. And, yes, we do have good-looking men in Ireland."

I was beginning to like Caitlin. She seemed personable.

Mel gave me a little nudge. "Check them out. The

blond guy is cute. Don't you think?" She nodded toward the two guys that grabbed her attention when we sat down.

"Not really."

"What do you mean? I think he's cute."

"The guy's young, and the way he's wearing that brown baseball cap sideways makes him look like a little kid." There was a noise to my right. I turned to find Caitlin trying to stifle a snicker.

Mel crossed her arms in front of her, displaying a defiant look. "I think we should move to those empty seats across the bar and join those two guys."

"You promised to behave, remember?" I looked at Caitlin. "Mel has a knack for dragging me into awkward situations and trying to set me up with random guys, although I've said a million times I'm not interested. She's supposed to behave this trip."

"It sounds like Mel might be finding herself a friend. I have a dinner reservation with my family and three others. You should join us, Liz. It might be safer."

"Dang. Those guys are leaving the bar. I'm too late." Mel looked frustrated as she watched the two guys walk away.

"In that case, you're both welcome to join us. The more the merrier." Caitlin suddenly beamed, focusing on a group of four people walking toward the bar. She waved at them, a burly dark-haired man waving back. "Here comes my cousin and his friends along with my husband. I wondered where he was."

Caught entirely off guard, I traded glances with my gift shop rescuer from Miami. I winced as Mel's elbow contacted my ribs.

"Ladies, I'd like to introduce you to my family and friends. This is my cousin, Shane." Caitlin motioned toward the man in the green shirt. "Next to him is Dylan and Dylan's wife, Margaret. They're good friends of Shane's. The big handsome man standing in the back is my husband, Patrick." Caitlin turned toward Mel and me. "These two ladies are Liz and Mel."

Dylan was a sandy-haired man of medium height and a slim build. He wore a pair of brown-framed eyeglasses. Margaret was slightly shorter with a shapely figure, her blond hair pulled back into a braid.

"Hello." Dylan slipped an arm around Margaret's shoulder as he greeted us.

"Hi. It's nice to meet you," Margaret said.

Patrick nodded at us, the grin that had appeared when Caitlin called him handsome still there.

"Hello." Shane addressed Mel. "I remember you from the Miami airport."

"I remember. You were at our gate."

"Liz. It's a pleasure to see you again," Shane said with an amused grin. "It looks like you took me up on my recommendation. I'm sure you'll find this resort pleasant."

"It's nice to meet you. Our previous encounter didn't exactly call for an exchange of names, and, yes, this hotel seems much better than our original resort. Thank you for the recommendation." Shane's voice intrigued me just as it had in the gift shop. The deep, husky tone and Irish accent created a sense of pleasure that ran right through me. I caught myself focusing on his neck as he stood there, the fragrance of his cologne a sensual memory. Part of me wished he'd move closer, so I could breathe in his scent again.

"You two have met?" Caitlin stared at Shane.

"We met in one of the stores at the Miami airport. Liz was trying to find an unusual book, and we stumbled across one another."

"I've asked these ladies to join us for dinner. Our reservation is in ten minutes, so we should head to the restaurant. Where's Anna?" Caitlin said.

"She went to the salon. She chipped a nail and went to get it repaired. She'll be joining us later," Shane said.

Caitlin muttered under her breath at his comment.

Patrick led the way to the restaurant and approached the host at the podium when we got there. "We have a reservation. It's under the last name of Burke. There's going to be eight of us instead of six."

"Yes, sir. I have your reservation. We have a table that will seat eight out on the patio. Please follow me." The man grabbed a stack of menus and led our party outside. He walked around the table, handing them out as we sat in our chairs. "George will be your server this evening. He'll be right with you to take your drink order."

Another employee was immediately at the table, filling up our water glasses.

I scanned the dining area while I sat there. String lights stretched across the open space above us, and decorative lanterns perched along the perimeter walls. Navy-blue linens, elegant-looking dinnerware, and an assortment of stemware adorned the tables, with candles in miniature metal lanterns the centerpieces. With the sun going down, the ambience was delightful. I peeked at Shane sitting next to me as a strange sensation came over me. There was a familiarity of some sort between us. Rather than a stranger who I'd recently met, Shane seemed like an old friend that I hadn't seen in a while. Confused, I couldn't make sense of what I was feeling.

"Liz, where are you from?" Patrick was looking at me from the head of the table.

"I'm from San Diego. I was born and raised there, specifically in the North County. I'm in one of the beach cities."

"Sunshine and beaches? How horrible. You must hate it." Shane turned toward me, feigning a look of distaste.

"I do. It's so hard to get up in the morning with the sun shining and the sky a beautiful blue. I fight against it constantly." Our conversation was fun. Shane seemed an easygoing person, besides being quite attractive.

"Good evening. My name is George. What can I get you to drink?" Our server was standing next to Patrick.

"Oh, before you take our order, could I get you to take a picture of us?" Caitlin held up her cell phone from the other end of the rectangular table. She appeared unconcerned by the scowl on Patrick's face.

"Certainly." George took the cell phone from Caitlin and took several steps backward. "Everyone smile." He took several pictures. Then he handed the phone back to Caitlin and waited for her to check the photos.

"They look nice. Thank you." Caitlin put her phone facedown on the table and smiled at George. "I suppose you should start by taking my husband's order first. He's the grumpy one at the head of the table. He gets that way when he's hungry." She winked at me when George walked over to Patrick.

"Does everyone know what they want to order? We might as well order our food with our drinks." Patrick glanced around the table, his gaze settling on Caitlin.

Shane leaned toward me. "Patrick is an impatient man and doesn't beat around the bush."

"He's just efficient," I whispered, browsing my menu.

"I'll have the prime rib, cooked medium, and a glass of the house cabernet sauvignon." Patrick handed George his menu.

"What can I get you, sir?" George was looking at Shane.

"I'll have the Caicos lobster and a glass of the Cambria chardonnay." Shane closed his menu and handed it to him.

"And you, miss?" George had come to my end of the table and stood between Caitlin and me.

"I'll have the same as him." I nodded toward Shane.

"Copycat." Shane spread his napkin in his lap as he glanced at me. "You seem intent on following my lead. First, you trail me into the store at the airport. Then you book yourself on my flight, and now, you copy my choice for dinner. It makes me wonder what's next." The corner of his mouth twitched, and he had a sparkle in his eyes when he glanced at me.

"If the waiter had gone around the table in the other direction, I'd be saying the same thing about you."

"That was a snappy response. You're good at this." Shane let out a small chuckle. "So, are you searching for any more unusual book titles? That last one of yours was a best seller." He took a drink from his water glass, an amused look on his face.

"I am. The new title I'm searching for is *How to Bring an Arrogant and Overly Confident Irishman Down a Notch*."

Shane started choking on his water. He grabbed his napkin and covered his mouth as he tried to cough up the liquid that appeared to have gone down his windpipe. After his coughing subsided, Shane cleared his throat and set his napkin back in his lap. He turned to look at me. His eyes were watery, and his face pink. "I need to stop asking you about your reading wish list. Your titles are killing me."

Caitlin burst out laughing. She shifted her gaze from Shane to me. "The two of you are adorable. You go back and forth like a married couple."

A warmth spread across my cheeks at Caitlin's comment. At a complete loss on how to respond, I fidgeted with my water glass.

"So, Mel. How long have you and Liz known each other?" Margaret said.

"Liz and I have been friends since preschool. We had a habit of getting into trouble together when we were growing up. I have a funny story about the first time it happened. It was during naptime in preschool."

"Please don't. No one wants to hear about this stuff." I hung my head. This discussion was going sideways fast.

"Sure we do. Mel's already said too much to stop. So,

go on," Margaret said.

"You can tell it, or I can." Mel cleared her throat. "Liz?"

"Fine. I'll tell it. Although, I have no clue why you think the story is funny." I took a deep breath. "The not-so-funny incident happened on my first day of preschool. My mom had sent me to school with a Sleeping Beauty blanket so I'd be a good girl and take a nap like the princess. I remember spreading my blanket out and lying down, just like the teacher told us. The super-talkative and mean-spirited little girl next to me wouldn't shut up or leave my blanket alone. To cut a long story short, Mel and I ended up on a timeout in the corner. I cried and cried, but not because of the timeout. I was upset because I didn't get to take my nap like Sleeping Beauty. To this day, I'd swear Mel traumatized me because I can still remember the pink, yellow, and white blanket."

"Wow. That wasn't nice. I was not a mean-spirited little girl. Well, at least not at four years old." Mel glowered at me.

Shane was chuckling along with the others at the table. "That was cute. I can picture the two of you bickering with each other. It sounds like you've had quite a few years of delinquent behavior together."

"We're both thirty-two, so we've had a few years together. Although I wouldn't exactly call them delinquent," I said.

"Liz was also the star player on our high school's volleyball team." Mel shrugged when I glared at her. "I thought I'd embarrass you a little more."

"Volleyball?" Dylan leaned forward in his chair, an

eager look on his face as he pushed his glasses up the bridge of his nose with his index finger. "Liz, you'll have to play a game of water volleyball down at the pool with us. And don't let Shane tease you. He was a troublemaker in college. He and I met when we roomed together at Columbia University. After graduating and passing the bar exam, we moved to Washington, D.C., to take attorney positions with different companies. My specialty is corporate law, while Shane's is employment law. The way he behaved, you'd never expect him to be a lawyer for the government. He spent far more time at the pub around the corner from the campus than he did on his studies or attending class."

"Hey, no changing the subject. We're talking about Liz's delinquent childhood, not my college years." Shane leaned back in his chair. "So, Mel. Are there any other stories you'd like to share?"

"There's Anna," Caitlin said with a hint of displeasure in her voice as she interrupted Shane. "It looks like she's decided to join us."

George followed behind Anna, carrying a large tray with our dinner plates.

Shane stood up to greet her, pulling out the empty chair between him and Patrick. He returned to his seat after assisting her. "Anna. I'd like to introduce you to our guests. Next to me is Liz, and across from her is Mel. Caitlin met them earlier. They're here from San Diego." He glanced at me and then at Mel. "Ladies, this is Anna."

"Nice to meet you," Anna said, the tone in her voice indicating otherwise.

"Same here," Mel said.

Shane partially blocked my view of Anna, so I leaned forward and turned to look at her. "Hello. It's a pleasure to meet you." I couldn't help it. I disliked her. It was like she was intruding on the fun I was having with Shane. Alex and I used to banter with each other, and I missed it. The teasing at our table this evening was comforting and reminiscent.

George had distributed the dinner plates while Shane made the introductions. Now, he stood by Patrick's chair. "Does anyone need anything?"

"You should probably order your dinner," Shane said, turning toward Anna.

"I already did, inside the restaurant. I figured you were eating by now. I ordered the lobster salad and a glass of Moët and Chandon Imperial."

I caught my breath. The price of the champagne on the menu was exorbitant.

Shane turned to George. "We'll have a glass of the Cambria chardonnay instead."

"I want champagne," Anna said, pouting.

"You're welcome to have champagne as long as it comes with a separate bill." Shane arched a brow at Anna in response to the angry look she gave him.

George looked at Shane, and he shook his head.

"I will bring a glass of the Cambria chardonnay. Thank you, sir." George hurried off.

That was extremely odd. I could understand and agree with not ordering the champagne based on its price, but the underlying friction between Shane and Anna was palpable. It wasn't what I expected from a couple on a gorgeous tropical vacation.

A low mutter floated to my ear from the seat to my right, the only words identifiable being *gold digger* and *princess*. I turned my head slightly, spotting Caitlin's hardened face.

"I have your lobster salad and chardonnay." George placed a bowl and a glass of wine on the table in front of Anna. "Can I get you anything else?" He stood next to her chair, waiting while she stayed silent and ignored him.

"Thank you, George. We're fine." Shane's shoulders tensed as he answered for Anna.

After checking on us several times, George returned and started picking up plates as we finished our meal. Seeing several nods when he inquired whether anyone wanted dessert, he hurried off, returning with a stack of dessert menus. Starting with Caitlin, he went around the table, taking our orders. He ended with me.

"Miss, did any of the desserts interest you?"

"Could I have the sticky toffee pudding, please? I've never had it before, and it sounds interesting."

"You've never had sticky toffee pudding?" Caitlin sounded aghast at the thought. "We grew up eating it. You'll have to try it. It's deadly."

I stared at Caitlin, confused by her comment. I started to open my mouth, then shut it.

"Liz, the look on your face is priceless." Shane's laughter rippled from his chest. He cleared his throat. "Caitlin meant deadly as in the dessert is great. Not deadly as in eating the pudding will kill you."

I stared down at my lap. It was my night to get teased.

"It isn't that funny," Anna said, snapping at Shane.

I looked over at Mel as she started to say something. I shook my head at her and kicked her under the table.

"Ouch." Caitlin glared at me. Then it appeared to dawn on her that Mel had been my target. She picked up her napkin and covered her mouth while her shoulders shook with silent laughter.

"Are you all right?" Shane raised a brow at Caitlin.

"I am." She cleared her throat. "I accidentally kicked the leg of the table." She bent down to rub her leg after Shane turned away, a snicker spilling from her throat.

George brought the desserts to the table and dispersed them.

I looked down at the sticky toffee pudding on my plate and hesitantly took a bite. I quickly took another one. It was delicious.

"I guess it didn't kill you." Shane kept his voice low as he peeked at me.

With the background noises and distractions all around us, plus Patrick's deep, booming voice as he told everyone a story, no one else but me seemed to hear him.

"Not yet. But if I do keel over, no mouth-to-mouth. I want to die in a sugary ecstasy." As soon as I whispered the words, I visualized Shane doing CPR on me. I froze, mentally berating myself for my slip of the tongue.

"All right. But I certainly wouldn't want you to die."

I relaxed in my chair, thankful he hadn't taken my comment and made something out of it. I needed to be more mindful of my choice of words in the future.

We finished dinner, and Patrick paid the bill.

"Patrick, what do I owe you for our dinner?" I said.

"Nothing. It's our treat. We're going next door for a few scoops, and you're welcome to join us."

"He means drinks, not ice cream." Shane grinned at me.

"I appreciate the explanation, especially since ice cream didn't seem fitting at the moment." I turned to Patrick. "I'm afraid we'll have to decline. Mel and I are going to head back to the poolside bar. Thank you for dinner. I enjoyed meeting everyone." I didn't want to intrude any further on Caitlin's group. Besides, it was best to avoid Shane at the moment. The image of him rescuing me with mouth-to-mouth resuscitation was still too vivid in my mind.

There was a round of goodbyes as Mel and I got up and left the table.

The bartender working our side of the bar earlier was still there, only now he didn't appear to be as swamped. He came over to take our order. "Hey, you're back. Sorry I couldn't get to you before you left earlier. What can I get you?"

I read his name badge. "It's all right, Carlton. We weren't here that long. How about a glass of the house chardonnay and a rum and Coke?" I turned my attention to Mel after Carlton walked away to make our drinks. "I enjoyed dinner. They're nice people, and I thought it was fun."

"Yeah, it was nice. But I would have had more fun if that blond guy had stuck around. You know, you and Shane look cute together."

"Excuse me? How can you say that? He isn't exactly alone."

"Geez. Don't get upset. I didn't say anything was going on. I'm just saying you two would make a cute couple. You looked happy, and I saw you laughing and having fun. You don't do that very often. Besides, I saw how you two were whispering back and forth."

"Seriously? You heard us?"

"No. I couldn't make out anything you said. But I did see the sideways glances you were making towards each other. What was up with that?"

"Here you are. One rum and Coke and a glass of chardonnay." Carlton set our drinks down in front of us. He slid the bill over to me to sign, charging the drinks to our room.

I signed it and slid it back to him, adding a small amount for a tip. I was thankful for his interruption as I preferred to keep my CPR comment to myself. Shane stirred something in me that I hadn't felt in a long time, and I wasn't about to share that knowledge with Mel. If she knew, she'd be relentless in trying to push the two of us together, and that couldn't happen. Besides my knowing nothing about him, Shane was here with Anna. Fortunate enough to have shared thirteen years with a man I deeply loved, I valued monogamy and respected others' relationships.

The band that had been setting their equipment up when we arrived began to play.

"Let's go dance." Mel grabbed my hand and dragged me out onto the dance floor.

We danced to song after song, periodically returning to the bar to sip on our drinks and order a shot. After several rounds and a load of dancing, we retreated to our seats.

"What can I get the two of you?" Carlton stood in front of us, a younger bartender with cornrows weaved into a zigzag pattern standing next to him.

"I'd like another rum and Coke and two more shots of tequila," Mel said.

"No tequila for me, please." I put my hand in the air. "I'm good for now."

"Ah, come on, Liz. Have another shot. We're on vacation."

"No. I'll pass. I've already had three shots. That's enough for me."

"Suit yourself." Mel shrugged.

"This is Christopher." Carlton motioned toward the man next to him. "He'll be taking care of you. My shift is over for the night." He gave us a nod and left the bar.

"One rum and Coke and one shot of tequila coming up." Christopher walked away to make Mel's drink.

"I'll be back." I touched Mel's arm. "I need to use the restroom." I left her at the bar and strolled toward the facilities. I was on my way back when I noticed one of the shops was still open. After browsing the boutique's window display, I went inside to look around. They had lovely pieces of jewelry and an assortment of beachwear. Seeing nothing compelling to purchase, I decided to head back to the bar. I couldn't find Mel when I got there.

"I think your friend has had too much to drink." The middle-aged lady sitting next to me pointed to the dance floor.

I swiveled in my chair, spotting Mel near the pool. She was dancing with an older gentleman in a Hawaiian print shirt. The man leered at her as he inappropriately brushed his body against hers. His male friends shouted encouragement, causing the man's actions to grow bolder.

I got up from my chair and worked my way across the dancefloor toward Mel. "Excuse me." I pushed my way between the man and Mel.

"You came to dance with us." Mel's speech sounded slurred, and she weaved on her feet.

"No. I came to take you off the dance floor." I took hold of Mel's arm. "You promised me you were going to behave, remember? Come on. I think we should go back to our room."

"I'm having fun. I don't want to go." Mel tried to push me away and stumbled backward a foot or so. Recovering, she grabbed the man's arm and started dancing with him again.

The man put his hands back on Mel.

"Take your hands off my friend," I said, my voice tight as I glared at the man.

"Your friend likes it, so butt out."

I clenched my jaw as I took a step toward him. "Take your hands off my friend, now, or I'll call security over here. She's drunk and doesn't know what she's doing."

The man scowled at me and gave Mel a little push to detach himself from her arms.

Mel tripped over her feet, stumbling down the concrete as she tried to stay upright. She plowed into a man standing next to the pool, sending him flying into the water. Then she crashed to her knees on the cement and landed on her shoulder.

The man in the pool flailed around as he yelled obscenities, calling Mel a choice name or two.

"Oh, shit. Are you okay? Mel, talk to me. Are you hurt?" I rushed to Mel's side.

Mel rolled onto her back and tried to sit up, collapsing back down on the concrete. After a second attempt and my help, she managed to get into a sitting position. She stared at me and then started laughing. "Did you trip me?"

"No, Mel. I didn't trip you. Come on. Let's see if you can stand up." I draped her arm around my shoulder and tried to get her on her feet. She was like a dead weight, and I couldn't move her.

A voice came from behind me.

"Miss, I think you're going to need some help."

I turned, spotting two men watching me, one blond, the other dark-haired. They looked to be in their early to mid-thirties. "If you could help me get her to our room, I'd appreciate it."

"No problem. It looks like your friend went well past her limit. I hope she doesn't do this too often." The blond man shook his head at Mel.

"I don't know what happened. Mel's a partier, but she usually holds her liquor much better than this. I stepped away from the bar for a little bit. When I came back, I found her in this condition."

The two guys got Mel on her feet. With one on each side of her, they followed me as I led them from the bar.

"Excuse me," Anna said smugly, coming out of no-where. She stepped in front of me, blocking my path. "I see your friend has a bit of a problem. Before you run away to play babysitter, I should give you this." Anna extended her hand, my driver's license in her grasp.

"How did you get my license?" Startled by what she had in her possession, I glanced at my purse. It had come open, my license falling out when I tried to help Mel.

"You dropped it. In my experience, people who change their names usually have something to hide. What are you hiding, Alyssa?"

"I'm not hiding anything, and it's none of your business," I snapped, snatching my license from her hand. Anna's comment that I had changed my name was ridiculous, especially since Liz was a common nickname for Alyssa. It appeared she was trying to make something out of nothing. Irritated, I quickly scanned the bar area, looking for Shane. He was nowhere around. That was odd. Why would Anna be here by herself?

"We'll see," Anna said with a sneer on her lips. She turned and flounced away, an exaggerated swing of her hips gaining the attention of several men nearby.

I turned toward the two men helping Mel. "I'm so sorry for the interruption."

"No problem," the blond man said. "She seems like a piece of work."

"It seems so." I glanced in Anna's direction, spotting her taking a seat at the bar, her seductive smile directed at a young-looking man seated beside her. Confused by her animosity toward me and her behavior at the bar, I couldn't help but wonder what was going on.

"Hang on." The dark-haired man looked at his friend. "Let me have her. She's small. It'll be easier if I carry her." He took Mel from the other man and picked her up in his arms. He followed behind me while his friend trailed behind the three of us.

"You're a hottie. Where are you taking me?" Mel

started giggling.

I swung around to face her. "We're going to our room, Mel. It's bedtime for you." I led the two guys down the corridor on our floor and opened the door to our suite. "Could you please take her to the bedroom on the left and lay her down on the bed?" I walked behind the man carrying Mel to ensure he safely deposited her in her room.

"There you go. Your friend is safe, but I don't think she'll feel too good in the morning." The dark-haired man took a step back, his gaze on Mel sprawled on the bed.

Mel moaned and rolled onto her side.

"I'm sure she's going to feel horrible. Thank you, both. There's no way I could have gotten her up here by myself. I'm sorry. I didn't even ask your names. I'm Liz."

"I suppose we bypassed that part." The blond chuckled. "I'm Rick, and my friend over there is Steve."

"Well, it was nice to meet you, although I wish the circumstances were different. Next time I see either of you, I'll have to buy you a drink to thank you for helping us out."

"Sounds good. At least your girlfriend was entertaining, although I doubt she'll remember much of it. Have a good night," Steve said.

I walked him and Rick to the door and then checked on Mel, finding her passed out. I slipped her sandals off her feet, dropping them on the tile. Then I covered her with a blanket I retrieved from the closet. After closing her bedroom door, I retreated to my room. I hoped tomorrow would be better. I'd had enough chaos for the night.

CHAPTER 3

TROUBLE ON THE HORIZON

DISORIENTED, I GLANCED around the bedroom in the darkness. Worried when nothing seemed familiar, I quickly reacquainted myself with where I was, my hotel room in Providenciales. I sat up and slid to the edge of the bed, swinging my feet onto the cold tile floor. According to the clock on the table next to me, it was five o'clock in the morning. I sat there for a moment, trying to collect my thoughts. The dream had awakened me again; the people, place, and event were always the same. They'd started when I was in my late teens and, until recently, only occurred every once in a great while. Now, it was monthly.

I'm getting married to a man whose identity stays hidden from me in the dream. He's a tall man, dressed in a gray suit, and I sense we love each other deeply. The officiant is male, his face also hidden, but I somehow know him. We're under a tent decorated with pink, white, and purple flowers, and the two of us are facing the side of an old castle, a garden with beautiful red roses and hedges in front of us. In each occurrence, a tattoo is visible on the groom's left inner wrist as he holds my hand in his palm. I always wake when he slips the wedding ring on my finger.

I shook my head in a useless attempt to clear the images from my mind. Rising from the bed, I wandered into the kitchen and made myself a cup of coffee. Then I strolled out to the balcony and sat in one of the chairs, a nutty aroma wafting from the steaming cup to my nose. The sun was starting to come up, the air outside warmer than the air-conditioned coolness of my room. I leaned back and took a sip of the dark liquid, relishing the solitude of the early morning.

DYLAN WAS WAVING and yelling at me from the swimming pool. "Liz, we're going to play a game of volleyball. We need you on our team."

"Are you going to play?" Mel lifted her head from the lounge chair and peered at me over the top of her sunglasses.

"I am. I haven't played in years, but it should be fun. We'll see if I'm still any good at it." I sat on the edge of my chair and took a drink of water. "So, how about you? Are you going to play?"

"Nah. My head is still splitting, and my stomach is nauseous from last night. I'm going to lie here and bake." Mel rolled onto her back.

I got up and walked to the edge of the pool. I stood at the net, checking out the teams on each side. Dylan's team was on my right, and they had him, Margaret, and six others. I looked around for Shane, spotting him getting up from a lounge chair on the other side of the pool. Anna was lying on her stomach on the chair next to him. I had a tough time turning away. Even from this distance, I could see Shane was gorgeous, with a superbly built chest and well-defined abdominal muscles and arms. He jumped into the pool, joining Dylan's team. I scanned the other side of the net and counted players, finding that team was short one person.

"Get in here. We need you." Shane was looking up at me from the swimming pool.

The blond man that had helped me with Mel last night stood in the water, staring across the net at Shane. "No way, man. You already have nine players. We get Liz." He looked up at me and grinned. "Get in. You'll be our ninth player."

"It's nice to see you again, Rick." I quickly looked him over. He was a good-looking man, tall and nicely built with bright blue eyes. He also had a wedding ring on his finger. "All right, I'm coming in. I still owe you one for helping me out last night." I jumped in the water and turned to face the net while Rick moved to the back row to serve. "Sorry, Shane. It looks like they need me more than you do."

"You're going to play. That's cool." Steve, the other man who'd helped me with Mel last night, gave me a high five from the spot on my left. "How's your friend? Last night was a little crazy."

"She wasn't doing too well this morning and is still feeling nauseous. Thanks again for helping me. I couldn't have managed without you two."

"No problem. I hope we don't have to do it again."

Shane raised a brow at me while moving toward the

net. "What happened last night? Why did you need those guys to help you?"

"Mel caused a scene at the poolside bar. Trust me, you don't want to know the details. So, are you going to play against me at the net?"

"I am, so be prepared to get your butt kicked."

"Ah, such big words. We'll see how far they carry you." I put my hands up as Rick got in position to start the game.

Rick served, and we volleyed back and forth several times. The ball came to Dylan in the back row, and he sent it to Margaret at the net next to Shane. Margaret tapped it across the net towards me. I jumped up and spiked the ball back to Dylan. He missed it, and our team got the point.

"You got lucky. It won't happen again." Shane had a hand on his hip as he taunted me.

"You go ahead and keep thinking that." I grinned at Shane.

After a moment of yelling and fist pumps amongst our team, Rick served the ball again. It went to the opposite team's server, and the lady managed to return it across the net. There were more volleys back and forth, and then Rick called my name, sending the ball my way to spike it. We gained another point.

"Come on, Liz. Knock it off, or we'll ban you from playing," Dylan yelled at me from the back row, causing chuckles across the pool.

My team gained two more points before missing the ball. It was now the other team's turn to serve. A man in our front row, next to Steve, tried to toss the ball to the opposing team's server. It was a poor throw, and the ball flew past her and landed on the concrete. One of the players on Shane's team climbed out of the pool to retrieve the ball. After pulling it from underneath a lounge chair, the man tossed the ball to their server. Then he cannonballed into the pool. A shriek pierced the air as a wave of water splashed the row of chairs.

"You idiot. You got my hair wet," Anna yelled. She stood next to her chair, glaring at the man that had done the cannonball.

"Hang on a minute." Shane held up his hand to stop the game from starting again. He climbed out of the pool and ran over to Anna. After an animated discussion, he jumped back in the water while Anna picked up her towel and beach bag and left the deck area.

We continued to play, with Shane's team gaining a point now and then, although my team consistently maintained the lead. I was in the middle position when a contentious volley went back and forth for quite some time. The tension started to build in the pool, with players yelling and whooping it up each time the volley successfully crossed the net. The ball came flying across the pool, and I jumped in the air to hit it. A colossal body suddenly landed on me, submerging me under the water.

"Dammit, are you all right?" Shane had pulled me from under the water and was trying to stand me on my feet. "Talk to me. Can you breathe?"

My right arm draped over Shane's left shoulder while my head rested on his chest. I coughed up water as I tried to catch my breath. After a minute or so, my coughing started to subside.

Shane tilted my head up and brushed my wet hair out of my face. "You're already getting a black eye. Damn, that scared me."

I looked into Shane's eyes. "That was a hell of a typhoon. I didn't expect such monstrous weather in the pool."

Shane blinked at me, and then the corner of his mouth twitched. "I take it you're all right?"

"Other than my head hurting? Yes."

"Is she all right?" Dylan was standing behind Shane.

"For the most part. But Liz is going to have a nasty black eye. I need to get her out of the pool and put ice on it."

"I can take her back to her lounge chair," Rick said. He was standing next to Shane.

"No, I'll take care of her." Shane's voice was terse as he responded to Rick. He escorted me from the pool and over to my chair.

"Dang. That guy nailed you." Mel looked me up and down as I started to lie down.

"All I know is I jumped to hit the ball, and a second later, I was under the water." I looked down at my right thigh. My skin was starting to turn black and blue.

"The big drunk guy playing in the back row behind you tried to take your ball and landed on top of you. He must have elbowed you in the face." Shane touched my arm. "I'm going to get you some ice. I'll be right back." He took off in a hurry toward the bar.

"Dang, Liz. I've never seen anyone move so fast. Shane was at your side, trying to rescue you before you even went underwater." Mel gave me a sly smile. "That man likes you."

"Please don't start. He has a partner. Entertaining the idea that he likes me will cause nothing but problems. I think at this point, I need to avoid him."

"Why avoid him? Just go for it. Neither one of them wears a wedding ring, and I'll bet you a million dollars that Anna is nothing but an arm decoration and he's not serious about her. I see the way you look at him too. Whether you like it or not, your eyes devour him whenever he's near you."

"Stop it." I turned on my side to face her. "I don't want to cause any problems between them. Besides, you're only guessing how Shane feels about Anna, and I don't need the drama. My life is peaceful. Let's leave it that way."

"The bartender put some ice in a bag for me." Shane kneeled next to me. "Turn over. I need to put the ice on your face."

"Ow." I rolled over, putting pressure on my bruised thigh. "The guy must have kneed me in the leg."

"I can see the bruise. The guy got you pretty good. Here. I'm going to put the ice by your eye." Shane leaned forward and gently placed the bag on my bruised face.

I swallowed hard. Shane's muscular chest was only inches away from me. A stirring sensation began to spread through my lower body. Oh, God. Why was this happening? I found him so tantalizingly attractive I couldn't seem to help myself. I needed him to go away.

"What else do you need? I can get more ice for your leg if you want."

"I'm fine." I mustered a small smile, determined not to let on how he affected me. "I appreciate your help, but you don't need to stay. I'm sure your team needs you back in the pool."

"You're sure you're okay?"

"I'm sure. I'll be fine. I promise."

Shane stood and gave me one last look before walking away.

I expelled a deep breath. Heaven help me. Shane was dangerous with the way he made my body react. I needed to be careful. No, I needed to do more than that. I needed to stay far away from him.

"I told you he likes you."

I rolled onto my back, holding the bag of ice to keep it from falling. I looked at Mel, catching the smug expression on her face. "Believe me. Nothing is going to happen. I'll make sure of it." I adjusted the bag as the ice started to melt. "So, whatever happened to Anna? I saw her get up and leave while I was playing volleyball."

"She moved behind the hedges that were next to her chair. I guess she didn't want to get her hair wet again."

I glanced across the pool at the hedge. Shane was standing on the other side of it, talking to someone. It had to be Anna, hidden by the wall of vegetation. I turned back toward Mel. "I'm going back to our room. I need to take something for this headache of mine. What do you think about going to Kiki's for dinner? I can call and try to make a reservation for six o'clock."

"That sounds cool. I'm going to stay here a little longer and try to detox. I'll come up to the room in a while."

"All right. I'll see you in a bit." I picked up my towel and other belongings and headed back to our room.

CARS, TRUCKS, AND scooters packed the parking lot at Kiki's, the place bustling with activity and much busier than I'd expected. The restaurant looked welcoming, with twinkle lights wrapped around the surrounding palm trees and more of them hanging from the building's eaves. The outside dining area seemed quiet and relaxing even though patrons filled every table. The inside dining area had a more energetic vibe, a din of voices carrying through the air as we entered. After the glowing review from our driver, Thomas, we hoped the place lived up to his comments.

"Hello." A young woman in a white blouse and black pants stood at a small podium inside the door and greeted us as we approached her. She let out a small gasp when she saw my bruised face.

"You should see the other woman. She's a mess." Mel gave the woman a defiant look.

"Knock it off, Mel."

"She was staring at you. I couldn't help it."

"What do you expect? My face doesn't look pretty right now." I addressed the host at the podium. "I'm sorry about that. It's just the two of us. We have a reservation for six o'clock under the name Liz Whalen."

"I see you on the list. It'll be five to ten minutes. You're welcome to wait here or sit at the bar." The woman motioned toward a casual-looking bar stretched along the right wall of the establishment.

Spotting available seats, I turned back to the host. "Thank you. We'll wait at the bar."

"We'll get you when your table is ready."

I led the way toward the bar, stopping midway when I recognized our driver, Thomas, behind the counter. "I don't believe it."

Mel followed my gaze. "I'd say the transportation company fired him, or he's a jack-of-all-trades. What a surprise."

We took the two available seats at the far end of the bar. Thomas was waiting on a couple at the other end. When he finished, he meandered our direction, picking up glasses and wiping down the counter along the way.

"Hello, Thomas," I said.

Thomas appeared startled when I said his name and snapped his head toward my voice. "Oh, man. Did you get in a fight? Your black eye is pretty bad."

"It's from a water volleyball game this afternoon. A drunk guy elbowed my face."

"Wow. I'd say so." Thomas winced. "Well, I'm glad you decided to check the place out."

"You gave it such a good recommendation. We couldn't resist. Now I know why." I leaned back in my chair, waiting for Thomas to make a comment or two.

"I couldn't help it." Thomas chuckled. "The food here is excellent, and the bartenders are cool. Marie, I'm pretty cool, huh?" he called out to one of the servers as she walked by the bar.

"Of course you are. You're the best." Marie laughed as she rounded one of the partitions and disappeared from our view.

"See? You came to the right place."

Mel started giggling.

"All right, I can see you're a comedian too." I shook my head. Thomas was more personable and humorous than I'd expected. "Now tell me, what's with the two jobs. Are you a driver during the day and a bartender at night?"

"I'm not a driver."

"Excuse me? You did pick us up." I eyed Thomas suspiciously.

"I was helping my uncle out. It's his company. Something happened to your booking, and he couldn't afford a negative review. He hasn't been in business that long."

"What do you mean, something happened to our booking?" I shot a glance at Mel. "See? We did have another reservation mishap. Only we didn't know about it. So far, this vacation has been like none of our others."

The host appeared behind me before Thomas could answer. Our table was ready, and she waited to escort us to it.

I got up and turned back toward Thomas. "We'll be back. I want to finish our conversation and hear what happened."

"No problem. I'll see you after you have dinner."

Mel and I followed the host to our table. She took us to a dining section at the back of the restaurant with a beautiful view of the marina.

"Here you go. I hope you don't mind a booth. I thought you'd enjoy the view." The host handed us menus. "Your server will be with you shortly."

"I swear I heard someone call your name." Mel scanned the dining room. She fixed her attention on a table behind me and started laughing.

I turned to look and spotted Caitlin and her group sitting at a table against the adjacent wall. "Well, isn't that a surprise? And it looks like Caitlin is motioning for us to come and talk to her. Come on. We better go."

"So much for avoiding Shane." Mel sounded amused. She gave me a little nudge when we got up and walked across the dining room to Caitlin's table.

"Jesus, Mary, and Joseph. Shane told me one of the volleyball players collided with you in the pool, but it looks worse than I thought." Caitlin was staring at me with a mixture of shock and concern.

"Your face looks brutal. What happened?" Patrick said.

"Our water volleyball game this afternoon was a bit vicious. It was going okay until I tried to pretend I was Captain Ahab, and Moby Dick submerged me." I winced as I brushed my hair from my cheek.

There was a round of chuckles at the table from my comment.

"A big guy playing behind Liz tried to steal her ball. He came crashing down on top of her, submerging her under the water." Shane was studying my face as he explained what had happened.

"Liz was the best player in the pool too. She racked up most of her team's points before leaving the game." Dylan looked at Mel. "I can see why Liz was your high school's star player." He pushed his glasses back up his nose as he grinned at me.

"I told you she was good." Mel glanced over her shoulder at our table. "Oops. Our server is waiting for us."

"We better go before our server leaves. Enjoy your dinner." I caught the frown on Shane's face when I turned to walk away. I couldn't tell if it was because of the condition of my face or because I was leaving. Hopefully it was because of my black eye.

"Enjoy yours too. I'm sure we'll bump into each other around the hotel," Caitlin said.

Mel and I went back to our booth, catching our server before she walked away.

"Hi. My name is Darla. I'll be your server this evening. What can I get for you?" A young woman was looking at Mel.

Mel opened the menu and quickly scanned it. "I'd like the shrimp scampi and garlic mashed potatoes. Could I get a glass of the house chardonnay to go with it? Oh, and a glass of water."

"No problem." Darla jotted down Mel's order and then turned her attention to me. She flinched when she noticed the bruises on my face. "What can I get you?"

"I'd like the herb-crusted snapper. A glass of the house chardonnay is fine for me as well. No water." I closed my menu and reached over for Mel's. I stacked them together and handed them to Darla.

"I'll be right back with your water and wine." Darla tucked the menus under her arm and scribbled something down on her pad. Then she hurried off toward the kitchen.

"You ordered wine. I'm surprised." I peered across the table at Mel.

"I don't want a mixed drink right now. After last night, I'll stick with something light."

"I don't blame you. You didn't look so great this morning. Did you look at those brochures I left on the coffee table in our hotel room? I was hoping you'd pick out a couple of excursions for us to book."

"Here you go." Darla returned with a tray in her hands, setting our glasses of wine, Mel's water, and some bread and butter on the table.

Mel took a sip from her glass. "Huh. The wine's not bad. Anyway, yes, I looked at the brochures. I'm game for the island jeep tour and the snorkeling tour."

"I was hoping you'd pick those. We can stop at the concierge desk in the morning and book them."

Darla brought our dinner plates to the table. "I have the shrimp scampi for you." She put the plate in front of Mel. "The herb-crusted snapper goes to you." She set my plate down next. "Can I get you anything else?"

"No, we're good. Thank you." I took a roll from the basket and cut it open with my butter knife. There were two types of butter. I scooped what I hoped was the garlic butter out of a small dish and spread it on my roll.

"Shane's been sneaking glances at you the whole time we've been sitting here. It's cute."

"Don't start, Mel."

"Fine. I was just sharing."

We finished dinner. I slipped cash into the check folder Darla left on the table and gave Caitlin a quick wave goodbye. Shane watched me as we left the dining room and headed back to the bar.

"You're back for the story. What can I get you before I start?" Thomas folded the towel in his hand and placed it on the counter behind him.

"Two glasses of the house chardonnay," I said.

"You got it. Coming right up." Thomas poured two glasses of wine and set them down in front of us. "Okay. The story. My uncle's new reservation clerk got the email with your revised pickup time and flight number. The problem was she entered it in their system wrong. When my uncle checked your flight status, he realized your plane had already landed."

"So, how did you get involved?" I said.

"That was easy. No one else was available. My uncle called me and asked if I'd help him out. I had to borrow my brother's suit, grab one of my uncle's cars, and head to the airport." Thomas glanced at a couple at the other end of the bar and then at us. "You'll have to excuse me. I need to take care of them." He strolled down the bar, wiping it with the rag.

"I'm going to run to the restroom. It feels like I have a piece of food stuck between my teeth. I'll be right back." I got up and went to the powder room by the front entry. I was standing in front of the mirror checking my teeth when the door opened.

"It's you." Anna glared at me with hatred in her eyes. "Just so you know, Caitlin told me Shane was planning to propose to me. So stay away from him. He's not yours."

"Look. I don't know what you think is going on, but I can tell you nothing is happening between us. I'm not interested in Shane, and I'm quite happy with my life at the moment."

"Keep it that way." Anna's eyes were like daggers as she turned and went into one of the stalls.

I leaned against the sink and expelled a deep breath. Shane was already causing me trouble. I'd only been on the island for a little more than a day, and it was far from peaceful. I tossed my paper towel in the trash and left the bathroom.

"Besides your black eye, you don't look too good. What's up?" Mel leaned back in her chair as she studied my face.

"Anna just caught me in the ladies' room and told me to stay away from Shane."

"No way. What did you tell the witch?"

"I told her nothing was going on between us, and I wasn't interested in him. What am I supposed to say? I told you I needed to stay away from him." I retook my seat and rubbed my forehead, a headache beginning to develop. "On top of that, I'm just tired. I woke up early this morning. I had the dream again."

"Seriously? You're having them all the time now."

"I know, and I'm not sure why. Besides frustrating, it worries me."

"I heard dreams can have hidden meanings. What if yours is some weird omen or something? Are you positive Alex isn't the groom?"

"It isn't Alex. The groom has a tattoo of an elf on his left inner wrist. Alex had tattoos, but nothing like that."

Thomas had finished tending to a group of new arrivals at the far end of the bar and was working his way back to us.

"Thomas, I have a question for you. Yesterday, you mentioned you knew one of the bartenders at our hotel. You said his name was Kip. By any chance, is Kip a nickname for Christopher?" I said.

"Yes. Why? Was he working at the bar yesterday?"

Mel hung her head and stared at the floor.

"Yes, Kip was working there last night. Mel woke up with a vicious hangover this morning."

"I warned you," Thomas said, snickering. He shook his head at Mel.

"Yes, you did. But the name tripped us up. You should have told us his name was Christopher," I said.

"Yeah. I should have. Sorry about that."

Mel pursed her lips as she looked at me and then Thomas. "At least I know which bartender to keep an eye on. Too bad for Kip. We're now at war." Mel grabbed a straw from the container in front of Thomas and pointed it at him like a sword. "You need to tell your friend to watch out. It's payback time."

CHAPTER 4

THURSDAY NIGHT FISH FRY

MEL AND I decided to spend the evening at the fish fry at Bight Park. According to the flyer we'd stumbled across at the concierge desk, it was a weekly event hosted by the tourist board, exhibiting food and craft vendors, bands, and cultural performers. Having walked along the beach from our hotel to the park, we hiked up a sandy path framed by clumps of beachgrass to the parking lot where the event was taking place.

"This place is cool. It's like a big street fair. Look at all the vendor tents and the smoke from the barbeque grills. Dang. The food smells good." Mel talked to me over her shoulder as she stepped in front of me to make room on the path for a group of people walking toward us.

"The event's bigger than I thought it would be." I moved aside for two men rushing past me, appearing in a hurry to get to the event. "Let's hang a left at the first vendor tent and loop around the area before deciding where to eat."

We stepped off the path into the parking lot. The vendors lined its length, and a stage was at the far end to our left. Locals and tourists alike milled about, filling the open space between the rows of tents. The two of us strolled through the lot. The aroma of grilled fish, lobster, shrimp, chicken, and barbeque ribs was incredible. The sun was starting to set, and there was a light breeze. It pushed the smoke and tantalizing array of smells from the onslaught of barbeque grills across the event area.

"Hang on, Mel. I want to check out the jewelry."

Mel turned around and joined me at a table full of beaded jewelry, handmade dolls, and an assortment of trinkets. "Ooh. I love the turquoise color of these beads. I want this bracelet." Mel handed the woman standing behind the display table payment for the piece of jewelry. She slipped it on her wrist and held up her arm so I could see it.

There was suddenly a male voice next to me.

"How's it going, Liz?"

I turned, finding myself staring at Rick. "Hey. Fancy meeting you here. I'm fine. You?"

"I'm great. Steve and I thought we'd check out the fish fry. The food's good. Have you tried any of it yet?"

"Not yet. I'm still debating on what I want."

"Here. Try a conch fritter." Rick stabbed one with his fork and held it out so I could take a bite.

"Oh, that's good."

"Liz! What a welcome surprise." Steve walked up to us and stood next to Rick.

"Excuse me. How about introducing me to your friends?" Mel stood with a hand on her hip as she eyed Rick and Steve.

"Mel, this is Rick. The guy next to him with the

delicious-looking plate of jerk chicken and rice is Steve. They're from our hotel."

"Ah, you're sober and functional. That's a nice improvement," Steve said.

"What is that supposed to mean?" Mel glared at Steve, her voice snappy.

"Whoa. Don't get testy." I held my hand up. "Remember the other night at the bar when you had too much to drink? These are the two guys that escorted you to our room. To be completely honest, Steve carried you."

"Oh my God. You are such a liar. You told me the two guys that helped me were old and chubby." Mel looked daggers at me, her face turning pink.

"Old and chubby? I've never heard anyone call me that before." Rick shook his head as he let out a chuckle.

"If I told you the two of them were adorable, you'd bug me until I introduced you to them. I couldn't put these guys through something so horrible." I laughed as Mel smacked my arm and stamped her foot.

"Liz, take a bite of my jerk chicken before I finish it." Steve held out a piece of his chicken so I could try it.

"That's delicious. I need to get a plate. Where did you get it?"

"Come on. I'll show you." Rick took hold of my arm and led me down the row of vendors. "Where's Irish? I'm surprised he's not with you."

"Irish? Are you talking about Shane?"

"Yeah. I guess that's the guy's name."

We stopped at one of the tents. Buffet-sized chafing dishes lined the table in front of us, and two large barbeque grills were against the backside of the stall, the aroma from the chicken as it cooked drifted toward us.

"What do you want, Liz?"

"I want a piece of the chicken, some rice, and a couple of the conch fritters."

A woman dressed in a turquoise-colored T-shirt and a white pair of pants nodded at me and started to put together my plate. Her male coworker, also dressed in a blue T-shirt and white pants, took a bunch of chicken off the grill and put it in one of the chafing dishes.

I opened my purse to pull out some money.

"I got it." Rick waved his hand to stop me. "Can you hold my plate so I can pay her?"

"Sure." I took Rick's plate when he held it out, eyeing the remnants of his lobster.

Rick paid the woman and took my plate from her. "Let's go over there behind those tents to get out of the way." He nodded toward an area on our left.

I followed Rick to an empty spot behind the vendor tents. Mel was ordering her food with Steve at her side when we walked away.

"Thank you for paying for my food. That was sweet of you. Can I try your lobster before I hand your plate back?"

"Sure. Just don't eat it all. I want another bite."

I took a small bite. "The lobster is good. So far, everything I've tried has been delicious." I switched plates with Rick. "So why would you think I'd be with Shane?"

"He's crazy about you, and I thought the two of you might have gotten together by now." Rick rubbed his chin. "The guy seemed pretty upset when that man slammed into you in the volleyball game and then a little bent out of shape when I offered to take you back to your lounge chair. I don't think he wanted me near you. Of course, he had no idea you're not exactly my type."

"Excuse me?" I stared at him for a second, trying to comprehend why he'd make a blatant statement like that. I might not be drop-dead gorgeous, but I wasn't unattractive either. Then it dawned on me. "Rick—are you gay?"

"Do you have a problem with that?"

"No, not at all. Honestly, it makes me more comfortable. Anyway, about Shane. There's a bit of a problem with your theory. He has a girlfriend."

"Not for long. Irish's bundle of eye candy is one of those high-maintenance, shallow women who like to hang on a man's arm. I honestly can't see him keeping Barbie around for too much longer."

"Barbie? Damn. Remind me never to get on your bad side. The bottom line is he's in a relationship, and I have no intention of becoming a home-wrecker. I'm not going to fight over a man either. So, if he's interested in me, he'll have to be unattached to get my attention." I took a bite of my rice. It was just as good as the rest.

"I need to get something to drink. Walk with me over to the beer tent." Rick motioned to Steve, who was several yards away, carrying on a conversation with Mel. "Hey, Liz and I are going to get a beer. Are you staying or coming with us?"

"We'll join you." Steve walked with Mel as they followed us down the row of vendors.

"I have to say, you and Irish look good together. You

fit like two pieces in a puzzle." Rick tossed his empty plate in a trash can as we walked past it. "The two of you remind me of my husband and me. He's flying in tomorrow to join me for a couple of days. Steve's leaving in the morning. He and I came here on business to negotiate the purchase of a parcel of land. We finalized the sale yesterday, so there's no reason for Steve to stay."

"Ah, you're a savvy businessperson. And I thought you were just here on vacation. There's more to you than I thought. Of course, the ring on your finger was a giveaway you had a spouse." I chuckled at Rick's raised brow. Then it hit me. Alex used to look at me like that. A pang of sadness crept over me as I stared at Rick.

"What's with the sad look on your face?" Rick stopped at the beer tent and glanced at me over his shoulder.

"The expression on your face and the way you raised your brow at me reminded me of my husband. He died in an accident three years ago."

"I'm sorry to hear you lost your husband. I'd be completely devastated if I lost mine. I can't imagine going through something like that." Rick put his arm around my shoulder and gently squeezed me.

"What can I get you?" The vendor stood in front of us, waiting for Rick's order.

Rick scanned the list of beers on a sign on the counter. "I'll have the lager." He turned toward me. "What do you want?"

"I'll have the amber ale." I finished the last of my rice and tossed my plate in the trash can next to me. I took the beer Rick handed me after he paid the vendor.

Rick turned around to talk to Steve, standing behind us in line. "We're going to walk over toward the stage. It looks like the band is setting up to play." After receiving a nod from Steve, Rick took my arm and guided me through a large group of people. We had almost gotten clear of them when Rick suddenly pulled me backward.

Startled, it took me a second to realize what had happened. "Okay, that was close. I didn't see the guy start to cut in front of me. Thanks for pulling me back."

"No problem." Rick scanned the crowd in front of us and started laughing. "Speaking of Irish, he's up ahead of us by the stage and has his eyes on you. He doesn't look too happy to see us together."

I followed Rick's gaze, spotting Shane in the crowd. "Based on the scowl on his face and the way he's looking at you, I think you're right."

"Come on. Let's watch the group on stage. They're getting ready to start." Rick led us toward the performers, dodging around people as we moved closer. He stopped about fifteen feet away, so we could watch without being in the crush of people standing directly in front of the musicians.

The five-person band started playing. The music had a danceable rhythm, and I couldn't help swaying my hips to it. I glanced to my right, spotting Shane about twenty feet away from us. Rick was right. He had his eyes on me. I couldn't help noticing how handsome Shane looked, dressed in khaki shorts and a short-sleeved shirt. He smiled at me, and I smiled back, wishing he were the one at my side. Caitlin, Patrick, Dylan, and Margaret were with Shane, but I didn't see Anna. Just when it seemed she had stayed behind, she walked up and stood next to him. She must have been off somewhere getting a drink because she was holding a pineapple with the top half cut off and a straw sticking out of it.

Mel and Steve joined us and stood next to Rick. Steve had his arm around Mel, and she had a look of contentment on her face. The sun had gone down, and a row of streetlights illuminated the crowd, which had gotten thicker as darkness filled the sky.

"The band is wonderful. Dance with me, Rick." I stepped in front of him, moving my body in rhythm to the Caribbean music.

"Hmm. I'd say you're causing quite a commotion." Rick took my hand and started dancing with me. "Irish is feasting on you as if you were a mouthwatering banquet, and Barbie is glaring at you." Rick spun me around. "Where did you learn to dance like that anyway?"

"I learned it in the dance classes I take. It's great exercise and tones the body. I have to say, you've got some nice moves yourself. I'm impressed." The music stopped, and I stood next to Rick.

Mel reached out and grabbed my arm when the music started up again. "Ooh, the Caribbean slide. We have to go up front and dance. Rick and Steve have to join us." She grabbed Steve's hand and pulled him through the crowd toward the area in front of the stage.

"You have to dance too. There's no getting out of it." I took Rick's hand and followed Mel through the crowd, getting in line with Rick on my left and Mel and Steve on my right. I peeked over my shoulder at Rick while he danced. "You're good at this."

"My husband likes to dance to the electric slide and always makes me join him on the dance floor."

We made another turn, and now Shane, Anna, Dylan, and Margaret were in front of us. I focused on Shane as he danced to the music, his steps light and relaxed besides being incredibly sexy.

Rick leaned toward me. "You look like you're going to start drooling. I'd recommend taking your eyes off his ass."

"Oh, shush." I reached out and smacked his arm, making him laugh.

The music stopped, and the band started playing another rhythmic dance beat. I started dancing next to Rick again.

"Liz, how do you get your hips to move that way?" Margaret was watching me from a few feet away.

"It's not hard. It just takes practice. Here, I'll show you. Start by moving your hips to the right, to the back, to the left, and then to the front. See? It's easy. You can go the other direction too." I demonstrated the movement for Margaret, going in both directions. "Now, do it smoother and faster in combination with the steps. Just shift your weight from your left foot to your right foot. Barely lift your foot off the ground and bend at the knees. Move your hips as you do the steps." I did another demonstration for Margaret. "Now, you try it."

Margaret stood next to me, and we danced side by side. She wasn't half-bad for her first try. Dylan gave her a high five as she moved, pleased with her performance. Shane and Anna stood off to the side, watching us, while

Mel and Steve danced together a few yards away.

"Now try it with side steps. Step to the side with your right foot, then step in place with your left foot and bring your right foot back to join your left. Then go the other direction and do it with the hip movement." I glanced at Shane while I showed Margaret how to dance the steps to the music, catching him staring at my hips. I winced as Anna suddenly hit him in the ribs with her elbow and appeared to scold him.

Shane looked upset as he leaned over and said something in Anna's ear. Then he walked away, leaving her standing there, staring at his back.

Anna stormed over to my side and glared at me. "I told you to stay away from Shane. Next time, I won't be giving you a warning." She hit me with her shoulder before marching off.

Shocked, I stood there as she flounced away.

Mel must have seen what happened because she was suddenly in front of Anna, blocking her path. Mel looked livid as she pointed her finger at her and then pushed her shoulder. I was about to rush over to the two of them to intervene when Anna suddenly swung around and disappeared into the crowd.

"She must feel threatened by you. Are you okay?" Rick said from his vantage point behind me.

"I'm fine. Anna caught me off guard, that's all." I turned to Margaret and Dylan, finding them frozen in place. "What was that all about?"

Dylan slowly turned his head toward me. "I have no idea. I didn't see you do anything wrong. All I know is Anna's been difficult since they got here, and Shane wishes he hadn't let her come."

The music started up again. But this time, it was a different beat and coming from the opposite direction. There was cheering from the crowd, and then a costumed dance troupe appeared, weaving through the onlookers. Dylan and Margaret came over and stood next to me, and Rick moved to my other side. We watched the troupe perform in front of the stage. A small group of them beat on drums while the others danced. It was vibrant, rhythmic, and colorful, the costumes festive and in bright tones.

The music stopped, and Margaret leaned toward me. "I remember your friend from the water volleyball game. His name is Rick, right?"

"Yes, that's right. Have you met?"

"We introduced ourselves when we played against each other at the net. He seems like a nice guy. Are you two together?"

"Oh, no. We're not together. We're just keeping each other company while Mel and his friend, Steve, seem to be hitting it off."

Rick turned to face me. "Steve's motioning to me that he and Mel are heading back to the hotel. It sounds like they have plans. Do you want to stay here or head back to the hotel with them? I'll keep you company either way."

"I don't mind heading back. But I'll warn you. I'm not ready to call it a night, so you're going to be stuck having a drink and dancing with me at the poolside bar when we get there."

"It's a deal. We'll go to the bar." Rick swung his

attention to Margaret. "Hi, I'm Rick. I played against you in the volleyball game. You're Margaret, and your husband is Dylan. Am I right?"

"You are. I'm surprised you remembered." Margaret let out a little laugh. "I guess I'll see you two later since you're taking off."

Shane was suddenly next to me. "You're leaving? I wish you'd stay. I was hoping we could talk and dance a little bit."

I turned, Shane's nearness and the scent of his cologne causing me to catch my breath. "We're heading back to the hotel." I forced myself to speak, my voice sounding strained. I wasn't sure if the rhythmic dancing under the streetlights or the balminess of the Caribbean evening caused it, but I wanted him. My gaze strayed to his lips, and I had the urge to kiss them. I looked away and rubbed the back of my neck. I needed to stop having these thoughts about him. I turned back to Shane. "I'm sorry. I can't stay." I briskly walked away.

"Hey. Wait up." Rick caught up to me. "What was that quick departure all about?"

"Don't you dare laugh or make fun of me, or I swear I'll punch you. I get all googly-eyed when Shane's near me. I had the strongest urge to kiss him right now. I had to leave."

"I knew that guy got to you. I could see it in your face." Rick busted out laughing and playfully bumped me while we walked toward the exit.

Mel and Steve joined us when we reached the street. Taxis were dropping people off and picking others up at the curb.

Steve walked up to one of the taxis and talked to the driver. Then he motioned for the three of us to get in the car. "He'll take us back to the hotel."

I climbed in the back seat with Steve and Mel, and Rick took the front seat. I looked back at the parking lot as we drove away. I wanted to stay with Shane more than anything, but I knew I couldn't. Frustrated, I leaned my head against the window and closed my eyes.

"Thank you," Rick said as he paid the taxi driver and climbed out of the car, shutting my door after I got out of the back seat. He looked at Steve and Mel when they came around the back of the car and joined us. "So, you two are taking off?"

"Yeah. Mel and I are going back to my room. I'll catch you in the morning." Steve slipped his arm around Mel's shoulder and looked down at her, his height a foot taller. "Are you ready to go?"

"Yep, let's go." Mel peeked at me, a grin on her face as the two of them walked away.

"Well, I guess it's off to the bar for us. Cheer up. You look like someone died." Rick gave me a playful little nudge.

"I'm just frustrated. You have no idea how much I wanted to stay with Shane. Damn, that man has gotten under my skin, and there's nothing I can do about it. Why are the good guys always taken?" I shook my head at my bad luck.

"I'm telling you, Barbie isn't going to be around for much longer. You're a keeper, she's not, and I doubt their relationship is serious anyway."

"I'm not so sure. I ran into Anna at dinner the other

night. She told me Shane was going to propose to her, so their relationship has to be much more serious than you think."

"She lied to you. She had to. I'm telling you, there's no way Irish would marry her." We had reached the poolside bar, and Rick pointed toward the deck area near the band. "How about a table instead of sitting at the bar?"

"I'd like that." I followed Rick to a table and sat down when he pulled my chair out.

"What can I get you? I'll go up to the bar and get our drinks."

"I should stick with beer. How about another amber ale?"

"You got it. I'll be right back."

I let my mind wander while I sat there listening to the band. The situation with Shane was becoming complicated. I liked him and found myself immensely attracted to him. Based on his actions, I assumed he cared for me too. Anna was the barrier between us, and I had to respect their relationship. The best thing I could do for all involved was to stay away from Shane. I didn't want to, but I had to.

"How about a spin on the dance floor? You look so gloomy. It might cheer you up." Rick set my beer down on the table and stood over me, studying my face.

"Sorry. I can't help it." I took Rick's hand as he escorted me to the dance floor. I was going to have fun and put Shane out of my mind. I only had to avoid him for one more day. Mel and I were flying home the day after tomorrow.

CHAPTER 5

AN AFTERNOON EXCURSION

M EL SHIFTED HER attention to the yellow-and-white catamaran anchored in the surf. "We're not late, are we?"

"We're on time. The snorkeling tour starts at one o'clock, and we still have five minutes. The hut we're supposed to check in at is up ahead." I was looking forward to our afternoon of sailing and snorkeling, having a love of water sports and the ocean. I scanned the beach as we hurried toward the hut, surprised to spot Shane, Caitlin, and the others waiting in line to board the boat. There was something different about Shane. He stood by himself with Anna near him but not too close, and they didn't appear to be talking to each other. Anna kept glancing at Shane over her shoulder and then looking away. Something had to be going on between them.

"Dang. I don't believe this. You've tried so hard to stay away from Shane, and there he is. Now, you're going to be stuck with him all afternoon. Ah, poor you," Mel said, snickering.

"Please don't start. Avoiding Shane the last few days was the best option, especially after Anna's comment at

Kiki's and the fish fry. He'll drag me into the middle of whatever is going on between them if I don't stay away from him. Anna's here. That should make keeping our distance from each other fairly easy."

"Somehow, I doubt that."

We reached the small wooden hut, and I stepped up to the counter. "Hi. We booked the snorkeling tour. The reservation is for Liz Whalen and Mel Bradley."

A man with shoulder-length braids checked a list for our names. "Gotcha. I need you to read and sign the disclosure agreement." The man placed a clipboard and a pen in front of me. "What size swim fins do you need? It'll be whatever shoe size you normally wear."

"I wear a size eight." I scanned and signed the agreement as the man looked for swim fins in my size.

"Here's a size eight. If the fins don't fit, we can switch them for another size." The man placed the fins on the counter. He reached into a bin and pulled a snorkel and mask from it, placing them next to the fins. Then he removed the paper I signed from the clipboard and put it in a plastic file box.

"Thank you." I picked up my snorkeling equipment from the counter and stashed it in my canvas beach bag. Finished checking in, I moved off to the side and waited for Mel to sign the paperwork and get her equipment.

A man dressed in black swim trunks and a long-sleeved fluorescent green T-shirt with long braids pulled into a ponytail walked up to us. "Hi, I'm Marcus. It looks like you're the last two. We're about ready to leave, so I'll take you to the boat." Marcus led us to the catamaran, the front of its body resting in the sand. He helped us climb the ladder to the deck.

"Welcome. I'm Captain Frank." A man of medium build wearing a straw hat addressed us when we climbed on board. He pointed to the man standing next to him in another fluorescent green T-shirt. "This is Ryan, and you've already met Marcus. Ben is assisting some passengers in the cabin. They're members of my crew. Take a seat anywhere on the boat. We'll open the bar once we get underway."

"Thank you," I said before turning away.

Mel and I stepped down onto a small sundeck framed with bench seating. Behind this section was the covered cabin. It had seating along both sides and a U-shaped bar in the middle. Cutouts in the fiberglass sides created large glassless windows that allowed the breeze to flow throughout the cabin. Stairs at the back of the boat led to a large upper deck, the captain's chair, and several groups of people visible above us from where we stood. The third crew member, Ben, wore the same fluorescent green T-shirt and talked with several passengers near the bar.

"Dang, Liz. Check them out. The blond guy in blue swim trunks and the redhead next to him by the stairs are from our hotel. They were at the bar when we met Caitlin. Oh, this is cool. I'm going to have more fun on this tour than I thought."

"Whatever you do, don't drag me into it. You promised, remember?"

"Geez, you're such a killjoy. Fine. I won't try to push you into anything." Mel watched the two guys disappear up the staircase. "I'm going upstairs. You're welcome to come with me."

"No, you go ahead. I'll sit in the cabin with Caitlin and Patrick."

"Suit yourself. I'll come back down in a while." Mel hurried off to the back of the catamaran and climbed the stairs to the upper deck.

I sidestepped a group of people standing in front of me and sat with Caitlin by the bar. Patrick was standing at the back of the boat, talking to Dylan and Margaret.

"Where have you been the last few days?" Caitlin leaned back, her fingers working her auburn hair into a bun on top of her head as a small gust of wind pushed a wayward strand across her cheek.

"Mel and I have been staying busy. Besides spending time at the beach, we've explored the downtown area, took an island jeep tour, and did some kayaking around Mangrove Cay." I scanned the cabin, looking for Shane while I stashed my bag under the bench. He and Anna weren't anywhere around.

"You have been busy. With all your excursions, it's no wonder we haven't had a chance to chat since dinner at Kiki's earlier in the week. I did see you at the fish fry last night but never got a chance to talk to you. Shane told me you left early. If I didn't know better, I'd say you were trying to avoid us."

"To tell you the truth, I've been trying to stay away from Shane. Things started to get a little complicated, especially after the comments Anna made to me."

"Anna? What in heaven's name did she have to say? I know Shane likes you, but that's none of her business."

"I'm confused. Why would that be none of Anna's

business? I thought they were getting married."

"Where on earth did you hear that?" Caitlin stared at me, her mouth gaping open.

"Anna told me. She caught me in the bathroom when we were at Kiki's and told me that you had informed her Shane planned to propose to her. She warned me to stay away from him."

"Well, isn't she a bloody liar? I said no such thing to her, and it's pretty far from the truth. Shane and Anna aren't together. They were but broke up a month ago. They didn't date that long, and it wasn't serious. At least for Shane, it wasn't. The two of them had this vacation already booked when they broke up. Since Anna had already paid her share of the trip, Shane agreed to let her come if they did it as friends only. They're not even sharing a room at the hotel. So, she has no reason to say anything to you about Shane. Although I'm pretty sure Anna was using this trip as a way to get back together with him."

Stunned, I stared at Caitlin. This revelation changed everything. Shane was single, and his relationship with Anna was strictly platonic, albeit her presence here and their agreement were a bit odd. It was no surprise she'd made those comments to me if she hoped to use this vacation to get Shane back, especially since I was messing up her plan. Not that I was going to throw myself at Shane, I wouldn't do that for anyone, but I no longer needed to avoid him. I could gracefully express the feelings for him that I was trying so desperately to suppress and see where it took us. Since Alex's death, no man had gained my interest or attention as Shane had.

When he was near me, he invoked feelings I'd thought were long gone, and I couldn't help thinking about him when he wasn't around. He seemed intelligent, responsible, humorous, well-spoken, and kind, the type of man that could make me happy, and I wanted to try.

The engine started up, and a few minutes later, we were sailing along the coast to our first snorkeling stop at the barrier reef. The catamaran cut through the water in a rhythmic bobbing motion, a sea breeze blowing softly through the cabin.

Patrick took a seat next to Caitlin. "Marcus said they'll open the bar in a few minutes. Are you going to want anything?"

"A bottle of water if you don't mind." Caitlin patted Patrick's knee. "Thank you, love."

"How about you, Liz? Can I get you something when Marcus opens the bar?"

"Thank you, Patrick. I'd love a rum punch." I turned to look at him, catching sight of Anna storming toward us. I held my breath, waiting for her outburst, but she simply glared at me as she hurried past us. Surprised by her lack of commentary, I was glad she stayed silent.

"That woman is a piece of work." Caitlin kept her eyes on Anna as she took a seat at the front of the boat. "I'll be glad when she's completely out of the picture. Besides being greedy and manipulative, she's caused Shane countless moments of grief."

Anna leaned back on the bench seat in a skimpy white bikini, pushing her chest out so any male watching her would get a good show. I wasn't surprised by Caitlin's comments. Anna seemed like the type of woman that attached herself to men of substance, using them until she got what she wanted, then moving on to the next victim. And sadly, Shane was still her target. I'd already observed Anna enough to conclude she had a need for attention, specifically from men. I was also sure she could be vicious, which meant I needed to be careful. It was best to be discreet in my interactions with Shane, at least for now.

Marcus went behind the bar and looked at the three of us. "Can I get any of you something to drink?"

"That you can. We'd like a beer, a rum punch, and a bottle of water." Patrick jumped up and stood next to the bar while Marcus got our drinks.

Shane came down the stairs and headed toward us. He beamed when he saw me.

Suddenly nervous, my heart started pounding in my chest. Now that I understood the situation between Shane and Anna, everything was different.

"I'm glad you're here. You've made my afternoon so much better," Shane said, sitting next to me.

"I wondered when you were going to say hello. I was debating whether you were being rude or just ignoring me."

"Neither one. I knew you were here. I've been talking to Mel and her two friends on the upper deck. She's a little spitfire."

"Oh, no. Mel isn't getting out of hand, is she?" I playfully wrinkled my nose at him. "I don't have to go up there and tie her up, do I?"

"No. Mel's not that bad." Shane shook his head and chuckled. "She's just a ball of energy and has those two boys mesmerized. She'll have them wrapped around her little finger before the afternoon is over. Liz, I have to tell you. The freckles on your nose and cheeks are adorable. Has anyone told you that before?"

"My mother when I was a little girl."

"That was a nondisclosure type of answer."

"And that was a comment typical for a lawyer."

The two of us laughed, and my heart skipped a beat when Shane smiled at me.

"You're different, Liz. You seem down-to-earth and honest, and I like that in you. I get the impression I can talk to you about anything, and you'll understand." Shane looked down at the deck and shook his head. "I can't believe I'm babbling and saying this stuff to you. Anyway, I'm just glad you're here." Shane smiled and put his hand over mine on the bench.

The boat stopped, and Marcus and Ryan went to anchor it.

"I need to get my snorkeling equipment and bag from the upper deck. I'll be right back." Shane walked to the back of the boat and disappeared up the stairs.

Marcus stood in the middle of the deck. "This is the barrier reef. Anyone wishing to snorkel or swim is welcome to leave the boat. You can use the diving board and the slide if you're hanging around here instead. The reef is behind the boat for those snorkeling. Please be careful not to touch any of the coral or sea life. We'll be here for ninety minutes. If you need help with anything, let Ryan, Ben, or me know, and we'll help you."

Shane returned from the upper deck, accompanied by Dylan and Margaret. He took his snorkeling equipment from his bag and then shoved the bag under the bench.

"Are we ready to snorkel?" Dylan looked back and forth between the group as he stood in front of Patrick.

"Caitlin and I are ready. Let's get going," Patrick said.

Patrick and Caitlin stood with their snorkeling equipment in hand and followed Dylan and Margaret to the cutout in the side of the boat. They put on their gear and eased into the water one at a time down the ladder.

Shane removed his shirt, tossing it down on the bench.

I couldn't help it. My gaze went instantly to Shane's chest and moved downward across his stomach to his lower region. As I fought to quell the image in my mind, he turned toward me. I quickly put my head down. I had no intention of letting Shane catch me checking him out.

"Aren't you going in?"

I looked up at Shane. "I am, but I thought I'd wait for Mel. I imagine she'll be coming down from the upper deck any minute."

"I'll see you out there, then." Shane walked over to the side of the boat. After putting on his gear, he eased into the water.

After waiting a little while, Mel still hadn't come down from the upper deck. Not knowing her plan, I decided to go out by myself. I put on my fins and shuffled over to the side of the boat. Looking out toward the reef, I spotted Shane and the others. I thought it best to go in another direction since Anna would be watching from the upper deck. Getting ready to go in, I looked down at the water. It was wonderfully clear, the bottom appearing so close it seemed as if I could reach out and touch it. After putting on my mask and snorkel, I jumped feetfirst from the deck, the salty liquid cool against my skin as I came up to the surface. Taking a moment to get my bearings, I swam toward the reef.

The view in front of me was spellbinding. I took my time as I explored, the ocean floor alternating between flat sandy spots and ridges of colorful coral. After swimming around a large cluster of coral shaped like an elk's antlers, I found myself amid a school of yellow fish with thin horizontal blue stripes, their bodies darting back and forth around me. Something caught my attention off to my left. I dove to the bottom, finding a giant anemone. It had long white tentacles with tips a beautiful lavender, the arms waving gracefully with the current. Finished exploring the seabed, I came across a turtle as I swam back to the surface, the pattern on its legs resembling an artwork of black mosaic tile.

I was treading water when I caught a movement next to me. A wave of terror hit me as I swiveled in the water, coming face-to-face with a long, snakelike fish with two rows of fang-like teeth. It was staring at me with the evilest eyes I'd ever seen. I identified the creature as a barracuda, having researched reef fish in the area before the trip. Fear bubbled up inside me as the tidbits of information I'd learned about them swirled inside my head. These fish were ferocious and opportunistic predators. They hunted by sight rather than smell and, on occasion, attacked humans. Shiny objects attracted them—the items mistaken as the fish's prey.

I swam along the surface, trying to escape the predator, but it stayed next to me. I slowed down, and it matched my speed. With panic threatening to overtake me, I dove under the water and swam around the coral, hoping the fish would get distracted and leave me alone. But when I surfaced, it was still at my side. Only now, it was closer.

"You've gone out kind of far. Are you okay?" Shane was suddenly next to me.

"Oh my God. I have a barracuda following me, and I can't get it to go away." My heart was pounding as I turned to face Shane.

"Oh, shit. Where is it?"

I spun around in the water and pointed. "It's over there." The barracuda was five feet away from me and eyeing me like I was its meal.

"Okay, we have to get back to the boat. Let's see if it'll leave if I swim next to you."

We started swimming towards the boat, Shane placing himself between the fish and me as we swam. Trying to get my attention, Shane grabbed my arm. Pointing to his left, he was trying to tell me the creature was gone. I shook my head and pointed in the other direction. The barracuda had gone underneath us and come up on my right side. Now, it was only three feet from me and pacing us.

Shane motioned for me to stop. "It isn't going away. We have to figure out what's attracting it. They like jewelry. Are you wearing any?" His eyes darted back and forth between the fish and me.

I shook my head, keeping a wary eye on the barracuda. "No, I don't have any jewelry on me." My eyes suddenly grew wide. "It's my swimsuit."

"I don't understand." Shane stared at me, wrinkles stretching across his forehead.

"There's a silver ring on each side of my bikini bottom. I have another on the front of my top." I touched the ring between my breasts, the metal hard underneath my fingertips. "You'll have to try to cover them up."

"Okay. You'll have to explain to me how to do that."

"The rings have material gathered tightly at each side. You'll have to spread the material out to cover up the metal. My hands are shaking so badly, I don't think I can do it."

Shane put his head under the water. His hands were on my hip as he worked at spreading the material out around the ring. After a minute or so, Shane moved to my other hip and did the same thing. He surfaced in front of me and reached for the one between my breasts, stopping just short of touching it. "Are you sure you want me to do this?"

"The barracuda can eat me, or you can touch my chest. Which would you prefer?"

"I don't think it's going to eat you."

"Are you sure? Did you see the way it's looking at me? I think there's a menu printed on my backside that says breakfast, lunch, and dinner."

"All right. I'll fix it." He spread the material out around the ring, careful not to touch my breasts. "Okay. It's covered up. Let's see if this works." Shane looked for the barracuda. It was still a couple of feet away from me.

We started swimming back to the boat. Shane placed

himself between the fish and me once again. This time, when he signaled the barracuda had disappeared from his side, I confirmed it was gone from mine as well. Finally reaching the boat, I climbed up the ladder and stepped onto the deck. Shane climbed up behind me. We walked over to Caitlin and Patrick and sat on the bench next to them. Neither one of us said a word.

"What on earth happened out there?" Caitlin's eyes darted back and forth between Shane and me. "Everybody came back except you two. We could see you out there, but we couldn't begin to guess what you were doing."

"Liz had a barracuda following her, and she couldn't get it to go away." Shane ran his hand through his wet hair and leaned back against the fiberglass wall.

"A barracuda? No way. Are you serious?" Dylan put his arm around Margaret's shoulders as she walked up and joined him.

"I'm very serious," Shane said. "The damn thing stayed next to her regardless of what she tried."

"How did you get it to go away?" Margaret had a horrified look on her face.

"I finally figured out it was after the rings on my swimsuit. Shane helped me spread the material around them so they were no longer visible, and the barracuda took off." I shivered, picturing the evil-looking predator taking a bite of my flesh. "I'm sorry. You'll have to excuse me. I need to sit in the sun." I left the group and went to the front deck, wanting to be alone.

Marcus and Ryan pulled anchor, and we motored to our next stop to look for conch. Several people joined the two of them in the water to try their luck at finding the mollusks in the seagrass. Only here for half an hour, I decided to stay on the catamaran and observe. Mel and her two friends came down from the upper deck and joined me.

"Liz, this is Greg." Mel pointed to the man sitting next to her, his arm around her shoulder. Then she nodded toward the freckled redhead sitting next to me. "That's Greg's cousin, Brandon. These guys are from Charleston. They came here for a friend's wedding."

"It's nice to meet you." I looked at Mel. "Did you go snorkeling earlier? I waited for you and then went out by myself."

"I went snorkeling with these two. I didn't see you when we came down from the upper deck. You must have gone out to snorkel already." Mel laid her hand on Greg's leg. "We heard about your escapade with the barracuda and how Shane rescued you. It pissed Anna off like crazy. You should have seen her pacing back and forth." Mel snickered. "What was that you said earlier about avoiding someone?"

"I've learned something new since then. I'll have to tell you about it later." I turned to the redhead. He and his cousin looked young. My guess was their early twenties. "Brandon, what do you do in Charleston?"

"I'm a senior engineer at Air Alliance. I'm the youngest person there in that position. Normally, you hire in as an assistant engineer, but they saw I was overqualified for entry-level and hired me two positions above that." Brandon seemed to look down his nose at me while he talked.

I was about to ask him how long he'd been employed with the company when he began another round of bragging.

"My company hired me right out of college. They jumped on my employment application since I was top of my class. I've only been there for two months, but it should be easy to work my way into management." Brandon's face flushed, and he stuck his chin in the air as he boasted about himself once again.

"Well, good for you." I couldn't help imagining a complete set of peacock feathers magically shooting out from his back. It would be fitting with the way he was preening. I cleared my throat to camouflage the chuckle that was trying to escape. "You'll have to excuse me. I need to talk to my friend." I returned to the seat next to Caitlin, now alone since Shane and Patrick were standing at the bar.

"Running away from Mel's friends, are you?" Caitlin raised a brow at me.

"Well, yes. I suppose. Those guys are too young, and the redhead is pretentious. They're not exactly my cup of tea."

Marcus stood in the middle of the deck to make another announcement. "Hey, everyone. This is Iguana Island, also known as Little Water Cay. The island is a protected habitat for the rock iguanas native to the area. We'll be here for about an hour. You're free to swim and snorkel in the area. Ryan will demonstrate how to open the conch we harvested earlier on the beach. Then we'll make conch salad and have some sandwiches."

Shane was still conversing with Patrick at the bar,

and Dylan and Margaret had now joined them. Not wanting to intrude on them, I decided to explore the island.

I turned to Caitlin. "I'm going to take a walk. I'll be back in a while." I stood and pulled my cell phone from my bag.

"We're going to watch the conch demonstration and go for a swim. We'll see you in a bit," Caitlin said.

I checked the time on my cell phone and disembarked from the catamaran, heading inland. After cresting a hill and crossing a patch of bushy vegetation, I walked across a vast stretch of white sand on the other side of the cay. Finally reaching the shoreline, I set my phone down on the beach and waded out in the warm shallow water. Alone, I began to relax. It wasn't long before I found myself thinking about Shane. Was he wondering where I had gone or even looking for me? Wanting to quell my thoughts, I dove underwater and swam for a short distance. Then I headed back to the beach.

I sat in the sand next to my cell phone, Shane back in my thoughts. I'd fallen for him. No, it was much more than that. The man had stolen my heart. There was a tightening in my lower body as I imagined him making love to me and holding me in his arms. I scooped up a handful of sand, feeling the grains slip through my fingers. Did he feel as strongly about me? Was I relationship material or just a passing fancy to him? I brought my knees to my chest and rested my head on them. I guess time would tell how serious this was.

I looked at the time on my cell phone. I'd been gone

for forty-five minutes and needed to get back. I stood and headed back toward the boat. When I reached the crest of the hill, I could see the crew was packing up. I hurried toward the beach.

"Hey, we wondered where you went. I have a couple of sandwiches left. Take one before I pack them away." Marcus pointed to a small folding table with leftover food on it. "I have to run down the beach and gather up some of the stragglers. I'll be back." He jogged down the sand toward a group of people in the distance.

"Liz."

I jumped and swung around to the voice behind me. "Shane. You scared me. I didn't hear you walk up."

"Sorry. I was coming from the other side of the cay. I was looking for you. I got worried when you didn't come back." Shane cocked his head at me. "Are you okay?"

"I'm fine. I just went for a long walk. Now I'm hungry. Marcus told me to eat a sandwich before he packs them away." I picked up a roast beef sandwich and started eating it—my stomach growling in the process.

"We should head back to the boat. Come on. I'll walk you back." Shane put his hand on the small of my back and escorted me across the sand toward the water. "So, where did you go earlier?"

"I found a shallow little inlet on the other side of the cay and went swimming. Were you really worried?" I peeked at him out of the corner of my eye, trying not to make it too apparent that I cared how he felt.

"Yes, I was worried about you." He chuckled and dropped his hand from my back. "Plus, I wanted to make sure one of Mel's little friends didn't try to steal you away from me."

I smiled to myself, my heart fluttering. Shane cared about me. Was it possible he felt the same way I did, our budding romance much more than a temporary attraction?

Anna was suddenly standing in front of us, blocking our path.

"I need to talk to you. Right now," she said, the tone in her voice angry and demanding. She stood there staring at Shane. "It's important. You can at least give me that courtesy." She focused her attention on me next, her lips tight and her eyes like the cold steel of a dagger. "I'm sure Liz won't mind giving us some privacy."

"I'm going to sit with Caitlin." I spun around and climbed the ladder to the catamaran's deck, a gut-churning feeling in the pit of my stomach as I tried to guess what she wanted. Whatever it was, it couldn't be good.

"You're back. Take a seat." Caitlin patted the bench next to her. Then she saw the look on my face. "What happened? You look upset."

"Anna stopped us when Shane and I got back to the boat. She said she had to talk to him, so I came here. Shane's with her down on the beach."

"That woman just doesn't give up. But that's all right. Once Shane gets home, she'll be completely out of the picture." Caitlin patted my hand and gave me a reassuring smile.

Shane walked across the deck a few minutes later, stopping next to one of the bench seats at the front of the boat. He ran his hand through his hair, a scowl spreading across his face as Anna approached him once again. They were in an animated discussion, and then Shane turned to walk away. Anna grabbed his arm to hold him back.

"Jesus, Mary, and Joseph. What is going on?" Caitlin appeared irritated, her mouth tight as she looked at Patrick.

"I don't know, but we'll find out soon enough since we've started sailing back to Grace Bay, and it's a short trip." Patrick slipped his arm around Caitlin's shoulder. "Don't get yourself all worked up either. Anna may be a conniving woman, but Shane can manage himself just fine."

I stared at Shane, feeling powerless. He looked upset, and I wanted to do something to help him. But I didn't dare get between him and Anna. I looked down at the deck as the catamaran cut through the water, its hull rising with the swells—the breeze cool on my warm face. I wasn't sure what to do.

CHAPTER 6

A PAINFUL GOODBYE

WE ARRIVED BACK at Grace Bay. After gathering my belongings, I joined the other guests and waited my turn to disembark from the catamaran. Shane was still in an animated conversation with Anna, only now they were at the back of the boat. Clueless as to what was going on between them, I decided to go back to my room and wait to find out.

"Thank you for booking with us. I hope you enjoyed the tour," Captain Frank said when I reached the front of the boat.

"Thank you. I did." I handed him a tip and then climbed down the ladder, Ryan assisting me when I reached the sand. I walked up the beach and waited for Mel next to the wooden beach hut where we had checked in for the tour.

Mel joined me, and she wasn't alone. Greg and Brandon were following her like a pair of puppies.

"These guys want to have a drink at the bar before we head to our room to clean up," Mel said.

"You go ahead without me. I'm tired and not in the best mood. I'll see you back at our room."

Mel eyed me suspiciously. "What's going on? I

thought you had fun on our tour. Anna didn't tell you to stay away from Shane again, did she? I saw the two of them arguing."

"It's a bit more complicated than that. I'll have to explain later." I'd forgotten that Mel hadn't been with me when I'd found out that Shane and Anna were no longer a couple.

Brandon took a step forward from his place next to Mel. "Come on. Have a drink with us. It'll cheer you up. Besides, I'd like to get to know you, and I'm good company. I promise."

Caitlin walked by us at that moment and asked Patrick to stop. "We're heading back to our room. Liz, you might as well walk with us since Mel's going to the bar." She gave me a little wink when no one was watching.

"Thank you." I turned to Mel. "I'm going to head back with Caitlin and Patrick. I'll see you later." I left Mel and her two friends standing on the beach, Brandon's eyes on me when I turned to walk away.

"What are you and Mel doing this evening?" Caitlin reached over and touched my arm as I walked beside her toward our hotel. "If you don't have plans, we'd love for you to join us for dinner. We have a reservation in the hotel's restaurant at seven o'clock."

"Thank you, but I'm not sure what Mel's plans are for this evening. And, frankly, I'm not sure what's going on with Shane either. I thought we might be getting together, but now I'm not sure. Something is going on between him and Anna, so maybe I should discreetly back away."

"That's nonsense. This afternoon was a hiccup, that's

all. Shane made the mistake of dating Anna once. He won't do it twice. Besides, you're the one that has captured his heart. I see the way he looks at you."

Patrick spoke up from his spot on the other side of Caitlin. "If you can't make it for dinner, you're welcome to join us afterward at the bar next door. There's a jazz entertainer performing tonight, and Caitlin is forcing us all to watch. I'd rather listen to an old Irish sea shanty and wouldn't mind your company." Patrick flinched and then let out a loud, booming laugh when Caitlin smacked his arm. "Woman, watch that hand of yours."

"I will when it hits you one more time. Keep it up, Patrick Burke." Caitlin turned toward me and flashed a sweet smile. "Now, where was I before I was so rudely interrupted? Oh, yes. This evening. We're leaving tomorrow. Patrick and I are flying to Washington, D.C., with Shane. We're spending a couple of days with him before flying back to Ireland. So you'll have to stop in this evening to say goodbye. Promise me you'll do that."

"I'll try, but no promises. Mel and I are flying out tomorrow too." I paused for a moment, unsure whether to broach the subject of Shane again. Then again, I had nothing to lose. "If Shane asks about me, could you tell him I'm in room four ten? He's welcome to come and find me." I pulled a pen and an old receipt out of my purse, writing my cell phone number on the back of the slip of paper. "If you could give him my phone number too, I'd appreciate it."

"I'll tell him and give him your number." Caitlin led us up a short concrete staircase and down a walkway leading to the guest complexes at our hotel. She stopped a short distance from the stairs where the walkway split, one segment continuing straight ahead while the other branched off to the left. "Patrick and I are in the complex ahead of us. Which building are you in?"

"I'm in the first building on the left, so I need to head the other way. Thank you for letting me and Mel join you this past week. I had fun and enjoyed meeting all of you."

"It was our pleasure. But, before you go, I want to give you one of our business cards." Caitlin held out her hand toward Patrick. "Can you give me one of the cards from your wallet?"

"Sure." Patrick pulled his wallet from his shorts pocket and dug a card from it. He handed it to Caitlin.

"We own a hotel in Kilkenny, Ireland. If you ever come to visit, I want you to look us up. We're in a wonderful location right off the Medieval Mile, so we're close to the main tourist area." Caitlin handed me the business card.

"Thank you. I'll keep that in mind. Who knows, Mel and I might make a trip there one of these days. I've always wanted to see it."

"I hope so. Now, give me a hug before you take off on me." Caitlin reached over and hugged me. Then she stepped back so Patrick could say goodbye.

"We've had a grand time and enjoyed your company. But don't forget—I expect to see you for jazz night. The first whiskey is on me since I'll need a few of them."

"Oh, you." Caitlin slapped Patrick's arm. "The music isn't going to kill you."

"If it doesn't, you will with the way you keep slapping me."

"Okay, I better go. Thank you for everything." I gave them a quick wave and turned away, hurrying up the walkway toward my building.

Reaching my room, I showered and dressed, putting on a short floral skirt and a plum-colored sleeveless blouse. I sat out on the balcony and waited for Mel. I assumed we were going to dinner, but the later it got, the more unlikely it sounded. After retrieving a box of water crackers and a tray of salami and cheese from the kitchen, I returned to the balcony to have my makeshift dinner. It was the best I could hope for at this point. Finally, spotting Mel come through the door, I went into the living room and sat on the couch.

"Sorry, I was having fun at the bar. Greg and Brandon completely sidetracked me. They're coming over here in an hour," Mel said.

"Seriously? Did you have to invite them over here?"

"Geez, don't get your panties in a bunch. They're coming over to hang out. If it turns into something else, so be it—no harm in that. I'm not forcing Brandon on you, either. You don't have to talk to him or stay."

"I have no desire to hang out with Brandon. He's a braggart and a kid. Besides, I was hoping to see Shane."

"I thought you were avoiding Shane. What changed?"

"He and Anna aren't together. They used to date but broke up about a month ago. They're here platonically since they split up after having already booked this vacation."

"Geez. Are you serious? Well, that changes things. He's available, and you finally figured out he's the guy for you. Wait a minute. That must mean you've fallen for the guy. I knew it. I swear, I could tell something was up with the way you looked at him. Dang. I've been waiting for the day you're finally interested in another guy." Mel suddenly cocked her head and peered suspiciously at me. "Hold on. Why weren't you with him on our snorkeling tour if they broke up? You sat with Caitlin or stayed by yourself most of the time."

"Anna's already displaying enough animosity toward me. I didn't want to hang out with Shane and blatantly throw it in her face. That would only make it worse, although my concern for her feelings may have backfired on me. She's trying her darnedest to reclaim him."

"Well, you're a lot nicer about it than I would be."

"Too nice, and that will change if Anna doesn't back off."

"Good. Like I said days ago, you and Shane are cute together."

"Thanks. I hope it works out. Anyway, I'll leave before Greg and Brandon arrive and go to the bar or something. I plan to join Caitlin and Patrick later this evening to listen to some jazz, and I'm hoping Shane and I can continue our conversation from this afternoon while I'm there. That is unless Anna somehow changed things. I have no idea what was going on between them earlier."

"I'll keep my fingers crossed. Well, I better go clean up. You'll have to give me an update later." Mel turned on her heels and went to her room.

I waited forty-five minutes and then went downstairs. Caitlin and the others would be finishing dinner about now, so I went to the pool. I wanted to wait a little while before I met them for the after-dinner jazz. Since it was dark, everyone had deserted the area. I leaned back in one of the lounge chairs and listened to the sounds carrying across the pool deck. There was laughter coming from the bar and clinking dinnerware, along with a mingling of voices from the outside dining venue.

It wasn't long before Shane was back on my mind. I had hoped he'd call or stop by my room, but I had heard nothing from him. With my hopes starting to disintegrate, I questioned whether I should go to the bar for jazz night. If Shane showed up with Anna, it would be more than I could take right now. But if I let the night slip by without talking to him, I wouldn't know where things stood between us. I sat up and swung my feet to the ground, suddenly catching my breath. Brandon was walking toward me. I jumped up and hurried to the bar, slipping onto the nearest chair. I froze a moment later, sensing someone standing behind me.

"There you are. I was looking for you." Shane whispered his words into my ear. Then he pulled a barstool close to mine and sat down.

"Well, you found me." Elated he had come looking for me, I was also nervous, hoping we could pick up where we'd left off.

"Caitlin gave me your room number. I went there, but no one answered. I hoped you'd be here. Fortunately for me, I was right."

"Mel was going to have company, so I left. I assume she was a little busy when you showed up."

"Well, that makes sense why no one answered your

door." As Shane finished talking, a boisterous group of people across the bar broke out laughing and carrying on. "Would you like to go for a walk? We could go down to the beach. It'll be quieter than here."

There was a flutter in the pit of my stomach. Yes, I wanted to do that, but I didn't want to sound too eager. I gave Shane a coy smile. "I'd like that." Then I took his arm and walked with him out of the bar.

"I owe you an apology for this afternoon. Things got a little messy with Anna. I don't know if Caitlin mentioned anything to you, but Anna and I split up a while back and agreed to come here as friends since we'd already booked the vacation. She was trying to plead her case for the two of us to get back together. When she failed to sway me, it got a little ugly."

"Caitlin explained the situation, and I'm glad to hear your abandonment of me wasn't done on purpose." My voice sounded like I was teasing, but in a way, I wasn't. I had a deep-seated fear of people leaving me, the emotion cultivated over years of heartache. Snapping out of my melancholy thought, I peered up at Shane. "I want to thank you for helping me with the barracuda today. I got worried when I couldn't get it to go away."

"That was pretty insane. I've seen barracuda before, but never one so persistent. I'm glad I swam over to you when I did. I originally came to check on you since you'd gone out so far."

"I'm glad you did too."

We strolled arm in arm along a dimly lit walkway framed by palm trees and tropical plants. It was quiet out, most guests either out on the town or at one of the hotel's venues for the evening. I leaned toward Shane, enjoying the heady scent of his cologne as it filled my nose. Finally reaching the beach, we walked toward the water. No one but us was there, the only sound coming from the waves as they lapped at the shore. A balmy breeze blew lightly across the water, the night sky lit with the glow of a full moon.

I slipped off my shoes, the grains of sand working their way between my toes. Then I waded into the water, letting it come up to my knees. A wave came, and I dashed toward the beach, trying to keep my skirt dry. When the water receded, I did it again, laughing as I played in the surf.

Shane stood on the beach, watching me.

Another wave came, this one larger, and I misjudged it. I squealed as it hit me, my skirt becoming soaked.

The sound of Shane's laughter drifted toward me.

"Okay, smarty. Show me how you'd do it." I stood there in the water, goading Shane to join me.

"Ahh, you want the expert to show you." Shane took off his shoes and rolled up his pant legs, joining me as a wave was coming. Rather than run, he grabbed my waist and held me back.

I shrieked, breaking free from his grasp. But, it was too late. The wave drenched me.

Shane doubled over with laughter. Catching his breath, he stood up and faced me. "I'm sorry. I couldn't resist since you taunted me."

"That wasn't fair." Cupping the water with my hands, I flung it at him. Hoping to wipe the grin off his face, I did it again.

"Okay, that's enough." Shane grabbed my hands and held them at my side as he stood in front of me. He was still chuckling. "You'll have me wet from head to toe if you don't stop. Come on. Let's go sit on the sand." Maintaining his hold on my left hand, he pulled me from the water and onto the beach.

We sat quietly for a minute or two, listening to the waves caress the shore, the moonlight reflecting off the water. Shane reached for my hand, holding it in his.

"I love that sound." I leaned my head back and stared at the stars.

Shane moved closer, his arm encircling my waist. "Come here," he whispered, his voice husky as he pulled me against him.

I lifted my face and looked into his eyes, the moonlight casting him in a sensual bluish glow.

Shane bent his head slightly, his lips tenderly caressing mine. They were as soft as I imagined.

I basked in the headiness of his kiss, my body beginning to ache. Oh God, how I wanted him. If he continued, I wouldn't be able to stop.

Shane's phone suddenly dinged, and he ignored it, his kiss deepening as his tongue explored mine. He was erotic and sensual, his body lighting mine on fire.

I could barely breathe, my pulse racing as his lips left mine, and he left a trail of kisses down my neck.

Shane's phone dinged three more times. Whoever was trying to get a hold of him was persistent, their unwanted interruption threatening to destroy our moment of passion.

"I'm so sorry," Shane whispered in my ear. "I have to

see who this is. It doesn't look like they're going to stop." He straightened up and pulled his cell phone from his pocket. His face began to tense as he read several messages. Then he abruptly got up. His body was rigid as he stood above me, his voice hard and bitter when he said, "Are you married?"

"What?" I stared at him, dumbfounded by his question.

"Are you married? Anna texted me, saying you're married to a man named Alexander Whalen. Is this true?"

I blinked, stunned by the implication of what he had done. Then the anger set in. "Did you investigate me? My God. How dare you."

"No, I did not. Nor do I condone it. Anna did it with the help of her brother, who's a lawyer with my agency. Regardless of that fact, the bottom line is you've tried to dupe me. To what end, I don't know. But you certainly didn't bother to tell me you're married, did you?"

I was so furious, I didn't want to give him an answer. Shane didn't deserve one, and my pride wouldn't allow it. How dare he assume I lied and that I was deviously planning something behind his back. And how dare that witch do something like this to me. I should have expected something unsavory to happen after Anna found my driver's license and commented about my name the night Mel got drunk. I could easily explain that I was a widow, but Shane didn't deserve that answer.

"I'm done here. I'll walk you back to the bar," Shane said, his voice tight with anger.

I shook my head, my tone bitter when I replied, "You believe her? That's not a smart move on your part. Just leave me alone. I don't need you to walk me anywhere."

"Give me a reason not to believe her," Shane demanded, his eyes coldly fixed on me.

"I'll give you nothing. Just leave." I brought my knees to my chest, wrapping my arms around them as I stared out at the water, tears threatening to spill down my cheeks.

"Have it your way." Shane stiffly turned and trudged away through the sand.

I laid my head on my knees and silently let the tears spill. Anger, resentment, hurt pride, and a sense of loss welled up inside me, with each emotion fighting against the others for dominance. The feeling of loss finally won, and I wondered what I had done.

CHAPTER 7

THE DATE

Ross Sullivan walked into my office and sat in one of the ruby-red-and-tan upholstered guest chairs in front of my desk. "How's the special project going? Sorry about dropping it on you at the last minute. The annual transportation audit has Chelsea swamped, so she can't work on it right now. You're the only person in the office besides her that knows how to pull the data and can complete the assignment in record time. You know management. They want it done by the end of the day too. I can get an extension on the updates you were working on if you need me to."

"That won't be necessary. I'll have the project done before I go home today and still be able to finish the updates by Monday afternoon. Just don't throw any more last-minute assignments at me, or I'll have to fire you as my boss. Oh, wait. I can't do that, can I? Damn." I feigned a look of disappointment as I leaned back in my chair. I enjoyed kidding around with Ross. We'd worked together for the last twelve years and had become good friends. Thankfully, there was no change in our relationship after he'd become my supervisor a year ago.

"You wouldn't fire me if you had the chance. I'm the

best supervisor you've ever had, and you know it." Ross chuckled. Our bantering always lightened his mood. He turned slightly and scanned the whiteboard on my wall. "When are you going to update your board and remove that vacation to Turks and Caicos? Wasn't your trip two or three months ago or something like that?"

"It was two months ago." I swiveled in my desk chair to face the board. "I should erase it, but I haven't been able to bring myself to do it. The trip to Providenciales was special, and I think about it whenever I look at my board. I'm sure that sounds silly."

"Special, huh? Care to talk about it? If there's one thing you learned about me over the years, I'm a great listener. Besides, now you've got me curious." Ross raised a brow in what seemed silent encouragement to divulge my story.

"It's personal, but I'll share. I've known you too long to keep this to myself." I straightened up, folding my hands across my lap. "Have you ever done something that you knew without a doubt went against your better judgment, but you went ahead and did it anyway? Something where you let your emotions take control and guide you to a response that wasn't necessarily the wisest one?"

"I can think of a time or two. What did you do?"

"I fell in love with a gorgeous Irishman when I was in Turks and Caicos, for starters. The whole thing was strange from the beginning. It was like we had some weird bond, and fate kept pushing us together." I paused a moment, remembering how Shane had seemed familiar to me, more like a long-lost close friend than a stranger. I shook off the thought. "I thought he was there with his girlfriend and tried to do the decent thing and avoid him. That strategy failed big-time, and I fell head over heels for the guy. After I found out the woman with him was his ex-girlfriend, we took a walk along the beach, and things started to get intimate between us. Then this bomb exploded and destroyed it all." Still feeling annoyed with myself, I looked down at my hands, unsure whether I wanted to go on. I'd thrown all my anger and blame at Shane when it was only partially his fault. Most of it lay on Anna's shoulders. He was her victim, just like I was. She played us both to get what she wanted—for Shane to stay away from me. Whether or not she knew I was a widow, I didn't know. But one thing was clear. I should have told Shane the truth that night rather than let my emotions get the better of me and stay silent. The consequence of my action, specifically of my hurt pride, was the loss of a man I cared for and our potential future together.

"Oh, don't stop now. You have to tell me what happened. What was this bomb?"

"The bomb was a particular tidbit of information that the ex-girlfriend deviously used to make me look like a manipulative liar. To be specific, the guy's ex saw that we cared for each other, and in her attempt to break it up, she had her brother do some investigating to find some dirt to use against me. Her brother discovered my marriage to Alex, and the ex-girlfriend conveniently texted my Irishman during our moment of intimacy on the beach that I was married. He was upset, of course, and confronted me about it. I was so shocked and furious at all of them that I refused to answer him. We argued, and he walked away. How's that for a story?"

"Wow. That's not what I expected to hear. Well, let's see. You called the guy 'my Irishman,' so you must still care about the man. And he was upset, so that makes me think he cared about you. Although, I'd bet the information angered him more because he thought you were using him. But, if you think about it, it could be worse. The ex could have told him you're an ax murderer or something like that." Ross put his hand in the air when he saw the look on my face. "Okay, okay. That's not helping. In all seriousness, I'd say it sounds repairable. Just call the guy and tell him the truth. Doesn't that sound better than letting your anger and pride get in the way and doing nothing? What have you got to lose at this point?"

"First of all, I don't have his number. I'd have to contact his cousin in Ireland to get it, and I'm not sure I want to involve her or that she'd even give me the number. Second, what if he doesn't want to talk to me? It's been two months, and I'm sure he's moved on. Plus, as you've already guessed, I'm still angry they investigated me and thought I'd cheat on a spouse. I'm not sure I can forgive that. Although I have to admit, my Irishman wasn't the one who did it. But he did believe his ex-girlfriend, which hurt."

"Let me ask you something, and be honest with me. Did the Irishman know you well enough not to believe the ex-girlfriend? Did he have a reason to believe you over her?"

I looked down at my lap as I fidgeted with the hem

of my blouse. "I guess not."

"Then get the guy's phone number from his cousin and call him. I'll repeat, what do you have to lose?"

"Fine. I'll think about it." I brushed a strand of hair from my cheek and looked at Ross. "All right. Enough of my drama. What's up? I know you didn't come into my office to talk about my whiteboard or a broken heart."

"No, I didn't. I came in here to let you know a bunch of us are going out for a drink after work, and you're welcome to join us. We'll be at Brindle's Pub if you're interested." Ross leaned forward, his forearm on my desk. "You might need a drink after you finish that project. There's tons of data to sift through."

"I can't go. I have a date, although Brindle's sounds more fun."

"A date? Who's the lucky guy?" Ross rubbed his chin as he cocked an eyebrow at me.

"He's a client of Mel's, a real estate mogul from what I understand. I don't know why I listened to her and let her set me up." I shook my head. I was having second thoughts about tonight. "Mel's company is doing a pricey remodel at the guy's house. He was in her office going over the plans when he saw a picture of the two of us on Mel's desk. He inquired about me, which led to Mel setting me up on the date. God only knows what I'm getting myself into tonight. Mel keeps telling me the guy is perfect for me, but her idea of perfect is typically different from mine."

"So, where's he taking you? Someplace special, I hope."

"He's picking me up at seven o'clock and taking me to Chez Maddison in Del Mar."

"That place is over the top. It's supposed to be one of the best fine dining restaurants in the North County. I better leave you alone, so you can work on that project and get out of here in time to make your date." Ross stood and walked over to my door. He started to leave and then stopped. "I want a full report on Monday morning on how your date went."

"Yes, sir." I chuckled and waved him out of my office. I needed to get back to work.

I JUMPED AT the sudden knocking on my window. Engrossed in my project, I'd lost track of the time. I swiveled in my chair, spotting Nicole waving at me from the walkway outside my office. Aware she was stopping by this afternoon, I motioned for her to hold on. Then I hurried to the employee entrance at the side of the building and opened the wood and glass door to let her in. "Thanks for stopping by. Do you have time to chat, or are you just dropping off my cookies?"

"I can chat. And before I forget, Gabby wanted me to thank you for your order. She was one of her troop's top sellers." Nicole handed me a plastic grocery bag full of Girl Scout cookies.

"Oh boy. Just what I needed. Tell my niece she's welcome and contributing to the delinquency of a chocoholic. I bet I eat a whole box by the time I go home."

"Better you than me. I've already had more than my share."

I led Nicole to my office. Although swamped with work, I was pleased to see her. It had been weeks since we'd talked. "So, how's my favorite sister-in-law doing? I haven't seen you in quite a while." I motioned her to the chair Ross had vacated two hours earlier and sat at my desk.

"You're in a quirky mood. I happen to be your only sister-in-law unless you've remarried and forgot to tell me about it." She pulled her long sandy-blond hair with the bright pink ends away from her face, tucking it behind her ears.

"Nope. No marriage for me, especially since I'd have to be in a relationship for that to happen. So, what have you been up to?"

"Not much, just the same old stuff. We're riding the motorcycles out to Borrego at the end of next month for Kurt's birthday. Everybody will be there, and I was hoping you'd join us. It'll be fun. You can come out for the day if you don't want to spend the weekend there. We'll be staying where we usually do at that motor lodge off the highway."

"Thanks for the invitation, but I can't do it. Being with the group again would bring back too many memories, more so since it'll be out in Borrego. That's the last place Alex and I were together, and he died on his way back from that weekend trip." The mere mention of the place started to bring back painful memories, so I knew I couldn't deal with seeing it again.

"Come on. I know you miss my brother. We all do. But it's time you moved on. Alex would want you to do that. So, at least think about it. Okay? Jesse said you could ride out with him if you decide to join us. You know he's been interested in you for a long time."

"I'm aware Jesse likes me and has since well before Alex died. He's made that abundantly clear, and I prefer to stay as far away from him as possible. I don't like or trust the man. He has a dark side, and I've seen firsthand how he treats his girlfriends. Your brother must be rolling over in his grave right now at your suggestion." I clenched my jaw, irritated at Nicole for even thinking I'd have anything to do with Jesse. He couldn't be more different from Alex, and Jesse's principles were far from acceptable. "Don't forget, I was on that motorcycle run with Alex when Jesse's girlfriend suddenly had a black eye and split lip after arguing with him the night before. I remember your brother asking what happened and Jesse offering up a lame story. I'm sure you recall how pissed off your brother was, especially when he told Jesse there'd be hell to pay if he touched another woman like that again."

"All right. I remember the incident." Nicole shifted in her chair. "But Jesse isn't all bad, and he wouldn't dare touch you. Call me if you change your mind, and we'll work it out."

"Nicole—I'm not going, and why are you pushing Jesse on me? What's up with that?"

"Nothing's up." Nicole shifted her gaze to the carpet, her hands fidgeting in her lap.

Something was going on, and she wasn't going to tell me what it was. If I had to guess, I'd say it had to do with her husband, Kurt, who was widely known as an asshole. There was an unspoken dislike between him and

Alex, with Alex only tolerating Kurt because he'd married Nicole. "Well, I need to get back to work. I have a deadline to meet on a project Ross gave me."

"No problem. I need to get going anyway. Oh, before I go, Kurt wanted me to ask what you plan to do with the Knucklehead? He said he'd be more than happy to take the motorcycle off your hands." Nicole shifted her gaze once again. This time she was staring out my window at the parking lot.

"I can't believe you. Besides the fact we've already had this discussion, you of all people should know I won't part with Alex's bike. Besides being a vintage motorcycle, it was his pride and joy. So, no. Kurt can't have it."

"I'm only asking because Kurt told me to. What are you going to do with the motorcycle anyway? It's not like you can ride it. Wouldn't you rather have Kurt take it out on the road and enjoy it than let it sit in your garage?" Nicole crossed her arms, looking defiant.

"First, you need to tell Kurt the answer is still a resounding no, and I'm not going to change my mind. Second, he better stop asking me."

"Fine. I'll tell Kurt what you said." Nicole appeared uncomfortable as she sat there.

"Please do. I'm tired of Kurt trying to pressure me. It won't work. I'm keeping the motorcycle." I stood and came around the side of my desk as Nicole got up from her chair. "Come on. I'll walk you out." I led her to the employee entrance and opened the door. "Make sure you tell Gabby I said thanks for the cookies."

"I will." Nicole hugged me and turned away.

I leaned against the door, watching her walk across the parking lot to her car. Nicole had been a sweet, caring person when we'd become friends in junior high school. She'd introduced me to her older brother, Alex, and I'd become part of her family several years later. But that Nicole was long gone. Now she was Kurt's puppet.

After she drove away, I went back to my office and continued working on Ross's project. It was a little after five o'clock when I finished. I emailed the completed spreadsheet and report to Ross and waited for his reply. He sent one back ten minutes later, telling me he liked what I had provided and needed no changes. That meant I could go home and get ready for my date.

MAGGIE GREETED ME at my front door when I got home. She was my tan-and-white smooth-coated collie, her appearance like Lassie without the long hair. I had gotten her as a puppy six months after Alex had died. Devasted and lost after the accident, I had barely been functioning. Maggie was the one thing that had helped me get through the grief and start to heal. She'd needed my attention, and I'd focused my energy on taking care of her. I had dived into training her, and she had become my companion, helping to fill the hole in my heart.

I fed Maggie her dinner and then went into my room to find something to wear. I wanted a dress that was both comfortable and elegant. Pulling a sleeveless black sheath dress from my closet, I tossed it on my bed and jumped in the shower. I didn't have much time to get ready.

Finished with the last touches forty-five minutes later, I looked at my image in the mirror. It was perfect. I chose a pair of black dress sandals with an ankle strap, a black clutch purse, and a silver-and-black silk wrap to go with the dress. My makeup had come out nice, and I'd swept my hair back into a sophisticated-looking bun. Hearing the doorbell, I checked myself one last time and then went to the door to meet my date.

"Hi, I'm Liz. You must be Cole." I had opened my front door to find a ruggedly handsome man in his late thirties to early forties standing on my doorstep. He looked stylish, dressed in a dark blue tailored suit, white dress shirt, and a dark blue tie with small burgundy polka dots.

"I am. It's a pleasure to meet you. Are you ready to go?"

"I'm ready." I stepped outside, pulling my front door closed behind me. I caught sight of Maggie sitting off to the side of the entryway as it shut. As she rarely barked unless alerting me to something, most people coming to my home never knew she was there. I had trained her early on to sit away from the door and observe my visitors. If she sensed the person was a threat, she'd growl or take further action. When there was no threat, Maggie watched the person and refrained from greeting them until I allowed it.

Cole led me to the black Mercedes-Benz sedan in my driveway and opened my door, shutting it when I was inside. He pulled out of my driveway a minute later and drove toward the restaurant, a jazz station playing on the radio. Cole turned the volume down and adjusted the air-conditioning. I could smell his cologne as I sat next to him, the scent floral and spicy. It was pleasant but didn't have a sensual undertone like Shane's. I hung my head. Why was Shane in my thoughts? Was it because of the discussion I'd had with Ross this afternoon? Regardless, I needed to get him out of my mind.

Cole escorted me into the restaurant after leaving his car with the valet. As we walked next to each other, I couldn't help but notice his height. I stood a good three inches taller than him with my one-inch heels. I hadn't had that happen before, and it made me uncomfortable. Alex and Shane were both tall men, which I preferred.

"Sir, do you have a reservation?" a middle-aged man dressed in a black suit addressed Cole from the reservation desk.

"I do. It's under Cole Payson."

"Ah, yes. I see it here. Please follow me." The man led us across a cozy dining room decorated in darker earth tones with soft ambient lighting coming from ornate wall sconces. He stopped at a table for two near the middle of the restaurant. "Here we are."

"This won't work." Cole frowned as he eyed the table next to us.

"Sir? Is there a problem?"

"You'll have to seat us somewhere else. There's a child next to us. I came here to have a nice dinner, and I don't want a noisy child to ruin my evening."

I scanned the table next to us. A couple was sitting there, a girl of seven or eight years old with them. The little girl looked perfectly behaved. I was a bit embarrassed when the woman stared at me, a look of irritation on her face. I mouthed I was sorry and turned away, unhappy with Cole's request. In my mind, it was completely unnecessary.

"Of course, sir. I'll seat you at another table." The man guided us to a quiet table across the restaurant. It was in the corner, next to a window, with an older couple seated near us.

"This is better. Thank you." Cole assisted me with my chair before taking the seat across from me.

"Here are your menus. Your waiter will be with you momentarily." The man handed me a menu and then gave one to Cole.

A young woman was immediately at our table, filling our water glasses.

"I don't understand why people bring children to a fine dining establishment. It irks me when I see that." Cole spread his napkin on his lap as he talked. He took a sip of his water.

"Do you have children?"

"None that I know of, and at this point, I'm enjoying my life too much to have any."

"Good evening. My name is Bernard, and I'll be taking care of you this evening. Did you have any questions about the menu?" A very proper-looking older man was standing next to Cole. He stood there waiting as Cole browsed the wine list.

"No questions. I'd like the Domaine Leroy Chambertin Grand Cru." Cole pointed to an item on the wine list as he ordered.

"Ah. Excellent selection. I'll be right back with your wine, sir."

"He didn't ask me what I wanted. That's odd." I looked down at the wine list, hoping to order a chardonnay.

"I ordered a bottle of French wine. So, Mel tells me you two vacationed in Turks and Caicos. Do you travel often?"

"We only started traveling together a year and a half ago, so we've only been to Mexico, Aruba, and Turks and Caicos."

"Your wine, sir." Bernard opened the wine bottle and poured a small amount into Cole's glass. He waited while Cole swirled the liquid and then smelled it, followed by a sip of the wine.

"Perfect. Thank you." Cole set his glass down, and Bernard filled both our glasses.

"Are you ready to order, sir?"

"Yes. We'll have the five-course tasting menu." Cole folded his menu and handed it to Bernard.

"Miss. Your menu, please."

I sat there confused for a moment, looking down at my menu. I'd never gotten to order. Cole had taken it upon himself to do it for me once again, and I didn't particularly like it. I handed Bernard my menu and took a sip of my wine.

"You should go to Europe. My two favorite cities are Vienna and Prague. I took my ex-girlfriend to Prague last year, and we had a fabulous time. We even went truffle hunting. I'd never done that before."

"That sounds different. Did you like it?"

"For the most part. But I didn't realize the truffle hunter used a dog. That took some of the pleasure out of it for me."

"I take it you don't like dogs?"

"Not especially. I can't say that I've ever wanted one. My ex-girlfriend had a little terrier. I hated that thing. The hair, the smell, and the barking were too much. I made her get rid of it."

That was it. Cole had failed, and he'd done it big. He didn't like children, he didn't like dogs, and I couldn't even order my meal. He was opinionated and overbearing, and far from the guy for me. I was too independent to put up with someone trying to control me. Alex had loved me deeply, had made me feel safe and secure, and had always been there for support. One thing he'd never done was tell me what to do. He might have made suggestions and tried to guide me, especially since I'd been so young when we'd gotten together, but he'd always let me make my own decision.

Bernard returned and placed a beautifully decorated plate in front of me. "We will start with amuse-bouche. Tonight we have yogurt fouetté."

I glanced across the table at Cole, my eyebrow slightly raised. I had no idea what was on the plate, although it looked too pretty to eat.

"For lack of a better description, it's a whipped yogurt. Amuse-bouches are bite-sized precourse appetizers. They're usually savory and packed full of interesting flavors."

I took a nibble of the yellowish yogurt molded into a flat, circular shape in the middle of my dish. "I like it. It has an interesting flavor. So, tell me about yourself. Mel didn't tell me much about you other than you live in Del Mar, and her company is doing a remodel on your house."

"Well, let's see. I own a corporation, Payson LLC. I deal in real estate with our current holdings consisting of industrial, retail, and residential properties, and I recently added two high-end boutique hotels to our balance sheet. I like to travel and entertain, which leaves no time for hobbies. Although I do like to take an early swim in the mornings to start my day."

"What would you describe as your perfect evening?"

"Wow. You're picking my brain here. I guess it would be an elegant evening out with a beautiful woman. Someone like you. You are stunning, Liz. The real you is far more beautiful than your picture, and the picture I saw of you was gorgeous."

"Thank you. I appreciate the compliment. So, no quiet romantic evenings at home for you? A glass of wine in front of the fireplace or making a special homecooked dinner for a lovely lady?"

"Unfortunately, no." Cole laughed and took a sip of his wine. "I'm not a homebody."

Cole struck out for the fourth time. He was a wealthy jet-setter who didn't have time for the small stuff or enjoy the ordinary things in life. Cole was far different from me. At this point, I was clueless as to why Mel thought we'd be a perfect match. "So, tell me about your travels. I have a huge bucket list I'm hoping to complete someday."

"As I alluded to earlier, Europe is my favorite."

I listened to Cole as he talked. Bernard occasionally interrupted his stories while he brought course after course to the table, each plate a small artwork unto itself. Cole was a handsome man. His teeth were perfect and brilliantly white, and his eyes a sparkling green. There was a touch of silver at his temples, so I suspected he was older than I'd initially thought. Besides the smattering of gray, his hair was mahogany brown, short, and neatly styled. He looked like he could be on the cover of *GQ* magazine, his looks and physique up there with the best of them.

After two hours of casual conversation, we finally finished dinner. I was both stuffed and tired. I'd had a long day before the date started and was ready to go home. I stood when Cole helped me with my chair, and we walked outside, waiting at the curb for the valet to bring his car around. Cole drove me home.

"I'll walk you to your door." His hand on my back, Cole escorted me across my driveway and down my plant-filled walkway to my front door.

After retrieving my keys from my clutch purse, I stood under the porchlight and unlocked my door. I turned back toward Cole. "Thank you for dinner. I had a lovely evening."

"You aren't going to invite me inside for a relaxing after-dinner glass of wine in front of the fireplace like you mentioned during dinner?" Cole gave me a suggestive smile, the whiteness of his teeth noticeable in the darkness.

"I'm sorry. I had a long day before our date, and I'm a bit tired."

"All right. Next time, then." Cole took a step forward and leaned in to kiss me.

I turned my face to give him my cheek, but his lips were on mine instead. The kiss started innocent enough but quickly changed. Arms pulled me against him, a tongue forcing its way into my mouth. Shocked, I pulled away.

"I apologize. I shouldn't have been so forward."

"No, you shouldn't have," my voice snapped as I wiped my mouth with the back of my hand. "I'm going to call it a night. Thank you for dinner." Shaken, I opened my door and stepped inside.

"Look, I apologized. Let's start over. One drink, and then I'll leave." Cole stepped across the threshold as I started to shut the door, his body blocking it from closing.

Immensely uncomfortable and feeling threatened, I wasn't sure what to do. Did I push Cole out the door? Did I try to talk him into acting like a gentleman and leaving? Would he back down or become even more forceful if he was used to getting his way? I didn't know what his personality was like, so I couldn't gauge how he'd react. Catching a movement to my left, I turned, spotting Maggie creeping toward Cole.

A low growl filled the air.

"Shit. You have a dog, and it looks like it's stalking me. It's showing its teeth and growling. You need to control that thing."

"Maggie's quite sweet unless I forget to feed her dinner, which I must have done tonight. She's also well trained. I taught her to attack when commanded. Would you like a demonstration?"

"You know. I believe you're right. We should call it a night." Cole nervously backed out of my house, hastily closing my front door when he was on the porch.

The sound of his car starting pierced the silence a minute later.

Relieved, I dropped to my knees in front of Maggie and hugged her, my hands petting her coat. "You are such a good girl, Maggie. You take care of momma, don't you." I kissed her head and scratched her chest. "Okay, girl. Let's get ready for bed. Come on."

Maggie followed me into my bedroom and lay down next to my bed. She was my security blanket and protector. I'd never needed her help like that before, and I hoped I never did again.

CHAPTER 8

CONFESSIONS

I SAT IN bed, staring at the stone fireplace across from me, a stack of plumped-up pillows wedged between my back and the headboard. I'd tossed and turned throughout the night, and now sunlight was starting to stream through the row of windows above my bed. I'd been unable to sleep, the incident with Cole still bothering me. I'd never had anyone treat me so aggressively, although my experience in the relationship department was minimal other than with Alex.

I shook my head at the irony of it all. Cole had wanted me, and I'd felt utterly disinterested. Yet I'd fallen head over heels for Shane, and he'd walked away, our argument on the beach that night like a painful wound that I couldn't heal. It was a recurring theme, the people I loved leaving me. My maternal grandparents had died when I was a toddler, and friction between my father and his parents had caused them to ignore me. Now that my paternal grandparents were gone, my existence felt as if it meant nothing to them. My mother had died when I was twelve, and my father had abandoned me in his grief. He'd died eight years ago, our relationship a mere shell of what it could have been. Then I'd lost Alex, and that was the deepest wound of all. He was everything to me, lighting up the darkness in my life. When I'd thought there could be no more pain, Shane had left me.

Saddened by my thoughts, I lay back down, pulling the bedcovers up to my neck. I was tired and needed to sleep. Just as I started to relax, my cell phone rang. Frustrated, I grabbed it from the nightstand and stared at the screen. I didn't recognize the number. Curious who would be calling me this early on a Saturday morning, I answered it. "Hello."

"Liz, it's Shane. I'm sure you want to, but please don't hang up on me."

I could feel my heart beating in my chest as soon as I heard his voice, his Irish accent warming me like a cozy fire on a chilly day. Taken entirely by surprise, I wasn't sure what to say. After a long pause, I managed to whisper, "I wasn't going to."

"Thank you. I've wanted to call you so many times, and I couldn't stand it anymore. I had to talk to you. The way we ended our last night together was horrible, and I'm sorry. I was angry and hurt, and I confronted you, never giving you a real chance to explain. It wasn't right. You said that night that believing Anna wasn't a smart move on my part, and I've never been able to get your words out of my head. Of course, it didn't help when Caitlin called me a bloody eejit to believe her and a fool to let you go." There was a pause, and then Shane sighed on the other end of the phone. "What I need to say is that I fell in love with you when we were in Providenciales, and I still feel that way about you. So, I have to know. Are you married to a man by the name of

Alexander Whalen?"

"Yes, I married Alex, so part of what Anna told you was true. What she didn't tell you is I'm a widow. Alex died in an accident three years ago." My voice sounded strained as I talked, our conversation becoming painfully emotional. It would be difficult to discuss, but now was the time to explain it to Shane.

"Liz, I'm so sorry." Shane's voice was full of agony. "I...I can't even put into words how horrible I feel. Nothing I could say right now would ever make up for what I did. Please forgive me."

"I forgive you," I whispered, my eyes becoming moist. "I have to because Anna played us both, and I was just as angry and upset as you were. My pride wouldn't let me explain it to you, especially since I didn't think you deserved to hear it. But I want to clear the air because I fell in love with you too." I gave a halfhearted laugh as I smiled ever so slightly into the phone. "Although I tried my damnedest not to."

"Christ, I can't tell you how much it means to me to hear you say that. And I agree. Anna played us. She tried to drive a wedge between us, and it worked. At least until now. Liz, if you don't mind, may I ask what happened to your husband?"

"It was a motorcycle accident." I shut my eyes as I reflected on that horrifying day. "We were on a getaway with friends. I drove my car that weekend rather than ride the motorcycle with Alex since I had brought all the beer and food. On the way home, we stopped for one last beer at a roadside bar." I paused for a minute, placing my palm over my eyes as I lay there in my bed, trying desperately not to cry.

Shane stayed silent on the other end of the phone as he waited for me to continue.

"I…umm…I left the place first. Alex and one of our friends rode out a few minutes later and passed me up a couple of miles down the highway. Alex rounded a blind curve on the winding two-lane country road and came upon a truck and trailer stopped in front of him. The driver was waiting for an oncoming car to pass before turning left onto a dirt trail. Alex saw the truck and trailer, hit his brakes, and managed to stop. His friend came around the curve and couldn't stop in time. He slammed into the back of Alex, catapulting him off the motorcycle and into the path of the oncoming car. He died instantly." I tried to brush away the tears streaming down my cheeks and held my breath, doing my best to suppress a sob. Laying my phone on my chest, I covered my face with my hands. Getting my emotions under a semblance of control, I put my phone back to my ear. "I'm sorry. I…umm…I reached the scene right after it happened and saw Alex lying on the road. I don't remember much after that."

"I don't even know what to say." Shane's voice was soft and comforting. "God, I wish I was there to hold you."

"I wish you were too." I sniffled as my tears continued to fall.

"I want to see you. I'm going out of town for a while in a couple of weeks, so I can't take any additional time off work until I get back. If it works out for you, can I fly out there for a couple of days at the end of May?"

"I'd like that."

"Thank you. I want to hold you and pick up where we left off before the interruption. I know it's still early in California, and I have an appointment in an hour, so do you mind if I call you again this afternoon? That way, we can talk some more and work out the details of my visit."

"That would be nice. I'll be here."

"Wonderful. I'll call you this afternoon."

"Okay. I'll talk to you then. Bye." I hung up my phone and stared at the ceiling, trying to put myself back together. As uncomfortable as our conversation had been, an enormous sense of relief filled me. The weight of the last two months lifted from my chest. As I lay there, I reflected on what Shane had said. Caitlin had not only given me the benefit of the doubt and defended me, but she'd also nudged Shane into contacting me. I needed to thank her and let her know we had worked it out. I retrieved the business card Caitlin had given me from my nightstand drawer and dialed the number on it. The time in Ireland was ahead by eight hours, so I assumed she'd be there.

"Burke House Hotel. This is Fiona. How may I assist you?"

"Hi, I was trying to reach Caitlin Burke."

"May I ask who is calling?"

"Yes. My name is Liz Whalen. I met Caitlin in Turks and Caicos a few months ago and hoped to speak with her."

"One moment, please. I'll see if she's available."

"Thank you." I was only on hold for a few seconds

when someone came on the line.

"Liz? Is that really you?"

"Caitlin? Yes, it's me. It's Liz."

"Jesus, Mary, and Joseph. I'm glad to hear from you. Did Shane call you?"

"Yes, we just got off the phone. That's why I'm calling. I wanted to thank you. It sounds like you gave Shane that extra little push to contact me."

"I did. It was obvious how the two of you felt about each other, and I knew what happened had to be a misunderstanding."

"It was, and we were able to work it out. Anna gave him part of the story, but not all of it. I was married, but my husband died three years ago. I'm a widow."

"Oh, Liz. I'm sorry to hear that. But I knew you weren't the type of person to play games and have an affair. That's not your personality. I have to say, I'm thrilled you and Shane worked it out. You're good for him, and I know he loves you."

There was silence on the other end of the line. "Caitlin, are you still there?"

"Can you come to Ireland? Shane will be here for his birthday in three weeks. You could surprise him. I know it's short notice and sounds a wee bit on the crazy side, but is there any chance you can be here? It would be the best birthday he's ever had, and we'd love to see you."

"I don't know. I'll have to think about it. So, when is Shane's birthday?"

"It's May ninth. Please try to come. I think surprising him would be worth the trip. I'm sorry. I have a problem at the front desk that I have to take care of right now, so I can't stay on the phone. Call me back when you get a chance and let me know if you're able to come."

"I promise I'll get back to you."

"Thank you. I'll talk to you soon. Bye."

"Goodbye."

I hung up my phone and lay there in bed. It was turning out to be an unexpectedly eventful and crazy morning. I thought about Caitlin's request. It sounded like it would be fun, and I did have vacation time on the books at work. I made my decision. I was going to fly to Ireland. It was still too early to call Mel, so I sent her a text message instead, asking if she wanted to go to Ireland with me. My phone started ringing as soon as I set it down on the nightstand. I picked it back up and looked at the screen, surprised when I saw it was Mel. "Good morning. Why are you up so early?"

"I just got home."

"Excuse me? From where?"

"I went out last night." Mel sounded tired. She paused for a moment to let out a huge yawn. "Oops. Sorry about that. I went home with a guy I met at a club. His name was Blake or Jake. I'm not sure which one it was."

"Whoa. You don't even know the guy's name?" I did a face-plant into my palm. I'd known Mel most of my life, and she still managed to surprise me.

"I knew his name last night. I forgot it, but it doesn't matter. He was a jerk, so I don't care. I got what I wanted, and I don't plan to see him again." Mel let out another yawn, this one more pronounced than the last.

"Sorry. I'm a little tired. Anyway, I got your message. When are you planning to go to Ireland? I assume it has something to do with Shane, although you did part on bad terms."

"We did, but he called me unexpectedly this morning, and we worked it out. He's planning to come out here to see me at the end of next month. Anyway, to cut a long story short, I called Caitlin to thank her for nudging Shane to contact me, and she informed me he's going to Ireland to celebrate his birthday. She wants me to come there and surprise him. His birthday is May ninth."

"May ninth? Dang. That's in three weeks. That's nuts."

"I know, but that's when he'll be there. I told Caitlin I wasn't sure if I'd go, but I want to see Shane."

"Hmm. It's pretty short notice, but why not? I still have a week of vacation, and my boss pissed me off. If he gets mad, I don't care. I've got another construction company trying to get me to come work for them, and I'm considering it."

"What's going on with your job?"

"The boss keeps giving me all the shitty projects that no one else wants. Hang on a minute. I just remembered about your date. What happened with Cole last night? He's a hot-looking guy, don't you think?"

"More like unpredictable. The date started nice enough. But it went south pretty quickly and ended badly. Cole doesn't like children, and he hates dogs. He's controlling and used to getting his way and tried to force himself on me when he took me home. Maggie had to rescue me."

"No. You didn't sic Maggie on him, did you?"

"I didn't have to. Maggie took him as a threat, growling and showing her teeth after she stalked him. I told Cole I had trained her to attack when commanded and asked if he wanted a demonstration. He left right after that. So, why did you think we were even compatible? We couldn't be more opposite."

"Well, it wasn't that I thought you were compatible. I thought you might like Cole since he's so good-looking and has tons of money. I remember you saying a long time ago that you longed for the feeling of safety, security, and comfort that Alex used to give you. I thought Cole could do that with his money."

"Oh my God, Mel. Those are things someone makes you feel deep down inside. You can't buy those. Cole's money may allow him to hire security personnel and live behind secure walls, but he wouldn't personally make me feel safe and secure or comforted. Alex was such a strong and commanding person. He was intelligent and street-smart but also tender and gentle, and I always felt protected when I was with him. I also knew he'd comfort me when I needed a shoulder to cry on or a word of support. There's an enormous difference between what money can buy and how a person makes you feel."

"Yeah, okay. I get it, but it doesn't matter anyway since it sounds like you and Shane are finally getting together." Mel paused, letting out another yawn. "I'm going to have to let you go. I need to take a nap. I have a date tonight."

"Another date? Who this time?"

"Some guy I met at my gym. I'm supposed to meet

him at a restaurant downtown for an early dinner at five o'clock."

"All right. I'll call you tomorrow."

"Sounds good. Bye."

"Bye." I hung up my phone and tossed it on the bed. That was an interesting conversation on a multitude of fronts. Mel could be so careless, especially sleeping around with all these guys. She needed to be careful.

SWEATY FROM MY jog, I walked Maggie up my driveway toward the garage. It was now late afternoon, and after my restless night, I was looking forward to a quiet evening at home doing nothing but relaxing on the couch. I stopped at the patio gate on the side of my home, its entry off the concrete drive. The secluded space was an inner courtyard, my house wrapping around it in a sideways U-shape. A place of comfort, it was my private retreat and favorite place to read an enjoyable book. I led Maggie through the courtyard and into the house through the unlocked sliding door. She took off, trotting down the main hallway toward the family room, the slap of the doggie door hitting the frame alerting me that she had gone into the backyard.

After showering and feeding Maggie, I headed into the kitchen to make myself a salad for dinner. I was about to sit down and eat when my doorbell rang. Expecting no one, I peeked out the long, narrow window in my entryway. Surprised to see Mel, I opened my front door. "What are you doing here? I thought you had a dinner date."

"I did, but the guy stood me up. I figured I'd come over here and drown my sorrows." Mel came into the house. She looked frustrated and had a distinct pout on her lips.

"I was just sitting down with a salad and glass of wine. You might as well join me."

Maggie was sitting quietly by the front door. Now she trailed behind us as we went into the kitchen, lying down on the rug in the family room where she could watch Mel.

"I'm amazed every time I see Maggie behave like that. My sister's dog jumps all over me and drives me nuts. I love her dog, but it obviously needs some training."

"Training does help. Maggie leaves everyone alone unless she senses they're a threat or I command her to act. Cole can certainly attest to that."

"Oh, he sure can. Too bad I can't train guys to do that." Mel gave a little snort. "No speaking until spoken to and having to follow all my commands. I'd have a blast." Mel finished making her salad and sat at the kitchen counter to eat.

I walked over to the cupboard and grabbed a glass, holding it out in front of me. "Do you want some wine?"

"I might as well. I finished off your bottle of rum last time I was here."

"So, what happened to your date?" I sat next to Mel at the counter and poured her a glass of wine.

"He didn't show up. I was supposed to meet him in the lobby of the Bayou Grill downtown." Mel took a bite of her salad. "This is hitting the spot. I haven't eaten anything since this morning."

"The guy didn't call you or anything?"

"Nope. He was a no-show." Mel took a sip of her wine and another bite of her salad. "I called him after waiting for twenty minutes, and he said he got busy. I could hear a woman in the background next to him. She was breathing heavily, and so was he. It sounded like I interrupted them. He cut the phone call short and hung up."

"The guy sounds like a complete jerk. But so did the guy from your date last weekend and the one from your date before that. Why do you keep doing this?"

"Why do I keep doing what? What are you talking about?" Mel put down her fork and turned to look at me.

"Dammit, Mel. You keep going out with losers. You don't seem to care who they are, and some of these guys are real sleazebags. You have one-night stands and kick the guy to the curb afterward. Don't you have any respect for yourself?" I was aware coming down on Mel like that wasn't the best move, but I was so tired of seeing a never-ending succession of men use and disrespect her. It was time to speak my mind.

"I have respect for myself, and what I do is none of your damn business." Mel was shouting at me, and her face was beet red.

"It is my business because I'm the one witnessing these guys hurt you. I care about you and don't understand why you keep letting it happen." I wasn't sure if Mel's vehement outburst was because I'd called her out or because her date had ditched her for another woman and it hurt her. Either way, we needed to air this out. Mel's personality had changed, and her behavior had gotten entirely out of control since her divorce. I didn't understand why, but it needed to stop.

"I do it because I have to." Mel jumped off the barstool and glared at me, her fists clenched. "I'll be damned if I'll get into another relationship and have my heart ripped out of my chest and stomped on until it's in a million shattered pieces. It almost destroyed me last time, and I won't let it happen to me again." Mel stopped yelling, and like the flip of a switch, she was suddenly silent. The look on her face was heartbreaking. She seemed lost and completely vulnerable.

"Dammit, Mel. What are you talking about?" Confused, I stared at her as she stood there.

Mel leaned against the kitchen counter, burying her face in her hands.

I got up and put my arm around her, guiding her to the family room. I had her sit on the couch. Then I went back into the kitchen, returning a minute later with a bottle of tequila and two shot glasses. I sat next to Mel and filled the glasses. After I handed one to her and kept the other for myself, we downed the tequila. Finished, I set the glasses on the coffee table and turned toward Mel. "Tell me what happened."

"When I told you four years ago that Mark and I were divorcing, I never told you the truth as to why. I led you to believe we had grown apart, and I didn't love him anymore. But that was a lie. I was too embarrassed to tell you what happened." Mel looked down at her lap, her voice shaky as she talked.

"I remember you told me the divorce was a mutual decision, and it was best for the two of you to split up. Although I always thought it strange that it happened so fast. I didn't even know you and Mark were having problems."

"What I told you was only a sliver of the truth. We weren't having any problems, at least not any major ones. I caught Mark cheating. When I say cheating, I don't mean I found out he had a girlfriend. I mean, I walked in on him screwing some bitch in my house, in my bed." A tear was falling down Mel's cheek.

"I'm listening. Go on." I hurt for Mel. She never cried. I put my arm around her and had her lean her head on my shoulder.

"I was visiting my sister and came home early. I didn't tell Mark I was coming home. I didn't think it mattered." She took a deep breath and slowly let it out. "I came into the house, and it was quiet. Then I heard voices from my bedroom. Walking down the hallway, I heard groaning and heavy breathing mixed with the voices. I felt sick, my stomach completely in knots. I stopped in the doorway of my room, in shock at what was going on in front of me. A woman I'd never seen before was on top of Mark. She was riding him, and they were going at it like two rabbits. The woman saw me standing in the doorway and smiled while she kept riding him. It was like she wanted me to see her enjoying my husband. I can still hear her saying, 'Look, Mark. We have company. Should we let her watch?' Then she laughed as Mark turned and saw me in the doorway."

"I'm so sorry." I was beyond shocked. My heart was breaking for her, and I didn't know what else to say.

Mel sat up and grabbed the tequila bottle. She poured a shot and downed it. After pouring another, Mel drank it more slowly this time and then sat the glass back down. She leaned back against my shoulder and took another deep breath. "I remember screaming at them both. I was hysterical. Mark jumped off the bed and grabbed my arm, dragging me into the living room. He told me I was causing a scene and needed to leave. Do you believe that? It was my home, and he was my husband, and he let her stay and told me to leave. He grabbed my purse and car keys, shoved them in my hand, and pushed me out the front door."

"What happened after that?" I leaned my head against Mel's and squeezed her hand.

"I tried to drive away but didn't get more than a block before losing it. I remember shaking uncontrollably, and it was hard for me to breathe or talk because I was gasping for air. I called some friends, a married couple we knew, and they had to get me." Mel sniffled and tucked a strand of hair behind her ear. "I was such an emotional wreck. I don't think I can fully explain what it felt like, other than the sensation of having my heart ripped from my chest. The anguish and devastation were so physical; I remember throwing up." Sitting up, Mel poured both of us another shot. Then she turned to me with cold eyes and a curled lip. "I swear. I'll never let anyone do this to me again. I date guys that mean nothing to me because I know it won't lead anywhere. Loving someone hurts too much." Mel's voice sounded deep, almost guttural, as she talked.

"Mel. If Mark could do something like that to you, he wasn't a decent person from the start. He didn't love you. A loving, respectable man wouldn't do that to you. These guys you keep dating don't care about you or respect you. They only want one thing from you. What you're doing isn't helping you. It's doing the opposite." I needed Mel to understand that her method to keep from getting hurt was making her life worse. She'd never find real peace or happiness this way.

"Such sound advice from someone who can't manage her own love life. Don't you think?" Mel gave me a mocking smile.

"Excuse me?" I stared at Mel, her comment startling me.

"You had Shane at your fingertips and lost him. All because your pride wouldn't let you answer a simple question."

"It wasn't a simple question. It was a demand for an answer and believing a conniving and untrustworthy person over me."

"Either way, two months later, you still hadn't fixed it, and it took Caitlin to intervene on your behalf. So, how's that for confronting a problem head-on and managing your love life?"

"Okay, I'm not the best example. But all I'm trying to do is help you. If I didn't care about you, I wouldn't bother."

Mel let out a long sigh and leaned back against the couch. "This is stupid—our arguing over guys. Neither one of us is perfect. You just screw up a lot less than I do." Mel shook her head, a snide smile on her face. "I'd swear Cupid has a messed-up sense of humor and aimed for our asses instead of our hearts." She picked up her shot glass and handed me the other one. Then she lifted hers for a toast. "To Cupid's arrow. Now that it's found your correct body part, may it someday hit mine." We tossed back the tequila. It was going to be a long night.

CHAPTER 9

A STEAMY IRISH NIGHT

M EL AND I were in Kilkenny, Ireland, having arrived here by train late this morning. We'd spent our first two nights on the Emerald Isle in Dublin since Mel had insisted on experiencing some of the city's nightlife. Now that she'd had her fun, it was time to surprise Shane for his birthday, which was why I had come. We'd spent the afternoon exploring the medieval city, built on the banks of a river, and were now finishing dinner in the dining room at Caitlin and Patrick's hotel.

Caitlin hurried toward our table, an air of excitement about her. "Shane just got here from my parents' estate in Kilcullen. He's heading to the bar with Patrick to get a beer, and then Patrick will suggest they go out on the patio. That way, you'll have more privacy when you surprise him."

"Oh, I can't wait for this." Mel pushed her empty dinner plate to the side and laid her scrunched-up napkin next to it. She suddenly cocked her head at me. "Are you nervous? You don't look so great."

Was I nervous? That was an understatement. I couldn't wait to see Shane, but a piece of me feared he might not like my surprise. We'd spoken on the phone numerous times over the last three weeks, and as difficult as it had been, I'd kept my trip to Ireland a secret. Now I hoped he wouldn't be upset that I hadn't told him. I took a deep breath and slowly exhaled. "Honestly, my stomach is doing somersaults. Talking to him on the phone is one thing. Getting to see him is another." I looked at Caitlin. "Shane has no clue I'm here in Ireland, right?"

"Not a one. We've kept it quiet as can be. Shane thinks we had him come down here to Kilkenny to see a school performance for my daughter, Glenna."

"Let's go, Liz. I'll keep that adorable bartender busy while you surprise Shane." Mel got up from the table and led the three of us to the bar.

"Liam, did Patrick and Shane go outside?" Caitlin said, addressing her bartender.

"Yes, they did." Liam smiled at Mel as she slipped onto the barstool in front of him.

"All right then, let's go take a peek." Caitlin took hold of my arm and led me through a doorway to the small dining room used for the breakfast buffet. She walked me past several tables and then over to a panel of windows and a glass door that faced the patio.

I made a little sound as soon as I spotted Shane, my hand instantly covering my mouth. I stood there devouring every inch of him as he sat at one of the tables with his back to me. The muscles on his shoulder blade flexed through his shirt as he lifted his arm and took a sip of beer from his glass. He set the dark liquid back on the table and ran his hand through his hair. It was much shorter than I remembered. The sides had been closely clipped, and the little wisps that had curled around his ears were gone.

"Why are you hesitating? Go on. Go out there." Caitlin gave me a lighthearted push toward the door.

"I will. I just want to look at Shane for a minute." My voice was low, almost breathless, and I couldn't take my eyes off him. Seeing him here, in front of me, knowing I could reach out and touch him, filled me with longing. Shane laughed at something Patrick said, and I wanted to see the smile on his face. I took several steps toward the door, suddenly gaining Patrick's attention.

Shane glanced over his shoulder toward the door and then froze in place. His eyes grew wide as the realization that I was standing there seemed to strike him. He slowly stood and turned to face me, his body rigid, his gaze fixed on me. Then Shane's expression appeared to change from disbelief to one of love and yearning.

With a lump in my throat, I grabbed the handle on the glass door, catching a glimpse of Patrick as he silently exited the patio through a side gate. Trying desperately to control my emotions, I pushed it open and stepped across the threshold. Then I lost it and broke into a run, launching myself into Shane's arms as he took several steps toward me.

Shane held me. His arms wrapped tightly around me, his head pressed against mine. "I can't believe you're here. God, how I've missed you."

"I've missed you too." I nestled my face into his neck, breathing his heady scent that I so lovingly remembered.

He pulled away, his eyes searching my face. "We've

talked so many times. Why didn't you tell me you were coming to Ireland?"

"It was supposed to be a birthday surprise. I hope you're not upset at my coming here."

"How can I be? You're the best birthday present I've ever had." Shane put a finger under my chin and tilted my face upward. Then, without saying another word, he leaned forward and tenderly kissed me.

I slid my arms around his neck, my body pressed tightly against him, as his tongue softly explored mine. I wanted to melt in his arms, his taste, touch, and scent mirroring the dreams I had of him night after night.

Shane pressed his forehead against mine and closed his eyes. Then he wrapped me in his arms once again. "I don't want to let go of you."

"And I don't want you to. But I suppose you'll have to eventually."

Shane laughed and kissed my forehead. "I suppose so. Come and sit at the table with me. I want to hear how this all came about." Shane guided me to a bench and sat down, his back leaning against the table behind him. He put his arm around me when I joined him. "So, what prompted this secret trip of yours?"

"I contacted Caitlin after you called me that morning to talk and clear the air. I wanted to thank her for intervening on my behalf. That's when she told me your birthday was coming up and you'd be here to celebrate it. It was her idea to come and surprise you."

"It seems I owe her another thank-you." Shane pulled me close. "I still can't believe you're here. The school performance must have been a ruse to get me down here. Am I right?"

"You are. Caitlin was sure you'd come without question if she said it was for Glenna."

Mel poked her head out the glass door and cleared her throat. "Now that you've had a chance to kiss and catch up, can we go to a pub and party? We are in Ireland, you know. We should be drinking right now."

Shane raised a brow at me, his arm still wrapped around my shoulder.

"Mel doesn't give up. We can go out somewhere for a beer and some music or listen to her pester us all night. I vote the three of us go out for a beer, so she'll stop."

"I agree. We can go out for a little while to satisfy Mel's need and then come back here so I can show you how much I missed you." Shane pushed some wayward strands of hair from my face and kissed me, his lips softly brushing mine.

"Well? Are we going out or not?" Mel came outside and walked toward our table.

"Yes, we're going out." Shane stood and pulled me to my feet. "There's a pub down the street that has live music. It's a small place but fun. Let me thank Caitlin for her hand in getting the two of you here and let her know we're going out. I'll meet you in the lobby." Shane walked away, disappearing through the glass door and into the bar.

"I take it everything is good between you two, and he'll be staying with you tonight?" Mel gave me a knowing look, a snicker escaping her.

"Yes, everything is fine. Shane's pleased with my surprise." I could sense my cheeks getting warm as Mel stared at me. "You need to knock it off. You're enjoying this way too much. I'm going upstairs to grab a sweater and my purse. I'll meet you in the lobby in a couple of minutes." I hurried inside and headed toward the elevator. I was already getting nervous at the prospect of Shane staying with me tonight. Quickly retrieving the items from my room, I joined Mel in the lobby, spotting her sitting in a yellow upholstered chair in the corner. "Where's Shane?"

"I haven't seen him yet."

Shane came rushing through the front door. "Sorry about that. I needed to pick something up from the pharmacy down the street before they closed." He hurried over to me and gave me a quick kiss.

"Really? What did you have to pick up?" Mel had an amused look on her face as she eyed Shane.

"Do I need to explain?" Shane frowned at Mel as he slipped his arm around my waist.

Mel started giggling. "No, I got it, and I have a box of condoms in my purse if you run out." Mel laughed as she jumped up from the chair and hurried out the door.

I hung my head, my cheeks burning. Mel was incorrigible.

The three of us crossed the street midblock and walked down the hill to the intersection. A cozy-looking pub sat on the corner across from us. Music and laughter streamed from the building each time the door opened.

"This is it." Shane led us across the narrow side street.

We entered the pub, finding two musicians sitting on barstools in front of us. One of them was older and white-haired, while the other man was much younger. They were entertaining a lively crowd. We stood there, looking around for empty seats. Finally, a man sitting at a table in front of the window motioned to Shane. He told us to take their chairs as his group was leaving. Taking the table, Shane and I sat with our back to the front window. Mel sat across from me.

"Where are you from, darlin'?" the older white-haired musician called out to Mel.

"We're from San Diego," Mel boisterously shouted back to the man.

"Welcome to Kilkenny." The man turned to the room full of patrons. "Folks, it looks like we have some people here from the United States." The man looked back at Mel with a grin on his face. "Darlin', I've got a song for you." He and the younger black-haired musician started playing an old country-western song.

Mel laughed, enjoying the attention and entertainment.

"Three Guinness, please," Shane said to the server when she approached our table. He paid for the beers when she returned and set our glasses down.

"Shane, what's the craic?" A tall, broad-shouldered man with red hair and emerald-green eyes came to our table.

Shane jumped up from his chair and shook the man's hand. "Conor, it's great to see you." He motioned to the empty chair next to Mel. "Why don't you join us. This is Liz and her friend, Mel."

"Nice to meet you both." Conor sat in the chair, giving a quick nod to Mel and me.

"It's a pleasure to meet you too," I said.

"You must be from around here," Mel said, her eyes raking Conor up and down.

Conor smiled at her. "I am. I moved here two years ago. Shane and I grew up together in Kilcullen. We've known each other since we were boys." He leaned across the table toward Shane. "I finally opened up a whiskey distillery. It's down on Bateman Quay."

"That's great. Congratulations," Shane said.

The two musicians started singing an Irish ditty. It was a catchy tune about a drunken man and his unfaithful wife. Conor hooted, and then he started singing. He looked at Shane, encouraging him to join in. Mel and I started laughing as Shane joined him, the two of them having fun with the song.

The musicians stopped playing, and the white-haired man glanced at Shane and Conor. Then he addressed the crowd. "Folks, it looks like these two gentlemen know the song. Why don't we have them get up and sing it to us?"

The patrons in the pub clapped and shouted encouragement as Shane sat there, shaking his head. Conor looked ready for the challenge. He got up from his chair and walked over to the two musicians. The three of them stood there, waiting for Shane. After a little more prodding from the crowd, Shane joined them. The musicians played their guitars, and Shane and Conor started singing. In no time at all, the patrons were roaring. The song finished, and Shane and Conor took a bow before leaving the floor.

"That was funny." Mel looked at Conor as he retook his seat.

"You should have joined us. You could have sung the chorus." Conor eyed the empty beer glass in front of Mel. "Can I get you another Guinness?"

"That would be great. Thanks."

Conor motioned the server to our table. "Two Guinness, please." He looked across the table at Shane and me. "Are either of you ready for another one?"

Shane shook his head. "No, I'm good. I'm ready to head back to the hotel if Liz is." He glanced over his shoulder at me. "What do you think?"

"I'm ready."

Shane turned to Conor. "We're going to call it a night."

"Liz, I'm going to hang out here for a while if Conor doesn't mind keeping me company." Mel turned toward Conor, raising a brow at him.

"I don't mind at all. I'd enjoy your company." Conor gave Mel a sweet smile and then turned toward Shane. "I'll make sure she gets back to her hotel safe and sound."

"Thanks," Shane said. He got up and escorted me from the pub, stopping at the corner. "Are you sure you're okay with going back to the hotel? I know it's still early."

"I was ready to go. Besides, with the way you were looking at me and had your hand on my thigh, I have a feeling there's something else on your mind."

"It was that obvious? After thinking about you constantly for so long, I fought to keep my hands to myself. I didn't quite succeed."

"In that case, I suggest a nice warm shower and some sensual foreplay, followed by hours of ardent lovemaking. Unless you plan to leave me again, and if you do, I swear I'll tie you to the bed."

"Well, I do have to leave soon. I had plans for to-night."

"No. You can't possibly be serious."

"I'm teasing. I thought it sounded fun to have you tie me to the bed."

"Oh, you are awful." I kissed him. "But so damn sexy. Take me to my room, Mr. Moore."

"With pleasure." Shane held my hand as we headed up the street. "I need to get my bag out of my car. I parked it in the hotel's parking lot. It'll only take a minute."

After he retrieved his bag, we entered the hotel lobby. I led Shane to the elevator, taking it to the third floor.

"I'm in room three twelve. It's at the end of the hall." I stepped off the elevator with Shane following behind me.

We reached my room, and I opened the door. After taking off my sweater and setting my purse down on the desk, I closed the curtains and turned toward Shane, my stomach suddenly full of butterflies. It had been such a long time since I'd been with a man, I wasn't sure how to act. Did I pretend to be coy and let him make the first move? Or did I boldly tell him what I wanted the way I used to do with Alex?

Shane started to remove the light jacket he had on, then stopped, pulling something out of the pocket. He tossed a box of condoms onto the table next to the bed and then slipped his jacket off, draping it across a chair.

"You certainly thought ahead. Should I be nervous?"

"No." Shane approached me and held me at the waist. He looked relaxed as he leaned forward and kissed me. It was a deep, fervent kiss, his tongue teasing mine.

I dropped my hands from his chest and took a step back. "After taking the train from Dublin this morning and exploring Kilkenny, I'd like to take a warm shower. Are you going to join me?" I grabbed the hem of my blouse and started to tug it over my head, suddenly feeling another set of hands helping me.

Shane tossed my blouse on the chair, his hands moving to the clip on the front of my bra. A second later, it fell to the floor.

My breathing quickened as his hands caressed my flesh, his lips on mine once again. A sound escaped me when his fingers teased my nipple. I pulled my lips away, my voice breathless in his ear. "If you don't stop, I won't make it into the shower. It's been years since someone touched me like that."

"Years?" Shane's hand froze.

"Since Alex. I've never been with anyone else. I was only sixteen when we started dating."

The look on his face seemed to change to one of tenderness. He touched my chin and tipped my head up. "We'll take it slow. A warm shower sounds nice."

"Thank you. I have to admit, I am feeling a little nervous."

Shane unbuttoned his shirt and tossed it on the chair. He sat to remove his socks and shoes and then watched me as I slipped off my pants and underwear. "You're beautiful."

"Thank you." I gave him a coy smile. "Give me a

minute in the bathroom, and then join me." I sensed his gaze on me when I walked away and stepped through the doorway. My hand was touching the stream of water from the showerhead, checking the temperature, when a quiet knock sounded on the door. I opened it, finding Shane standing naked in front of me, his body gorgeous. "Welcome to Liz's Spa, where a warm and steamy adventure awaits."

"I can't wait to see what the proprietor has in store for me." He stepped forward, his hands moving to my hips.

"I promise it will be more than pleasant." I wrapped my arms around his neck and kissed him. "Now, into the shower with you." I pulled away and stepped into the cascade of water, rinsing my body in its liquid warmth.

Shane unwrapped the small bar of soap and lathered up a washcloth. He took my hand and pulled me toward him. "You first." He gently began washing me, his hand sliding across my arms, breasts, and stomach. "Turn around. I'll scrub your back."

I complied, the soapy washcloth moving across my shoulders, down my back, and suddenly lower. I caught my breath as it slid between my legs.

Shane put down the washcloth and pressed his body against my back. His arms went around me, hands sliding across my soapy skin. He touched my thigh, his hand sliding upward, fingers teasing between my legs while his other hand stroked and teased a nipple. His mouth was on my ear. "How's the steamy adventure? Does it feel all right?"

"Yes." I leaned my head against his shoulder, my

eyelids closing, the darkness swirling with sensual pleasure.

"Your nipple is hard, and I can feel you swollen below. Do you want me to stop?" He breathed the words into my ear, lips caressing my neck.

"Oh God," I breathed, the pressure building, my body becoming tense. I suddenly cried out, my back arching as a wave of pleasure rippled through me. I leaned my body against him.

He turned me around to face him, groaning as I reached down and stroked him. "We need to finish. I don't want our first time to be in the shower. I want to take my time making love to you while I hold you in my arms. I've thought about you for too long to let it happen any other way."

A euphoria engulfed me. I stepped back under the water, washing my hair and rinsing my body as Shane watched me. Then I climbed out of the shower, drying off and brushing my teeth as he finished. I turned to study him, his body trim and muscular, while my knees still shook from what he had done to me. Leaving the bathroom, I lay down on the bed, waiting for him to join me. I feasted my eyes on him moments later as he stood in front of me, his desire openly displayed. I wanted him, my body longing for him to fill me.

Shane lay down beside me. He took his time, tenderly kissing me while his hands slowly caressed every inch of my flesh. After a prolonged period of sensual tenderness, Shane bent down, his mouth suddenly on my nipple while his hand slid between my legs. He moved lower, using his knee to spread my thighs. Then he lay down between them.

I gasped, Shane's tongue on me, flicking, teasing, and nibbling, the ecstasy of it rolling over me like a fog. The tightness inside me was building again, my body growing tense. My nipples grew to hardened points as a pair of hands suddenly pulled and pinched them. I moaned, writhing underneath him, the intensity steadily rising higher and higher. Then the wave crashed, the magnitude of my release overwhelming.

Shane came back to my side and kissed me, hands tenderly caressing my body.

I reached down, stroking and teasing him, reveling in the sounds coming from deep in his throat. I bent down and took his nipple in my mouth, sucking and nibbling, and he moaned again.

Shane pulled away, taking a condom out of the box and putting it on. Then he slid on top of me and eased inside, moving in a slow rhythm as he pushed deeper, the length of him filling me. Shane's pace suddenly quickened, and he began to plunge harder, his breathing coming in short pants. A small gasp escaped his throat, followed by a succession of moans as I wrapped my legs around him, tilting my hips, my muscles squeezing around his flesh as he thrust. His body tensed, and then he let out a long guttural sound as he released. Pulling away, he lay beside me, catching his breath. After a minute, he turned toward me, tenderly stroking my cheek with his thumb. "I can't even describe how that felt. I wondered so many times what you'd feel like."

"You thought about making love to me?"

"Constantly, mo ghra."

"What does mo ghra mean?"

"It means my love."

Deliriously happy and content, I snuggled into his chest.

I SAT UP in bed and scanned the darkness, trying to remember where I was. I jumped, sensing a movement next to me.

"Liz. Are you okay? It's two o'clock in the morning. What happened?" Shane reached out and touched my arm.

"I'm sorry to wake you. I had a dream."

"Come here." He pulled me to him. "A nightmare?"

I curled up against his chest. "No. It's this strange dream I've had off and on for years, but now they're more frequent."

"What's the dream about?" He brushed my hair away from my face.

"I dream I'm getting married, but I can't see the groom's face, although I can tell that I love him. The officiant is the only other person in the dream, and I can't see who he is either, but I sense we know each other. We're standing under a tent framed with flowers, facing the side of a castle, and there's a garden filled with red roses and hedges in front of us. I always wake up when the groom slips the wedding ring on my finger."

"That's an odd dream. You said you've had it for years?"

"Yes, it started when I was in my late teens. It was

right before I married Alex. I feel like it's supposed to mean something, but I have no idea what."

"Let's see if I can make you forget about this dream for now." Shane turned on his side and leaned over me. He kissed me, his hand caressing my breasts.

"It's working. I already forgot about it." I reached down and touched him. "Hmm. I'd say you want something. I believe this will be the third time since we've been here."

"Are you complaining?"

"Not in the slightest. I'm savoring every inch of you."

"Excuse me?"

I giggled as I slid under the covers, leaving kisses down Shane's stomach as I moved lower. I took him in my mouth, a moan piercing the air above me. I licked, sucked, and teased while working him with my hand, the sounds from deep in his chest growing more intense.

"Jesus, Liz." Shane's voice sounded strained and raspy, his breathing heavy. "Damn. That feels good." He threw the covers back, entangling his fingers in my hair as my mouth moved up and down his length. "Christ. You're going to make me come." His breathing became labored, his fingers tightening around strands of my hair. Then he let out a long groan as he spilled.

I sat up, wiping my mouth with the back of my hand.

Shane reached for me. "You are one wicked woman. Come here."

I slid back up to the pillow and curled up in his arms. "I swear it feels like I've known you forever. Please don't laugh, but I was so nervous when we came here last night, especially when you closed the door. Now, I'm so comfortable around you; I don't know what I was worried about."

"I feel strangely comfortable around you too. It's like we've been together for years." Shane squeezed me, his arms holding me tight. "So, I'm curious. What do you like about Ireland so far, and what do you want to see while you're here?"

"Besides the people, I like the country's history. One thing I'm hoping to see is a castle or two. They fascinate me. Mel's just interested in partying and finding herself a good-looking Irishman. Speaking of an Irishman, I hope it was safe leaving her at the pub with Conor."

Shane laughed. "I'd be more worried about Conor. He may be a big man, but he's a teddy bear at heart. I hope Mel didn't abuse him too badly." He leaned down and kissed me. "Since castles fascinate you, what do you think about staying in one tonight?"

"Are you serious? A real castle with turrets, hidden stairwells, and grand halls?"

"Yes, like that. There's one forty-five minutes or so away from here that dates back to the twelfth century. I can reserve a room for tonight if you want."

"Oh my God. Yes. I would love it." I frowned. "What about Mel?"

"It's up to her. She can stay here, or she can come with us."

"Okay. We can ask Mel when we see her at breakfast. In the meantime, I see a gorgeous chest that I'm dying to snuggle against." I laid my head in the crook of his neck and pulled the covers over my shoulder. I wanted to stay in his arms like this forever.

CHAPTER 10

PRINCESS FOR A NIGHT

SHANE AND I went downstairs to meet up with Mel. Besides being hungry and wanting breakfast, we needed to find out if she wanted to stay at the castle with us this evening. Sunlight streamed through the wall of windows facing the patio when Shane and I entered the hotel's dining room. Spotting Mel at a table for four next to the glass door, we joined her.

"Good morning. It looks like you've finished breakfast. How was it?" My voice was cheery as I eyed Mel's empty plate.

"It was good, and you almost missed it. The kitchen is about ready to stop serving breakfast." Mel looked me over and then grinned, appearing amused. "You're usually an early riser. Something must have kept you in bed." She snickered and glanced over at Shane. "Good morning, Shane. Did you sleep well?"

"I did. Thank you." The corner of Shane's mouth twitched as he got up from the table and pushed his chair forward. "I'm starving. I'm going to the buffet to see what's left and make myself a plate."

"I'm hungry too. I'll be right behind you." I slid my chair back and looked at Mel. "Try to behave."

"I can't help it. It's been a long time since I've seen you this way, and I'm enjoying it."

"Then try to keep it to yourself." I raised a brow at Mel and then hurried off to get breakfast. After filling my plate with scrambled eggs, sausage links, and several slices of melon, I left Shane at the buffet and went back to join Mel.

She leaned back in her chair, lightly tapping her fingers on the table. "Well, are you going to ask me how it went with Conor last night or not?"

"I was about to do that. So, go ahead and tell me."

"Nothing happened. We had a wonderful time at the pub, and Conor walked me back to the hotel. I had hoped he'd suggest going to my room or at least try to kiss me. But he didn't do anything, which was pretty frustrating. I thought he didn't like me until he offered to give me a tour of his distillery and show me around town. Now I'm confused."

"It sounds like he's a nice guy. Rather than worry whether he likes you, why don't you just enjoy his company? Sleeping with you isn't the only way to show it."

"Fine. I'll see what happens. Conor's supposed to call me later this morning."

"Did you ask Mel about tonight?" Shane set his plate down and joined us.

"No, but I'll ask her now. Shane's taking me to stay in a castle for the night that dates back to the medieval period. Did you want to stay here or come with us?"

"I'll stay here in Kilkenny since I have plans with Conor later today."

"It sounds like you two hit it off." Shane took a bite of his eggs and grabbed the blackberry jam.

"We did. Conor's naive but sweet. He's like a big teddy bear."

"I told you." Shane nudged my arm, a small chuckle escaping him.

"He told you what?" Mel stared at me, a defiant look on her face.

"Shane mentioned that Conor was a big teddy bear at heart. It's just cute you said the same thing. We hoped you didn't abuse him last night."

"I haven't yet." Mel flashed the two of us a mischievous grin, so well done it would have put the Cheshire Cat to shame.

"Since Mel's decided to stay here tonight, I'm going outside to call the hotel and make a reservation for the two of us." Shane finished off his sausage links and got up from the table. He went out the glass door to the patio.

Mel looked out the window at Shane. "I can't believe he's taking you to stay in a castle. Lucky you. I knew he was a keeper."

"Oh, he's a keeper all right. I didn't think I could ever fall in love with someone like this again, but I was wrong. When I saw him out on the patio last night, it hit me how much he means to me and how much I missed him. I think he's my Irish blessing."

"Oh, geez. Now you sound mushy. But I'm happy for you. I swear you're glowing this morning like you used to do when Alex was here. So, do you think he feels the same way about you?"

"I don't know." I brushed pretend crumbs off the table and looked at Mel. "I hope so. Honestly, I care for him so much; I'm ready for a commitment. I can see spending my life with Shane. God, I don't dare tell him that, though. I don't want to scare him off." I looked down at my lap, my face feeling warm. "He makes me want to melt every time he says, 'come here,' in his Irish accent and pulls me close."

"It's because you know what's coming next, and based on the way you're blushing, I'd say it must be pretty damn good." Mel chuckled, appearing to enjoy teasing me.

"I was able to get a reservation." Shane pulled out his chair and sat at the table. "The hotel had one room left in the castle, but only because they'd just had a cancellation. So, I booked us in one of their two suites."

"I'm so excited. I can't wait to go." I eagerly squirmed in my chair, hoping we could leave right away.

"I'm sure you'll like it. The hotel has quite the history surrounding it." Shane leaned over and kissed me.

"Dang. Will you two stop? I swear you can't keep your hands or lips off each other." Mel poured herself some coffee from the decanter on our table. "Liz, wouldn't that be weird if this castle had something to do with your dream and you could figure out who your groom is?" She made a face at Shane. "Sorry. I shouldn't have mentioned it."

"It's all right. Liz told me about her dream. I suppose it would be nice to know who my competition is."

"You don't happen to have a tattoo of an elf, do you?" Mel peered suspiciously at Shane.

"An elf? No, why?"

"I already looked. Shane has a tattoo in the same spot as the groom in my dream, but his tattoo isn't an elf. It's a Celtic cross." I turned toward Shane. "Can you show Mel your tattoo? Shane, why does your face look so funny? What's going on?"

Shane stared at me, his gaze intense. "Could the tattoo be a leprechaun rather than an elf?"

"Maybe. But the pointy ears and long white hair make it look more like an elf." I shifted in my chair and stared at him, uncomfortable with his sudden ashen color. "Why are you asking?"

"Christ." Shane leaned back in his seat and ran a hand through his hair. He stared across the dining room. After a minute, he turned toward me—an odd expression on his face. "My original tattoo was a leprechaun. I got it when I was a teenager, and the tattoo artist did a poor job on it. He put pointy ears and long white hair on the leprechaun, making it look like an elf. I hated it. It's expensive to remove a tattoo, and some procedures don't always work that well. So, I got the Celtic cross to cover it up." Shane rolled up his shirtsleeve and turned his arm over, displaying the tattoo on the inside of his wrist and forearm. The cross was much bigger than the tattoo in my dream and done in gray, black, and dark green.

"Holy shit. There's been something between you two since before you even met." Mel was wide-eyed as she stared at the tattoo.

"It seems you've been my destiny all along," I said, my voice breaking as I spoke.

"Come here," Shane whispered as he moved my chair

closer to his. He pulled me against his chest and kissed the top of my head, holding me as we sat at the table.

Mel leaned back in her chair, studying the two of us. "I have to say, if there's such a thing as destiny, you two are the poster children for it."

"Maybe so." Shane looked down at me. "Mo ghra, are you all right?"

"I don't know." I pulled away from him and smoothed a wrinkle in my pants. "It's all so strange. When I sat next to you at dinner our first night in Providenciales, I sensed a familiarity between us that I couldn't explain. Now I understand why."

"I sensed something between us too, but I could never put my finger on it."

Mel cleared her throat. "Well, I, for one, think this is exciting. The two of you should embrace it and consider yourselves meant for each other."

I turned to say something to Mel and spied Conor walking toward us. "Umm, Mel. You have company."

Mel turned around in her chair, her face suddenly beaming.

Conor stopped at our table and smiled down at her. "Good morning, Mel. I was hoping to find you." He turned his attention to Shane and me. "Shane. Liz. How's she cutting?"

"Good morning, Conor. It's nice to see you." I smiled at him, amused at his sudden appearance and apparent eagerness to see Mel.

"We're good. You?" Shane stood and shook Conor's hand. Then he retook his seat.

"I'm grand. I was at the bank down the street and

thought I'd stop by. Caitlin told me the three of you were in here." He turned back to Mel. "I've been up to ninety since early this morning, but I've got some extra time right now. Are you available to tour the distillery and let me show you around town?"

"I am." Mel giggled and looked across the table at Shane and me. "It looks like I'm taking off. Liz, call me in the morning."

"I will. You and Conor have fun."

Shane turned to Conor. "We'll catch you later. I'm whisking Liz away for the night."

"Bang on. I'll take care of Mel." Conor looked down at her. "Ready to go?"

"Yep, I sure am." Mel stood and grabbed her purse from the back of her chair. She smiled at me over her shoulder when they walked away.

"I have to take care of an errand before heading off to the castle. Do you mind going upstairs and packing? I'll be back in about an hour, and we can leave after that," Shane said.

"Sure. I can do that. What should I do with your toothbrush and stuff? Should I put them in your bag?"

"If you don't mind, that would be great. I'll be back soon." Shane kissed me when we stood. Then he disappeared through the dining room doorway.

I SURVEYED THE scenery as Shane drove to the castle. The villages we passed seemed so charming, and everything was so green. To call it beautiful was an understatement. Suddenly thinking about last night, I peered at Shane over my shoulder. "Caitlin told me you had come from her parents' estate. Why weren't you with your parents? Do they live farther away?"

Shane's expression changed, and it took a full minute before he answered. "My parents died when I was ten years old. My uncle Colin and aunt Neasa, Caitlin's parents, raised me. Caitlin and her brother, Niall, are more like my siblings than cousins."

"I'm so sorry. I didn't know. Caitlin didn't mention that you'd lost your parents. What happened?"

"They died in a train derailment. My parents had gone to Wales for a wedding. It was for my mother's cousin. I was sick, so they left me with my aunt and uncle. After the wedding, my parents took the train to London to stay there for a few days before heading home. They were on the city's outskirts when their high-speed passenger train collided with a freight train. My parents died in the crash."

"That's so horrible. I'm sorry." I peeked at Shane over my shoulder. I couldn't miss the sadness on his face, and his mood seemed suddenly pensive. "Was your mother from Wales?"

"She was. My father met her when he visited a friend there when he was a young man. He always said it was love at first sight. My mother was an only child but had many aunts, uncles, and cousins. Most of her family is in Wales. I have a fairly large family on my father's side here in Ireland. My uncle Colin is my father's older brother. There are two younger sisters. One is in Northern Ireland, and the other is in Dingle. I have cousins spread out all over the place. What about your family? Tell me about them?"

"There isn't much to say. My parents married when they were older. My mom was forty, and my father was forty-six. They had me a year later, and I was their only child. My mother died of breast cancer when I was twelve, and my father died from a heart attack eight years ago. We lost my mother's parents when I was a toddler and never saw my father's parents since there was friction between them and him. So I grew up with no family around me. I had a pretty lonely childhood. After my mom died, my dad was so grief-stricken he left me on my own. I lived with Mel for the most part until I got together with Alex."

"I guess the two of us know the pain of losing one's parents. At least I have a big family. It must have been rough for you."

"It was. My teenage years were tough, and they got worse and worse. Alex pulled me out of the abyss and got me feeling whole again. I'm used to being by myself, but I've never really liked it. When I was a little kid, I remember how jealous I used to get because all my friends had siblings, aunts, uncles, cousins, and grandparents, and I had none."

"You have me." Shane smiled and reached for my hand. He held it as we drove.

"How far away from the castle are we?" I scanned the side of the road, looking for a sign.

"We're coming up to the turnoff. See the cottage and the gate up ahead on our left? That's where we turn."

I strained forward, trying to see if I could catch a

glimpse of the castle, but I couldn't see beyond the line of trees framing the road. I wiggled in my seat, a burst of excitement hitting me when we turned onto the castle property and drove down a private lane lined with rail fencing.

"The clubhouse and rental lodges are ahead of us on the right. We'll veer to the left as soon as we pass them, and then you'll see the castle through the trees," Shane said.

"Have you stayed here before? You know the layout of the property fairly well."

"No, I've never stayed here. I attended a wedding here years ago. It's a beautiful place."

"I'm sure it is, and you're making me feel like a spoiled princess right now." I eagerly scanned our surroundings, bubbling over with anticipation when we reached the clubhouse. Then I saw it—a picture-postcard vision in all its glory. I held my breath, completely mesmerized by the view in front of us. The castle stood majestically between the trees. It was a weathered stone structure, four stories tall, with turrets crowning its top. I slowly let out my breath. "I don't know what to say. It's so beautiful."

"You don't have to say a thing. I just want you to enjoy it. Being with you makes my life feel complete, and I've never been happier. I love you, mo ghra."

"I love you too." I squeezed Shane's hand. I had always thought a love like what I'd shared with Alex only happened once in a lifetime if you were even fortunate enough to have that experience at all. Shane proved my theory wrong.

Shane drove through a stone archway into a small lot and parked the car near the hotel's entrance. I sat there as my eyes roamed across the structure. Tall, narrow windows climbed up its side, and a cross-shaped slit was in the wall above the door. Archers would have used the opening centuries ago, shooting their arrows through the slit while protected by the stone.

"Are you ready to go inside?" Shane had opened my door and stood there with his hand extended, waiting to assist me from the car. He beamed at me, his dimples an adorable sight.

I stepped from the car, turning in place as I scanned the grounds. A stone staircase was off to my right, leading to an area hidden from view. Strangely drawn to it, I slowly walked toward the stairs, a sense of déjà vu growing with each forward step. I reached them, my head spinning as I looked out over a garden, its red rose bushes and green hedges a familiar sight. I grabbed the stone pillar next to me to keep from falling. Recovering, I bolted down the stairs, Shane calling my name as he ran after me. I dropped to my knees in the grass.

"What are you doing, and why did you take off like that?" Shane bent over me, catching his breath. Worry lines wrinkled his forehead, and he sounded alarmed.

"My dream," I whispered, a chill sweeping over me.

Shane blinked several times as he stood there, staring at me. Then his eyes grew wide, and he sank to his knees next to me in the grass. "This is the place in your dream, isn't it?"

"Yes."

"We can leave if you need us to."

"No. We need to stay. I think we're supposed to be here."

Shane stood and pulled me to my feet. "You're cold, and your body is shaking. Come here." He gathered me in his arms, holding me close. "We should leave. You don't look well."

"No, please. I want to stay. I'm just overwhelmed and confused, and I'm not sure what else." I buried my face in his neck, feeling comforted by the rise and fall of his chest underneath my cheek.

"All right. We'll stay, but only if you're comfortable with it."

"I just need a minute to wrap my mind around it all."

Shane pushed a strand of hair from my face and tucked it behind my ear as he continued to hold me. After a few minutes, he finally spoke. "Are you feeling good enough to go inside?"

"Yes." I pulled away from him, my hands still on his chest. "When I saw the rose garden surrounded by the hedges, it was such a mental and emotional overload I couldn't think or breathe. It was a lot to take in."

"I understand, and as crazy as this seems to me, I agree with you and Mel when you said we were each other's destiny. Honestly, I don't know any other way to label it. And at this point, we should just accept everything that is happening to us. I mean, really. What else can we do? I can't explain it, and I don't think you can either. So for now, let's get our luggage and go inside." Shane put his arm around my shoulder and walked me back to the parking lot.

"Good afternoon. May I take your luggage?" A porter greeted us when we reached the car. He took our luggage from Shane and led us into the lobby, stopping at the reception desk.

"Hello. I have a reservation. It's under Shane Moore."

The slender young man behind the desk checked his computer. "Ah, yes, Mr. Moore. I see you've reserved a suite. I'll need you to fill out this card for me, and then I'll need to see a credit card we can put on file in case you decide to charge anything to your room."

"Here you go." Shane took a credit card from his wallet and handed it to the reservation clerk. Then he proceeded to fill out the paperwork. "Liz, did you want to book any of their activities for tomorrow morning? They have a list here of everything they offer."

"Do they have horseback riding?" I walked across the lobby to look at a picture on the wall that caught my attention.

"They do, but we should skip that one. I was hoping you wouldn't mind if I took you to meet my aunt and uncle tomorrow in Kilcullen. They own a stud farm, and I can take you horseback riding there."

I swiveled in place to face Shane, momentarily stunned by his plan. "You want me to meet your family? Are you sure you're ready to introduce me to them?"

"Positive. My aunt and uncle are wonderful people. They'll love you. Believe me. You have nothing to worry about."

"I didn't expect to be meeting your family so soon, but sure, we can go see them."

"Sorry about that." Shane turned his attention back to the reservation clerk.

"No problem, sir." The clerk handed Shane his credit card and our room keys and picked up the paperwork Shane had filled out.

I spun around to look at the picture. It was an old black-and-white photographic print of the castle with a couple posing by the entrance. The image looked to be from the early 1900s, and I assumed the people were the owners or members of the family. There was suddenly whispering behind me, the voices echoing in the hall. I glanced over my shoulder, catching Shane nod his head and the clerk grin at him, the two of them behaving as if they were up to something. Curious, I studied the two of them, hoping Shane would share with me later what was going on.

The porter led us to our suite on the third floor. "Here's your room, sir. May I?" He took the room key from Shane and opened our door for us.

I stepped inside and was more than pleased with the suite. The sitting area had several chairs, a fireplace with a carved mantel out of dark wood, and a large television installed on the wall above it. A desk with a coffee and tea station was against the wall. I continued down a hallway, discovering the bedroom to my left and the bathroom straight ahead. I walked into the bathroom, finding it oddly round in shape, with a tiled shower built inside a deep recess and an old-style footed bathtub to my right. Several tall, narrow windows framed the room.

"I like that bathtub. You think we'll both fit?" Shane came up behind me, wrapping his arms around my waist.

"I'm not sure, but I'm more than happy to give it a try." I turned in his arms and kissed him, my fingers sliding up his chest. "I love the way you feel and smell." I laughed. "It must be the Irishman in you." I squealed a moment later when Shane picked me up in his arms. "What are you doing?"

"This Irishman can't get enough of you." Shane carried me into the bedroom and deposited me on the bed. He quickly removed his clothes while I followed his lead and removed mine. Now naked, Shane lay down beside me. He tenderly brushed my cheek with his thumb, then he leaned down and kissed me, his hands sliding across my skin. "I want you. Every time I'm near you, I want you." He started to slide his body on top of mine and then stopped. "Damn. I need a condom. I'll be back."

"I'll talk to my doctor about getting on birth control when I go home. Otherwise, we'll have to buy stock in Trojan. We'll be using enough of them."

"Birth control would be nice." Shane returned to the bed, rolling onto his side. "I don't think either of us is ready for a mini-Shane or a mini-Liz." He let out a chuckle. "Although a dozen kids would be fun."

"You want children?"

"Well, not now. But it would be nice to have some eventually."

"You're serious." I stared at him. Alex and I had tried for nine years to have children. After our first couple of years with no pregnancy, we'd assumed I had a medical problem. A round of testing had proven otherwise. It turned out Alex had a low sperm count. Finally resigning myself to marriage without children, I could never get past the feeling I was missing something. I'd never shared my despair with Alex. I hadn't wanted him to think I blamed him. Shane's comment made me hopeful, besides the fact it also meant he was into our budding relationship for the long haul. Shane, children, a long-term commitment instead of a few fleeting moments, was everything I wanted.

"Don't you want kids someday?" Shane studied me as if trying to read my thoughts.

"I do, but not a dozen. I think it's more like three or four." I kissed his chest and then climbed on top of him, leaning down to whisper in his ear. "You are my everything, Mr. Moore." I kissed his lips, lightly nibbling on them.

"You are mine, mo ghra. I've never known what it was like to truly love someone and have them love me in return until you came along. You are everything I could have hoped for and more." Shane placed a supporting hand on my back and then flipped us over, so I was on the bottom. He kissed me, his hands sensually exploring my flesh.

I savored his touch as he caressed me. My muscles were taut, and my senses were at their peak when he stopped his foreplay and eased inside me. I craved him, pushing my body forward as he filled me, our passion exploding as our bodies merged as one. I tilted my hips, causing his length to touch me at just the right spot, the tightness inside me growing. The wave of pleasure built higher and higher as he made love to me. Then it crashed. I cried out, fingers of ecstasy spreading deliciously through me.

Shane frantically thrust several more times, and then his body tensed as he groaned above me. He relaxed, lying still on top of me, his voice at my ear. "You feel so good. I swear, I can't get enough of you."

Fulfilled and content, I leaned my head back as his lips softly kissed my neck and shoulder. Yes, Shane was my Irish blessing.

It wasn't long before Shane began to stir. "We should get up and get something to eat down at the clubhouse. I made a dinner reservation for seven o'clock, so we have several hours to go before then."

"Can't we have dinner earlier, say around five o'clock? We can snack if we get hungry after that."

"No. I don't want to have dinner early."

"But I'm not that hungry right now. I'd rather wait and have an early dinner. I doubt the hotel will care if we change the reservation."

"I'll care. I want to get something to eat now and leave the dinner reservation as it is. We can walk down to the clubhouse, grab something to eat, and explore the grounds. Oh, I forgot to ask you. Do you have a dress you can wear to dinner?"

"Yes, I have a dress with me. I always pack one just in case." I grudgingly got up, irritated at his reluctance to change the reservation. I didn't understand why it was so important, especially since I wasn't that hungry. After freshening up and changing into my jeans and a light pullover sweater, I let Shane know I was ready to go.

We left the castle and walked down to the clubhouse, following the same path we took to get here. By the time we reached the building, my irritation had subsided. The castle was so beautiful and Shane's treat so extraordinarily special, I didn't want to taint it with a bad mood.

The hours seemed to fly by as we had lunch, walked around the grounds, and then explored the castle. Nearing dinnertime, we went back to our room to clean up.

Finished dressing for dinner, I surveyed my image in the full-length mirror in the bedroom. I wanted to look nice for Shane and our special evening together.

"You look gorgeous." Shane came up behind me and slipped his arms around my waist as he kissed my neck. "I like your purple dress."

"Thank you." I swung around, my gaze running the length of him. Shane wore navy slacks, a white dress shirt with a burgundy-colored tie, and a navy two-button blazer. "You look quite handsome. Why don't we delay dinner for a few minutes?" I ran my hands up his chest and kissed him.

Shane took hold of my hands and took a step backward. "I appreciate the thought, but it will have to wait. I don't want to be late for dinner. If you have a shawl or something you can wear over your dress, you should bring it."

"You're up to something, aren't you? I heard you whispering to the reservation clerk when we checked into the hotel earlier."

"Yes, and it's a surprise, so you'll have to wait and see. If you're ready, we should go downstairs since it's almost seven o'clock."

"Is that why you wouldn't change our reservation?

You have a surprise planned?"

"Yes, and that's all I'm going to say."

"Fine," I said, excited at the prospect of what might be next, but frustrated he wouldn't tell me. "Let me grab a wrap out of my luggage, and then I'll be ready." I took a black wrap from my suitcase and slipped it over my shoulders.

"Perfect. You look beautiful."

Shane escorted me downstairs. A uniformed hotel employee was waiting for us when we stepped off the elevator. The man smiled when he saw us.

"Good evening. You must be Mr. Moore and Ms. Whalen?"

"Yes, we are." Shane didn't appear the least bit surprised at having an employee waiting for us.

"Wonderful. My name is Reginald. Please follow me, and I'll escort you to your table."

Shane took my arm as we followed behind Reginald. Rather than lead us to a dining room, he took us to the hotel bar. He didn't stop, crossing the room and heading toward the side door leading to the garden.

"Where is he taking us?" I whispered.

"I thought you might like a private candlelit dinner out in the rose garden. I hope you don't mind."

"Oh, I don't mind at all."

We exited the bar, stepping out onto a terrace. Reginald led us down a stone staircase toward the rose garden. A small tent was visible in the distance, with several torches illuminating the space and two men standing nearby to take care of us. I gasped when we got close. A candlelit table was underneath the tent with a champagne bucket on a stand next to it. One of the men wore a tuxedo, a violin in his hands. The other man wore a uniform and stood beside the champagne bucket with a towel draped over his arm.

"Please have a seat." Reginald assisted me with my chair. "Archie will be your waiter this evening." He motioned toward the man in the uniform. "I will leave you in his capable hands. Enjoy your dinner." Reginald nodded his head at us and then walked away.

"Good evening. Here are your menus." Archie handed one to each of us. "May I start you off with a glass of champagne?"

"That would be wonderful, thank you." Shane reached across the table and took my hand in his. "Do you like it?"

"Yes, and I'm borderline speechless. I can't believe you did all this for me."

"There's more to come."

I wanted to melt in Shane's arms with the way he looked at me from across the table.

Archie popped the cork on the champagne bottle and filled our glasses. He put the bottle back in the bucket and took a step backward. "May I suggest the smoked salmon tartare, the braised beef short ribs, or the cannon of lamb this evening?"

"Oh, I would love the smoked salmon tartare." I smiled up at Archie, my mouth already watering.

"Excellent choice." Archie directed his attention to Shane. "Sir. What may I get for you this evening?"

"I believe I'll try the cannon of lamb." Shane reached for my menu, stacking it on top of his, and handed them to Archie.

"Very good. Thank you, sir." Archie hurried off toward the castle.

The man in the tuxedo started playing his violin. The music was romantic and relaxing.

"May I have this dance?" Shane stood and extended his hand toward me.

"Yes, you may." I stood and took his hand, unable to put into words how I felt. No one had ever done anything this special for me before, not even Alex. I leaned my head on Shane's shoulder as we danced. The music, his cologne, and dinner under the stars were all so intoxicating.

Shane kissed my cheek, his mouth moving to my ear. "You are a woman like no other, and I've fallen in love with you. I want us to have children and grow old together." He pulled away from me and knelt on one knee.

"Oh my God," I whispered as I clapped my hand over my mouth.

"Liz, will you allow me to be your husband?" Shane pulled a small red box out of his pocket and opened it, displaying a beautiful diamond ring.

I knelt in front of him, tears running down my cheeks. "Yes," I sobbed, too overcome for more words.

Shane put his knee down and pulled me against him, his lips tender as he kissed me. Then he pulled away and sat back on his heels. "Let's put this ring on your finger and make it official." He took the ring from the box and slipped it on my finger when I held out my hand.

I stared at the ring. It was gorgeous. It was white gold with a large diamond in the middle and a smaller diamond on each side. The sides of the ring contained filigree scrollwork with a trinity knot in the center. The ring had a dainty look to it. I looked at Shane, my emotions a complete mess. "When did you decide?"

"The day I called you, and we reconciled. I knew then I wanted you as my wife. I bought the ring this morning when I went out on that errand."

There was a noise to our left. Shane and I turned simultaneously, finding Archie placing our dinner on the table. Our bread, butter, and salads were already there, although I didn't recall hearing anyone bring them.

"I guess we better get up." Shane chuckled. "We do have an audience." He stood and helped me to my feet, escorting me back to the table.

The violinist smiled at us and began playing another song.

"Congratulations. Based on the ring on your finger, I take it the answer was yes." Archie smiled as he refilled our champagne glasses.

"It was a resounding yes." I looked lovingly at Shane. I didn't think I'd ever been happier.

Shane buttered a roll and set it on my plate. "I guess I should warn you the trip to my aunt and uncle's estate tomorrow is actually to celebrate our engagement. Of course, that was with the hope you'd agree to marry me."

"When did you have time to tell your family you planned on proposing?"

"This morning. Caitlin went with me to pick out the ring. I'm sure they're all waiting anxiously to hear whether you said yes or no. I'll have to give them the news when we go back to our room later." He picked up his champagne glass and looked at me, his expression full of love and tenderness. "To a long and beautiful life together, a happy household, and plenty of children. I love you, Mrs. Moore." Shane held his glass toward me for a toast.

"I'm not Mrs. Moore yet."

"I'm practicing. I like the way it rolls off my tongue."

"I like the way it sounds too." I held my glass up. "To a long and happy life together and a house full of children. I love you, Mr. Moore." I clinked my glass against his and took a sip of the champagne. Gloriously happy, I tilted my head toward the stars, mouthing the words *thank you* to whoever was responsible for bringing Shane into my life. After years of heartache, I welcomed a future of tranquility and love.

CHAPTER 11

THE FAMILY

THE AIR WAS crisp and earthy as we walked across the castle grounds. We had gotten up early to explore the surrounding area and make the most of our time before checking out of the hotel. Returning from a hike in the adjacent forest, we neared the clubhouse as we headed back to the castle. I spotted a group of people in the grassy area next to the building taking archery lessons. Intrigued, I wanted to watch.

"Can we stop for a few minutes and view the lesson?" I said, pointing toward the group.

"Sure. I don't see why not."

We walked toward the archers and sat in the grass. We were close enough to get a clear view but not so close as to be a distraction. They stood in a single line with colorful targets on wooden stands a short distance away. There were six people, plus the male instructor. It looked like four of them were a family consisting of an older couple and a younger one. Standing at the end of the line closest to us was a man with a boy around eleven or twelve years old. I assumed they were a father and son based on their actions. The boy had missed his target, and the father was trying to help him. The man turned the boy to line him up sideways to the target and adjusted his arms as he held the bow.

"I think that's a father and son. They're adorable." I peeked at Shane over my shoulder. "That might be you one of these days."

"I'd like that. I look forward to having a bunch of kids, and we can start working on that after we get married. Speaking of marriage, do you have any thoughts on where and when? I'd prefer to wed as soon as we can manage it."

"Well, I already know I want the wedding to be here. I want it exactly as I've seen it in my dreams, under a tent in the rose garden with us facing the side of the castle. We can't have the wedding too soon because of the extensive planning involved, and I'm sure other couples have already booked the hotel for the summer and fall. Winter isn't the best idea, so that leaves next spring or summer. I'd narrow it down to April, May, or June. Are there any Irish superstitions about wedding months that we should be concerned with?"

"I don't know. I'll Google it and see if I can find out." Shane pulled his phone out of his pocket and browsed the internet. "I found a website with a wealth of information about planning an Irish wedding, and it lists some of the superstitions. Hmm. May is out of the question since it says those that marry in May will rue the day. These are better. It says if you marry in June, over land and sea you'll go, and if you wed in April, there will be joy for maiden and man. Those are interesting."

"That was easy. I pick April. What do you think?"

"I agree, mainly because it's sooner than June. Since

you want the wedding here, why don't we book everything before we leave? It beats trying to do it over the phone later."

"I like that idea. Can we see if someone's available to talk to right now?"

"Why not? Let's head back and see. Since you know what you want, it shouldn't take us that long to book everything."

Shane got up and helped me to my feet. We walked hand in hand back to the castle.

"Good morning," Shane cheerfully addressed the man standing behind the reception desk. "We were wondering if the hotel's wedding specialist was available. We'd like to see about booking your venue for next year."

"I'm not sure, sir. If you can give me a moment, I'll give her a ring and find out." The clerk picked up the phone and dialed a number. "Rowena, it's Peter. I have a couple at the front desk wanting to speak with you about booking a wedding. Okay. Yes, I can do that. Thank you." The clerk hung up the telephone. "Sir, Rowena has an appointment in an hour but can meet with you now. She'll be with you in a moment."

"That's great. Thank you." Shane joined me across the lobby as we waited.

"Hello. I'm Rowena." A middle-aged woman dressed in a skirt and blazer walked up behind us. She had her ginger hair neatly pulled back into a bun.

"Hello. I'm Shane." He shook Rowena's hand.

"I'm Liz. It's nice to meet you."

"It's a pleasure to meet you both. If you could follow

me, I'll take you to my office, where we can go over some of our wedding packages and options." Rowena led us to a door around the corner from the lobby. She opened it, revealing a corridor. Her office was on the left. "Please take a seat." Rowena motioned to two chairs in front of her desk. "Can you give me an idea of what you're looking for?"

"Certainly." Shane leaned back in the chair. "We're looking for a Saturday in April for the date. We prefer a civil ceremony under a tent in the rose garden and a reception immediately following. My best estimate of the guest count is somewhere around a hundred and fifty people."

I gasped. "Shane. That's a lot of people."

"I know, but I have a big family, and my aunt and uncle have a lot of close friends, both socially and through the family business. I did a quick count while we walked over here, and that's my estimate. We can adjust the count as we get closer to the date."

"Okay." I stared at him, still shocked at the thought of that many people.

"Wonderful. First, I'll need to check our availability for April." Rowena opened up a calendar on her computer. "You have a choice of the twenty-third or the thirtieth. To maximize the bride and groom's experience, we only allow one wedding per day. I can look at May if you don't like either of those dates."

"We prefer April. We'll go with the twenty-third." I glanced at Shane, and he nodded his head in agreement.

"The twenty-third it is, then. Did you happen to pick out a wedding package?"

"Not yet." I looked over my shoulder at Shane. "I supposed we should do that now."

Rowena took a binder off the shelf behind her and opened it. She set it down on the desk in front of Shane. "The binder lists our various wedding packages. Please feel free to look through them. The reception will have to be in our large hall based on your guest count. I can assure you it's quite lovely."

Shane scooted his chair closer to mine and opened the binder across his lap so we could both view it. He flipped the pages as we browsed the options. "I like the first package."

I caught my breath. Good Lord, it was expensive. With that large a guest count, the reception would cost a fortune. "It's a lot of money. We should pick a cheaper package."

"Yes, it is a little expensive. But it has everything from the arrival reception for our guests to the late-night reception with finger foods. It includes a five-course dinner selection, plus four hours of an open bar and a champagne toast. When you look at the other options, this one seems the best."

I took a second look at the other packages. As they got less expensive, they included far fewer things. Shane was right. The one he had chosen was the nicest. I placed the binder back on the desk. "It's pricey, but I agree with you. The package you picked has everything we'd want."

"I hoped you'd agree." Shane turned to Rowena. "We'll take the first package."

Rowena looked pleased with our selection. With the date and wedding package now selected, she went over some of the other items we needed to discuss. Forty-five minutes later, we had taken a quick look at the reception hall and signed the contract, and Shane had paid the deposit. Finished, Shane and I stood to leave. He grabbed the folder Rowena had given us containing our copy of the contract and a detailed wedding brochure.

"Thank you so much for your booking." Rowena stood and came around her desk to walk us out. "I always like to ask—what made you choose our venue for your special occasion?"

"I've always dreamed of having my wedding here. I'd seen images of it over the years." I caught Shane's smile at my choice of words.

"That's wonderful. We'll do everything possible to make the day a memorable one for you. Now, let me walk you back to the lobby." Rowena escorted us out of her office, stopping when we reached the lobby. "Thank you both, again. It was a pleasure assisting you with your special event. I'll be in touch once the date gets closer so we can finalize those last few items." She shook both our hands and then turned to greet a young couple sitting in a pair of high-backed chairs.

Shane and I went upstairs to our room. We had packed earlier, so Shane grabbed our two suitcases while I picked up my carry-on bag. It hadn't made sense to keep my room at the hotel in Kilkenny since we'd be here, so I had brought all my luggage with me.

"I got a text message. Hang on." Shane let go of the suitcases and looked at his phone. "It's Conor. He says he'll pick up Mel and meet us at my aunt and uncle's estate. I'm glad he could make it to our engagement celebration."

"Me too. It'll be fun to see Mel. She sounded so excited when I called her last night."

"My family sounded excited when I talked to them too. Speaking of my family, I should send my aunt a text to let her know we're getting ready to leave." Shane typed a message on his phone. "Okay. I told her we booked the castle for our wedding on the twenty-third of April and would be leaving here in a couple of minutes. Luckily, Kilcullen is only a twenty-five-minute drive."

We checked out of the castle, packed our luggage in the car, and headed north to Kilcullen. Butterflies swirled in my stomach as Shane drove. The prospect of meeting the rest of his family made me nervous.

"Which of your family members will be there today?"

"You'll be meeting my aunt and uncle, of course. I'll also introduce you to my cousin Niall, his wife, Tara, and their nine- and eleven-year-old boys, Michael and Ronan. Niall went on a business trip a few days ago, but my uncle expected him back this morning. Patrick and Caitlin will be there with their twelve-year-old daughter, Glenna, and that's it. It's supposed to be an intimate gathering with only my immediate family."

"That's not bad. I was worried you were going to introduce me to so many family members I'd have no hope of remembering their names."

"I'm saving that for the wedding," Shane said, giving me an impish grin. He turned his attention back to the motorway, his cell phone suddenly ringing. He pulled it from his pocket and answered it, putting the call on speaker. "Hello."

"Shane, it's Niall."

"Hey, you're back. How was the trip?" Shane laid his phone down on the console between our seats.

"I'm not sure yet. I've got our vet checking out the stallion we were interested in using for stud services. I'll know in a day or two whether we go ahead with the purchase or not. Anyway, that's not why I'm calling. Tara told me about your engagement, and I wanted to talk to you about it. I'm concerned your proposal might be premature. You haven't known Liz that long, and the caliber of women you've dated over the years hasn't been terribly impressive. Are you sure she's the right one and that you're not so enamored with her that you're jumping the gun?"

Niall's words floored me. Jumping the gun? Hadn't known me that long? Shane's choice of women hadn't been impressive? Who did he think he was to question my character like that? Besides feeling hurt, I was resentful of Niall's comments. I turned toward Shane, crossing my arms over my chest while I waited to hear his response.

"Now is not a good time to discuss this. We'll have to talk later." Shane's body was visibly tense, and he shifted in his seat, looking uncomfortable.

"I think we should discuss it now before it's too late. You're like my little brother, and I feel compelled to make sure you're not making a big mistake."

Shane's face flushed, and he cleared his throat. "Umm…Niall. We seriously need to talk later. Liz and I are in the car driving to the estate. We'll be there in ten minutes."

"Oh, damn. Sorry. I'll catch you when you get here."

"Thanks. I'll see you in a few minutes. Bye." Shane hung up his call and glanced at me over his shoulder. He looked thoroughly embarrassed. "I'm sorry you heard that, mo ghra."

"I am too." I stared out the window. I was so irritated that I wished I could confront Niall right now. I turned back toward Shane. "He already doesn't like me. That's not fair. And why would he question your marriage proposal and our relationship?"

"I swear, Niall isn't doing it to be mean or malicious. It's because he's being protective of me. You and I have only known each other for a few months. From Niall's perspective, we're rushing into a commitment. He doesn't know you, and I'm certain he'll change his tune when he meets you. He'll see right away that you're different and we're meant to be together. Trust me. There's no reason to be concerned."

"We'll see." I pursed my lips as I reached forward and turned up the volume on the radio. Music always put me in a pleasant frame of mind, and I needed to be at my best when I met Shane's family.

Shane exited the motorway and headed east along a two-lane road. After several more turns, he drove through a gated entrance and into a wooded area along a private lane. When we emerged from the trees, a large Georgian mansion was in full view in the distance.

I sucked in my breath, my gaze frozen on the palatial house. It wasn't anything close to what I expected.

Shane drove past rolling lawns and formal gardens. There was a pond on our right, a white wooden gazebo on its far side. As I turned my head, straining to see, I spotted a red footbridge spanning a fingerlike extension of the pond. It connected to a walkway that led to the gazebo. Shane continued driving toward his family's estate.

"Are all those buildings off to the side and behind the house part of the stud farm?"

"They are. Those are the stables, an indoor arena, equipment sheds, tack room, and paddocks. There are more buildings on the far side that you can't see from here."

"It must be a huge operation. I'm impressed."

"I'll take you on a tour of it later." Shane parked the car and turned toward me. "Are you sure you're comfortable staying here with me for the next two nights until you fly home?"

"I am. Your aunt and uncle sound like nice people."

"They are. You'll like them."

We toted our luggage up to the house, entering a foyer with a stunning double grand staircase. Off to our right was a parlor with yellow walls, French provincial furniture, and a bank of windows facing the front of the house. After depositing our luggage next to the staircase, Shane escorted me through an entryway underneath the stairs to a large living room. Patrick and Caitlin were sitting on a beige-colored brocade couch next to an ornately carved fireplace. An older couple sat on a second couch across from them, a coffee table between the pieces of furniture. A third couple sat in two chairs between the sofas. I assumed the man was Niall.

"It's about time you got here." Caitlin jumped up and hurried toward us. She gave me a huge hug. "I'm tickled at the news. I knew you two were meant for each other from the very beginning. Thank goodness my cousin finally figured it out."

"Hey, you better watch it." Shane gave her a mock scowl.

"That's what you get for making me wait for you to get here." Caitlin took me by the arm. "Come with me. I want to introduce you to my family." She walked me over to the sitting area by the fireplace and motioned toward the couch across from Patrick. "These are my parents, Colin and Neasa."

"It's nice to meet you both." I stepped forward as they both stood.

Shane's uncle was a tall man with an average build, brown hair interspersed with gray, and a kind-looking face. There was an abundance of laugh lines around his eyes. Shane's aunt was motherly looking, wearing horn-rimmed eyeglasses with her auburn hair pulled back into a tidy bun.

"It's about time someone got Shane to settle down. I like you already." Colin chuckled and shook my hand.

I turned toward Neasa and found myself suddenly wrapped in her embrace.

"Liz, I'm so happy to meet you. I've never seen my nephew happier. I can't wait to show you his childhood photos and tell you all his embarrassing stories." She gave a short, half-suppressed laugh as Shane came rushing toward us with a horrified look on his face.

"Auntie, don't you dare." He was looking at her as if trying to figure out whether she was serious or not.

"I'm Niall, and this is my wife, Tara. I figure I better

butt in and save you from my family before all this excitement gets them too carried away."

"Oh, don't mind my husband. He's always the serious-minded conventional one. The family is lovely," Tara said with a slight chuckle.

"It's nice to meet you." I smiled at the two of them. Tara was short with long red hair and reminded me of Mel. Niall was a younger version of his father and not the mean or evil-looking person I envisioned. Our eyes locked when I studied his face, wondering what other preconceived opinions he had of me.

Niall frowned and shifted his gaze.

"Liz, Shane—come sit next to me and tell me what you booked for the wedding." Neasa sat on the couch and patted the space next to her.

Shane and I joined her.

"I texted you the date, Auntie. We figured marrying in April would give us plenty of time to work out the wedding details, plus the weather should be decent." Shane handed Neasa the folder the wedding specialist had given him. "The ceremony will be outside in the rose garden, and the reception will be in their hall. The contract inside the folder details the wedding package we chose. You can look at it."

Neasa opened the folder and looked through the paperwork. "This is a very nice package. You still have a few details to sort out, like the musicians, photographer, flowers, and a few other things. Do you want help with any of this?"

"Liz and I would welcome the help." Shane glanced at me, and I nodded my head.

"Oh, this is going to be fun." Caitlin rubbed her hands together. "Mom, Tara, and I can work on anything you need us to take care of on this end."

"Thank you. We appreciate it." I was relieved to have help. Trying to plan it all from back home would be a challenge.

A stocky middle-aged woman in a uniform walked into the room. "Mr. Ferguson and Ms. Bradley are here. Shall I show them in?"

"Yes, Maeve. Please bring them in here." Neasa glanced at Shane. "We're all here. Tea should be ready in a few minutes." She turned toward Niall. "Can you round up the kids?"

"Of course." Niall left the room, running into Conor and Mel in the foyer. The sound of his exuberance at seeing Conor flowed to the living room.

Mel rushed into the room, followed by Conor. She hugged me and then Shane. "Dang. I knew it. I knew you two were destined to be together. I'm so excited for both of you."

"Everyone, this is Mel. She and Liz have been friends since they were children," Shane said. "Mel, this is my aunt Neasa, my uncle Colin, and my cousin's wife, Tara." Shane motioned to each person as he introduced them. "You met my cousin, Niall, out in the entryway. Of course, you already know Caitlin and Patrick."

"Hi, everybody." Mel gave a wave of her hand in response to their greetings.

"Conor, what a pleasant surprise it is to see you. It's been a while." Colin walked over to Conor and shook his hand. The two of them quickly engaged in conversation.

Two boys dashed into the room, running up to Shane. Niall was several steps behind them.

"Can we practice boxing since you're here?" The younger boy looked pleadingly at Shane as he bounced up and down with excitement.

"Not right now. We're getting ready to have tea." Shane ruffled the boy's hair.

"Shane spoils my boys." Niall stood next to me, smiling. "They get excited when they hear he's coming to visit. When Shane leaves, the boys want to know when he'll be back. The one with the disappointed look on his face is Michael. He's our youngest. Our older boy is Ronan. Boys, say hello to Liz."

"Hello," the boys greeted me in unison.

"Hello. It's nice to meet you both."

"Shane, you're here." A dark-haired girl came bounding into the room. She ran up to Shane and hugged him. "Can we take the horses out for a ride?"

"This is Patrick and Caitlin's daughter, Glenna." Shane put a hand on Glenna's shoulder and spun her around to face me. "This is my future wife, Liz."

Glenna rushed over to me, giving me a hug. "Can I see the ring? I heard my mom helped pick it out."

"She did, and it's gorgeous." I held out my hand and showed Glenna the ring.

"Shane spoils her too," Niall said, laughing.

"He does not," Glenna said, pouting.

"Tea is ready." Maeve made her announcement from the doorway. She stood off to the side, motioning everyone down the hall.

Shane led me into the formal dining room. It was

large and stately in appearance but uniquely comfortable, containing small personal touches that kept it from being stuffy and over the top. The table had been elegantly set with silver tea sets, and a row of tiered tea stands filled with finger sandwiches, scones, cakes, and pastries lined its middle. A congratulatory banner adorned the wall, and a cake inscribed with "Happy Birthday Shane" was on a table in the corner, the original celebration blossoming into much more. Colin took his seat at the head of the table while Neasa took the chair at the other end, motioning for Shane and me to sit next to her.

Maeve went to the sideboard to fill champagne flutes with something nonalcoholic based on the bottle's label. She walked around the table, handing out the beverage.

Colin raised his glass after everyone settled at the table. "Liz. On behalf of my family, it is with immense pleasure I welcome you and congratulate you and Shane on your upcoming nuptials. Would everyone please join me in a toast?"

Everyone raised their glasses. Neasa beamed at Shane and me while the children giggled.

"May you have love that never ends, lots of money, and lots of friends. Health be yours, whatever you do, and may God send many blessings to you." Colin glanced around the table. "To Shane and Liz."

There was a round of clinking glasses and cheers.

"Mo ghra. I look forward to spending my life with you." Shane clinked my glass, and then he kissed me.

"Ahh. Those two are so cute together. I knew it from the start." Caitlin smiled at us from the other end of the table.

The children giggled once again.

"Liz, I understand you live in San Diego." Neasa poured herself a cup of tea and selected a sandwich from one of the tea stands. "What do you do for a living?"

"I'm an investment manager for a government agency. I oversee their cash and investments." I stole a peek at Niall, sitting across from me, catching him raise an eyebrow at Shane.

"Have you been there long?"

"Twelve years. I started as an accountant and worked my way up." I turned in my chair toward Shane. "I just realized I don't know where you work. Dylan mentioned you were a lawyer for a government agency, but he didn't give any details. I assume you work for a city or state agency."

"Not quite. It's federal. I work for the Central Intelligence Agency."

"Seriously? You're not secretly a spy or something like that, are you?"

"No. Nothing colorful like that," Shane said, laughing. "I started there as an attorney in the Office of General Counsel, working on employment and personnel issues. Management promoted me to Deputy Counsel in the Office of Inspector General a year ago. Now I conduct audits, inspections, and investigations relating to the agency's programs and operations."

"Well, I'm impressed." I gazed proudly at Shane.

"Thank you. I'm impressed with yours."

"So, Liz. I understand the cost of living in California is extremely high. What's the average rent where you live?" Niall eyed me from across the table.

"I honestly don't know. I own my home." I suspected Niall's question was an attempt to draw information from me regarding my finances and stability. It made me wonder what he was going to ask next.

"Conor, I understand you opened up a distillery in Kilkenny," Colin said, switching the conversation over to Conor.

"I have. It took about a year to get the place up and running and the doors open. But the business is doing grand."

"Well, I'm proud of you, son. That's been your dream for quite some time."

"It has. I appreciate the kind words, Mr. Moore."

I took a finger sandwich and a scone from the tea stand, listening to the discussions around the table. Shane's family seemed like wonderful people, and I was delighted to become a part of it. After acknowledging Shane's birthday with the cake and a song, the children began to get restless. Glenna excused herself and left the room, and the two boys quickly followed suit. The rest of us continued our stories and conversation as the afternoon slipped away.

Conor pushed his chair back, gaining everyone's attention. "We've enjoyed the celebration, but Mel and I need to crack on."

"Are you sure? We've not seen you in a while. You're more than welcome to stay," Neasa said, looking disappointed.

"We'd like to, but Mel and I are going to a concert at Saint Canice's Cathedral tonight."

I snapped my head toward Mel, catching her grinning at me.

"Liz and I will walk you out." Shane stood and waited for me to join him.

Mel got up from her chair. "It was nice to meet everybody." She gave a little wave in response to the round of goodbyes and followed Conor from the dining room.

Shane and I walked them to Conor's car.

"Thanks for coming up here to join us." Shane shook Conor's hand.

"I wouldn't have missed it. Congratulations again." Conor clapped Shane on the shoulder, and then he stepped toward me. He gave me a huge hug, squeezing the air from my lungs. "Liz. Shane's a fine man, and I'm happy for the two of you. Mel and I need to head on, but I don't want you to worry. I'll take care of her." He gave me a sweet smile as he took a step back, waiting for Mel.

I couldn't help a grin. Conor was indeed a giant teddy bear.

Mel hugged me and whispered in my ear, "He wants me to stay with him tonight. I can't wait. I'll call you tomorrow." She pulled away and walked over to Shane, hugging him goodbye.

I waved as they drove away, thrilled to see Mel so happy.

"Check out the boys. They're playing by the pond and being mischievous like usual." Shane pointed toward the small body of water a short distance away. He laughed as the boys chased each other with Super Soaker water guns through a small stand of trees behind the wood gazebo.

Michael gave Ronan a good soaking and dashed across the bright red wooden footbridge as Ronan returned fire. He reached the concrete path on the other side and ran toward us with Ronan in hot pursuit.

"I need to ask the boys something. Hang on a minute." Before Shane could say anything, I hurried across the manicured lawn, reaching the boys as they chased each other around a group of bushes. "Ronan, can I borrow your water gun for a minute? I'll give it back."

"Okay." Ronan eyed me suspiciously as he handed me the water gun. "What are you going to do with it?"

"You'll see." I strolled toward Shane while pretending to examine the water gun. "Ronan says this thing isn't working right. Can you look at it?"

"Sure. But Ronan was doing pretty well with it." Shane reached out to take the toy.

I swiveled the gun in my hands and pointed it at him, hitting him with several blasts of water. Then I bolted across the grass, my laughter carrying through the air.

Shane stood there sputtering, looking completely surprised. Recovering, he chased me up and down the lawn as I kept dodging out of his reach. Finally gaining hold of me, Shane tried to pry the water gun from my fingers.

I tripped, taking him with me as I tumbled to the ground. I laughed as we rolled around the grass, fighting for the water gun.

Shane ended up haphazardly on top of me. He stopped moving and looked at me, his expression suddenly changing as he leaned down and kissed me.

I let go of the toy and wrapped my arms around his neck, ardently returning his kiss.

Michael squealed with delight, blasting me in the face with water as he let loose on us with his Super Soaker.

"Ow," I cried, covering my nose with my hand. I had jerked my head to the side to avoid the deluge of water right as Shane tried to block it, his hand hitting me in the face.

"Damn, are you okay? I swear. I didn't mean to hit you."

I touched my face. There was no blood, and I could wiggle my nose with my fingers without too much pain. "I'm fine. It just stings." I looked for Michael, spotting him running down the lawn with his back to us. "Umm. I think Michael's expecting you to chase him. You better go after him."

"Are you sure? I don't want to leave if you're hurt."

"I'm fine." I started laughing as Michael continued running down the lawn. "You better get him before he reaches the stables."

Shane jumped up, grabbed the water gun I had taken from Ronan, and ran after Michael toward the horse facilities. Their laughter pierced the air.

I sat in the grass, watching them chase each other around the property as they drenched each other with water. A shadow suddenly appeared on the ground in front of me. I turned my head, finding Niall standing behind me.

"May I join you?"

"Of course." I motioned to a spot on the ground next to me.

Niall took a seat on the grass and stretched his legs

out. "I owe you an apology."

"And why is that?"

"Because of what I said to Shane on the phone earlier. I know you heard me, and that was not my intention, nor was it to hurt you. And I have to say, in the short time I've witnessed you and Shane together, it's become pretty clear there is something genuine between you. It's also impossible to miss how much you love one another." Niall held his hand up before I could say anything. "But in my defense, Shane hasn't had the best history. He tends to get involved with women with an unsuitable character. And he's like my little brother, so I've become a bit protective of him."

"I'm not going to hurt him. If you're worried I'm in this relationship for some unsavory purpose, please get that thought out of your head. I have a career. I own my home, and I'm self-sufficient and independent. I'm not with Shane because I want something from him. I'm with him because I love him."

"I can see that now. So, if you don't mind, can we start over, and let me express my heartfelt congratulations and welcome you to the family?"

"I would like that."

"Thank you. Welcome to the family, Liz. And I truly mean that."

"I appreciate that, Niall."

"Well, I better go save Shane from my boys. They can be relentless." Niall got up and jogged across the lawn toward Michael.

I sat there, wondering if anyone else would voice reservations about our hasty engagement.

CHAPTER 12

GLENDALOUGH

S HANE AND I left the stables and headed back to the house after our morning horseback riding tour of his family's estate. Although a delightful excursion, I couldn't help feeling saddened by the knowledge that this was our last day together. Mel and I were flying home tomorrow while he was staying for another week. Resigned to the inevitable, I pushed my melancholy thoughts aside, determined to enjoy the day.

"I had fun on the horseback ride," I said, smiling. "Hopefully I wasn't too bad in the saddle." My skill level was intermediate, as I'd ridden horses occasionally since I was a girl. Although I looked more like a novice compared to Shane. It was evident that he was an expert on a horse.

"You rode pretty well. I could tell you've been on a horse more than a few times." Shane reached out and grabbed my arm, pulling me toward him. "Watch where you step. That pile on the ground would have made a mess of your boots."

"Thanks. I didn't even see it." I passed through a gate as Shane held it open for me. The front of the house was visible in the distance. "I didn't expect the property to be so huge. You said Niall helps your uncle run the stud farm. Do they also manage the acreage with the cattle and sheep? There was a good-sized house next to one of the fields."

"Colin does, with the help of a farm manager, Mr. O'Hara. He lives with his family in that house you saw on an eighty-acre parcel. I should mention that the house, livestock, and acreage are mine. I inherited it when my parents died in the train accident. It went into a trust that Colin managed until I reached twenty-one, and now I operate it with the help of Mr. O'Hara and Colin. That's one of the reasons I visit several times a year. I check on the property and the business."

"That's yours? Why didn't you say something when we were there?"

"I don't know. Would you have looked at me differently if I did?" Shane was eyeing me strangely as he asked the question.

"Of course not. But it would have been nice to know. Do you have any other surprises you'd care to share?"

"No. That was it. I don't have anything to do with the stud farm. It's all Colin's, which will go to Niall and Caitlin. The stud operation started at about the same size as my farm, but Colin purchased the surrounding land over the years and expanded. That's why I had to hire Mr. O'Hara. The stud operation got so big, Colin couldn't manage my property on his own anymore."

"I'm impressed but still clueless why you didn't tell me you owned the property when you showed it to me."

Shane stopped and turned to face me. "Honestly, mo

ghra, I didn't tell you at the time because of habit and a few bad experiences. I've learned the hard way to keep my finances private. When I was in college, I made the mistake of telling my girlfriend that I owned the farm. Not long after that, she kept trying to get me to marry her. I thought it was because she loved me. Then I realized it was because she wanted my property."

"That's horrible."

"It was, but that's the type of woman I seem to attract. That's why I'd never seriously been in love until you came along. I knew none of them truly cared about me. Sadly, I also made the mistake of letting Anna find out about my holdings here in Ireland, and as soon as I did, she changed. We went from a casual date here and there to her wanting to move in with me. It wasn't hard to figure out that all Anna wanted was a piece of my assets. That's why she was so desperate to hold on to our relationship."

"You don't think I'm that way, do you?" I fidgeted with the pendant necklace I was wearing, almost afraid to hear Shane's answer.

"Absolutely not. You're not that type of person and never could be. I saw you were different right away. You're honest and down-to-earth, and I adore that in you. We're partners in this relationship, and I want to spend my life with you. I've spent years trying to protect my privacy. Now, I need to learn to share."

"Yes, you do."

"All right. Enough said. How do you feel about taking a hike in the Glendalough National Park? It's a forty-five-minute drive from here. We can pack a picnic lunch and hike to the lower lake. What do you think?"

"That sounds like fun. When I was planning this trip, I saw Glendalough listed online as one of the must-see places in Ireland."

"I'm not surprised. It's breathtaking. Let's go in the house and see what we can pack for lunch."

Shane and I went into the kitchen, finding Maeve preparing a meal for the family. She seemed startled to see us, especially when Shane poked his head in the refrigerator.

"What do you think you're doing?" Maeve stood in the middle of the kitchen, wiping her hand on her apron as she gave Shane a pointed look.

"I'm taking Liz on a hike in Glendalough. I want to pack a lunch so we can picnic at the lake."

"Get that head of yours out of the refrigerator. I'll make it. Now, get out of here. Go on. Off with you." Maeve waved her hands, shooing Shane away from the refrigerator. She turned toward me and smiled. "Shane always was my favorite. He'd come in here and keep me company when he was a boy while I made dinner."

"You're kicking me out? So much for being your favorite." Shane jumped out of the way when Maeve reached out to swat him. "Okay. We're going." He grinned and took me into the living room. We took a seat on the couch as we waited for Maeve.

"It's so quiet in the house and quite different from yesterday. Where is everyone?" I said.

"The boys are in school, and Niall and my uncle should still be at the office over at the horse facilities. Tara is at work. She teaches history at the secondary school in Newbridge. My aunt should be in her office in the house's west wing. Today is one of her volunteer days with the Genealogical Society of Ireland."

"I packaged up some of the leftovers from tea yesterday and put them in one of Ronan's old backpacks with some bottles of water." Maeve was talking to us from the doorway. She had a black-and-red backpack in her hand.

"Thank you, Maeve." Shane got up and took the backpack from her. He gave her a peck on the cheek.

"Go on. Off with you, now." Maeve laughed as she gave Shane a lighthearted push.

"We're going. Liz, can you grab my car keys from the coffee table?"

"I have them." I joined Shane, and we left the house, heading to Glendalough.

Shane drove east for a little while and then headed more southerly, passing the charming village of Hollywood along the way. As lovely as it was, the place couldn't have been more different from California's urban area. Amused, I couldn't help but smile when I spotted a set of white-painted letters spelling out the village's name, installed in a kelly-green meadow with grazing sheep.

"This place is the original Hollywood. It was in existence centuries before your California city was even a thought," Shane said proudly.

"Really? I had no idea. Ireland is certainly full of surprises besides being my new favorite place."

Finally reaching Glendalough, Shane pulled off the highway and parked near the visitor center. He put the backpack on, and we walked across a wooden footbridge spanning a narrow river. We hiked along a paved path with grass, shrubbery, and trees on both sides. A lake was in the distance, off to our right. Shane cut off the main trail and hiked down a dirt path to the body of water. Once there, we walked along the lake's edge until we came to a small clearing. After finding a place to sit, we stretched out on the grass, enjoying the view of the lake.

"This area is the lower lake. It's a bit of a hike to get to the upper lake and a steep climb to get to the cliff walk above it." Shane unzipped the backpack and took out several plastic containers. He opened them, displaying finger sandwiches and some scones. Placing two of the small sandwiches and a scone on a napkin, he handed them to me. "Is this okay?"

"It's perfect. Thank you." I ate my lunch while enjoying our surroundings. It was beautiful and incredibly serene. The air had an earthy smell, and birds were audible in the trees with an occasional rustling in the bushy undergrowth a short distance away.

Shane tucked everything into the backpack when we finished. He stood and scanned the lake. "Let's take a walk along the shore. If we're lucky, we'll see some wildlife."

"Oh, I hope so. That would be fun." I got up and brushed several twigs and leaves off the back of my pants. Relaxed and content, I walked hand in hand with Shane along the shoreline.

He stopped and pointed to an area at the water's edge. "There's a rocky outcropping up ahead. We can sit on one of the larger rocks and check out the swans. I can see a few of them on the lake." Shane led me to the rocks, and we took a seat on a semi-flat one. He put his arm around my shoulder, drawing me close.

"It's so peaceful here. I love the way the trees surround the lake. It makes it seem private, like a secret little place." I leaned my head on Shane's shoulder and gazed at the swans, their majestic white bodies gliding across the water. Intrigued, I watched two of them swim toward us. They stopped next to a clump of reeds, their heads turning back and forth as if trying to figure out what we were. "I've never seen a swan before. They're beautiful."

"This place is Mother Nature at its best. I never get tired of a walk in the forest, seeing the bluebells, and listening to the birds in the trees." Shane kissed the top of my head and squeezed my shoulder. "We need to discuss our future and make a game plan for when you'll be moving in with me. Hopefully we can arrange it so it's soon. I don't want to wait until after the wedding to live together."

I sat up straight, my body suddenly tense. "Umm. We do need to talk because I hoped you'd move in with me. What made you think I'd be moving?"

"I don't know. I just assumed you would. I own my place and have an excellent job with the potential to work my way up the management chain. It would be hard for me to move. Plus, we plan to have kids someday, and the school system where I live is pretty good."

"I own my house too, although I think I'm more vested in mine than you are in yours." I resented his automatic assumption that I'd be the one moving. Why me? Why should I give up everything to join him? My roots and personal life were just as important as his. I crossed my arms in front of me as I faced Shane. "I grew up in my house. It was my parents' and mine after them. Alex and I put a lot of time and effort into renovating it after my dad died and left it to me. My job is also important, and I have a very nice income. Our school system isn't bad either, so I'd say we could just as easily live on the West Coast."

"Hang on. I'm not trying to get you upset. I just think it would work out better if you were the one that moved. Try to take a step back and look at it objectively. I have a career instead of a job, and I'd be a fool to give it up. Management promoted me a year ago, and there are already whispers that I have a chance to move up again as soon as I get enough experience under my belt. I'd also have to pass the California state bar to practice law in California. That's another hurdle on top of finding a job. Plus, the cost of living is cheaper on the East Coast. You have to admit, living in California is expensive."

"It is, but there are benefits in return for the cost. Wages tend to be higher, and the weather tends to be decent the majority of the year. At least it is where I live, and the mild weather causes people to be outdoors more often, which leads to more active lifestyles. I read a survey that said Californians are typically healthier. You can't deny that's a plus. We're also known for our relaxed attitudes, diversity, and tolerance of others. Wouldn't you want that for our kids?"

"You know what? We need to put this discussion aside for now. Today is our last day together for weeks, and I don't want to spend it arguing with each other.

How about if we revisit it after I've gone to California and you've come to Washington, D.C. We'll see where each other lives, including the environment and lifestyles, and go from there. Does that sound fair enough?"

"I can live with that."

"Thank you. So tell me. Do you want to hike to the upper lake or head back to the visitor center?"

"I prefer to head back." Besides getting late in the day for a long hike, I was still annoyed by our conversation and wanted to head back to Kilcullen.

After hiking back to the main trail, we strolled along the path to the visitor center, crossing over the river once again. Reaching the car, Shane drove us back to the family's estate.

My cell phone rang when Shane and I walked into the house. I pulled it from my purse and looked at the display. It was Mel. "Mel's calling me. I'll sit in the parlor while I talk to her."

"I'll see where everyone is. It should be dinnertime about now." Shane disappeared through the archway into the living room.

I sat on the couch and answered my phone. "Hey. It's about time you called me. I left you a message early this morning."

"I know. I planned to call you back, but Conor sidetracked me when he took me to breakfast and then around town to see more sites. We just got back from an early dinner."

"Can you at least send me a text message next time to let me know you're all right?"

"Dang. Don't get all worked up. Nothing is going to

happen to me. It's safe around here, plus I'm with Conor."

"Speaking of Conor, how are you two getting along?"

"Better than I hoped. After the concert last night, I stayed at Conor's, and he was well worth the wait. The man has some talent. That's for sure." Mel giggled on the other end of the phone. "I checked out of Caitlin's hotel, and I'm staying with Conor again tonight. He wants to drive us to the airport tomorrow. Can you check with Shane and see if it's okay if we pick you up at ten o'clock in the morning? Conor said he'll bring Shane back to Kilcullen after dropping you and me off at the airport."

"I'll ask him. He's walking into the room right now." I put my phone down and waited for Shane to reach me. "Mel says Conor wants to drive us to the airport tomorrow. He wants to know if he can pick us up at ten o'clock. He'll bring you back here afterward."

"I'm fine with it. Tell Conor he can pick us up."

I put my phone back to my ear. "Shane says he's okay with Conor picking us up."

"Cool. I'll tell Conor. I have to go. We're going out for a couple of beers. I'll see you in the morning. Bye."

"I'll see you tomorrow. Bye." I hung up my phone and stashed it back in my purse.

"Dinner is ready. We need to join the family." Shane pulled me to my feet, escorting me to the smaller, informal dining area off the kitchen.

Shane's family was already at the table when we joined them. Everyone was there except Patrick, Caitlin, and Glenna since they'd gone back to Kilkenny last night. Shane and I took the two seats on Neasa's right.

Maeve stood at the sideboard, ladling stew into bowls as a young woman set them down on the table.

"Maeve made stew for dinner." Neasa glanced at me and smiled. "It's one of Shane's favorites. You'll have to ask her how to make it."

I looked down at the bowl the young woman placed in front of me. It had a brown gravy with plenty of meat and vegetables and looked hardy. I took a bite, impressed by the savory flavor. As we ate, I listened to the conversation around the table. Shane shared how our day went, and Niall talked about the new stallion they had acquired.

"If you need nothing else of me, I'll be leaving." Maeve placed more soda bread and fried cabbage on the table.

"Thank you, Maeve. We'll see you in the morning."

Maeve gave the young woman helping her some instructions, and then she disappeared from the room.

"Play me a game of billiards after dinner, Shane. We'll see if your game has improved," Niall said, teasing him from across the table.

"Sure, and you'll lose like always." Shane looked at me over his shoulder. He had a grin on his face and a sparkle in his eyes. "Niall likes to goad me. He thinks it'll psych me out, but it doesn't help. He's still a lousy player."

"Hey, none of that. We'll see who beats who. Twenty euro says I kick your butt."

"Let me finish my dinner, and you're on." Shane finished his bowl of stew and took the last few bites of his soda bread. He looked at Neasa. "Do you mind, Auntie?"

"Boys will be boys. Go on." Neasa chuckled as she waved him away from the table.

"Liz, are you going to come and watch or stay at the table and chat?" Shane got up from his seat and stood next to me.

"I'll watch." I stood and accompanied Shane and Niall to the other side of the house.

The billiard room was huge, with dark paneling and a row of windows overlooking a garden. A large fireplace with a carved mantel was against the wall near the entrance. There was a leather couch and several over-stuffed leather chairs in front of it. The billiard table and several wing chairs were in the middle of the room, with a bar and an additional sitting area against the far wall. I sat in one of the wing chairs and watched Shane and Niall play. They appeared closely matched in skill, although Shane was slightly ahead.

"Who do all those trophies belong to?" I said, scanning the bookshelf behind me as Shane approached the table.

"They're mine." Shane hit the white cue ball and then stood back to watch it travel across the red felt surface of the oak table and hit a yellow ball, sending it into the corner pocket. He hit the cue ball again. It hit his intended target, but the angle was off, causing the ball to bounce off the edge of the side pocket. He scowled as he turned toward me. "I got them when I raced motocross when I was a kid."

"You ride a motorcycle?"

"You sound surprised." Shane took a step back, waiting for Niall to take his turn. "My dad had an old 1967

Triumph motorcycle, and from as far back as I can remember, he'd take me for a ride on it. I was around six years old when he got me involved in motocross, and I rode competitively for ten years. I tried Irish road racing a couple of times, but it was too dangerous for my taste. I haven't ridden a motorcycle since I sold mine five years ago. There wasn't much opportunity to ride between long work hours and living in the city."

"You were young when you started motocross. You must have been good at it since you have all those trophies."

"He was." Niall bent over the table and took his shot, sending the green ball into a side pocket. He took another turn, this time missing. "Shane was a daredevil on his bike. He used to scare my mother half to death when she'd watch his races."

"Really? A risk-taker on two wheels. If you like motorcycles, you might like what's in my garage at home."

"What's that?"

"A 1945 Harley-Davidson Knucklehead."

Shane was leaning over the table, getting ready to take his shot. He stood up, giving me a skeptical look. "Seriously? In your garage? That's a vintage motorcycle and a valuable one if it's in pristine condition."

"I know, and yes, it's in my garage. It was Alex's pride and joy, and he spent years lovingly restoring it." I glanced at Niall. "Alex was my husband."

"Didn't Alex have an accident on it?" Shane furrowed his brow as he stared at me.

"No. Alex was on his Softail Deluxe the day of the accident. He had two motorcycles and didn't ride the

Knucklehead that often. My sister-in-law's husband has been pressuring me to give him the bike for a while now. I keep telling him he can't have it, but he won't let up. It's like he thinks he's entitled to it."

"He doesn't threaten you, does he?" Shane walked over to my chair as he talked. He stood above me, studying my face.

"No, but he's getting more aggressive. When you come to San Diego, we can take the motorcycle out for a ride. If you enjoy it, it might help me out."

"Help you? How?"

"I intend on pointing out the many benefits of living in California while you're there, and riding a motorcycle in our backcountry is one of them. I'll keep it up until I get you to give in and move to the West Coast."

"Hmm. Ulterior motives, huh." Shane sat in the chair next to me. "What's good for the goose is good for the gander. Expect the same in return when you come to stay with me." Shane chuckled as he got back up.

"East Coast versus West Coast. This monumental problem sounds challenging to resolve." Niall glanced back and forth between the two of us.

"That's all right. I'm not worried. When Liz comes to stay with me on the East Coast, she'll see how nice it is." Shane leaned down and kissed me. Then he walked back to the billiard table to take his shot.

"We'll see." I smiled at Niall.

After a few more turns, Shane and Niall finished their game, with Shane winning.

"Another game?" Niall pulled a bill out of his wallet and handed it to Shane.

"No. I think we're going upstairs. Tonight is our last night together until I fly to San Diego in a few weeks." Shane put his cue stick away and then joined me as I got up from the chair. Without warning, he picked me up and flipped me over his shoulder.

"What are you doing?" I shrieked, shocked by his sudden action.

"I'm taking my damsel, otherwise known as the love of my life, upstairs to my chamber so I can make love to her all night long."

I giggled from my upside-down perch on his shoulder.

"You two are crazy." Niall busted out laughing.

"Maybe so." Shane laughed as he carried me out the doorway of the billiard room.

"Good night, Niall," I called out, giving him an upside-down wave.

Shane carried me up the back staircase and down the corridor to his room. He plopped me down haphazardly on his bed.

"At your service, madam. What else may I do for you?" Shane gave me an elaborate bow.

"I would be ever so pleased if you would make love to me, sir."

"Ah, no need to rush, my fair maiden. Do you want the shower first, or shall I go before you? Alas, there isn't quite enough room for us both unless you care to take a bath."

"Well, my fine sir, I'll wait here while you take a shower first." I giggled, having fun with our playful banter.

Shane removed his clothes and started to walk toward the bathroom.

I fixed my gaze hungrily on him, my demeanor changing with his nakedness. "God, you're so breathtakingly sexy."

"You need glasses, mo ghra."

"I can assure you I don't."

Shane went into the bathroom and shut the door. I rolled onto my back and stared at the ceiling. I hated the fact that this was our last night together. The following three weeks were going to seem like an eternity. I sighed, slipping my arm behind my head. It would be a challenge, but we needed to resolve our West Coast versus East Coast dilemma.

"Your turn. I'm done in the bathroom."

I got up and took off my clothes, tossing them on a chair.

"I know I don't need glasses. You drive me crazy every time I look at you." Shane walked over to where I stood and kissed me. "Hurry up. I want you."

I went into the bathroom and shut the door, the anticipation of what was to come already exciting me. I tried to hurry, climbing into bed with Shane, the uppermost thought on my mind. Finished, I exited the bathroom, finding him watching me from the bed.

"Come get warm." Shane threw the covers back, the space next to him looking warm and enticing.

Aroused, I got on my hands and knees in the bed, leaving a trail of kisses down Shane's chest and stomach. I swiveled in place, turning away from Shane and giving him a view of my rear. I kissed, licked, and teased, my tongue caressing him wildly, his excitement growing beneath my fingers. A burst of groans came from behind me when I took him into my mouth. Then I moaned as Shane stroked and teased me between my thighs.

"Damn, that feels good," Shane said between panting breaths.

I couldn't take it anymore, wanting to feel him inside me. I turned around, grabbing the condom Shane had placed on the bedside table. I handed it to him. "I can't wait. I want you."

Shane put on the condom and then reached for me. "Take the top."

I climbed on him, guiding him inside. Thoroughly aroused, I threw my head back, savoring the sensation of his abdomen rubbing against the sweet spot between my legs. I ground my hips as I rode him, leaning forward, so the angle was perfect. Desperately wanting to release, I began pushing harder, our bodies merging in an erotic sensual rhythm.

Shane took my nipples between his fingers, rolling, pinching, and pulling.

I moaned, his action pushing me toward the brink. Then I toppled, an eruption of pleasure sending waves of contractions spreading through my body.

Shane grabbed my hips, pulling me against him as he thrust, his rhythm frantic. A groan came from deep in his throat as his body tensed and then relaxed.

I collapsed in his arms, my body spent.

Shane slowly rolled us onto our sides. "My God. The things you do to me. The way you make me feel. I don't know if I can go three weeks without you."

"I know. I was thinking the same thing."

Shane got up to dispose of the condom.

I snuggled against him when he returned, my eyelids slowly closing.

I SAT UP in bed, trying to focus in the dark, jumping when a hand touched my back.

"Is it the dream again?" Shane said.

"Yes." I lay back down, curling up against Shane as he pulled me to him. "It's so frustrating. Now that we know you're the groom, why am I still having the dreams? I don't understand."

"There must be some meaning to it. In time, we'll hopefully figure it out. You still don't know who the officiant is, do you?"

"No, but I have such a strong feeling that I know him. I just can't figure out who it could be since no one I know officiates weddings."

"Whatever the meaning, there's nothing we can do about it right now. We need to get some sleep." Shane looked at the clock on the bedside table. "Conor will be here in five hours, and it's going to be a long day for you."

I nestled my head in the crook of Shane's neck. Yes, tomorrow would be a long day and a sad one for me once I got on the plane. There was no question about it. We had to resolve our dilemma of where we were going to live.

CHAPTER 13

A WEST COAST VISIT

I T WAS EIGHT o'clock in the evening, and Maggie and I were a couple of minutes away from picking Shane up at the San Diego airport. His plane had landed fifteen minutes ago, and I assumed he was retrieving his luggage by now. I couldn't wait to see him and take him home. I was signaling to take the exit to the airport's terminal two when a call came in.

"Hello?"

"Liz, it's Shane."

"Where are you?"

"I just got my luggage, and I'm walking outside. Are you parked at the curb?"

"I'm driving up the road to the front of the terminal right now. You should see me any minute. I'm in a dark gray Range Rover." I was ecstatic at the sound of his voice. The last three weeks had been lonely without him.

"Okay. I see you. You're pulling up behind the black Honda Civic. I'm hanging up and walking over to you right now."

I craned my neck, looking for Shane, spotting him walking toward me. I hit the tailgate release button, and he put his luggage in the back of my car. He saw Maggie right away.

"Well, hello. You must be Maggie. Aren't you a pretty girl?"

Maggie had watched him walk toward the car. Now she was wagging her tail at him, her behavior unusual. She didn't typically respond to strangers that favorably.

Shane greeted me with a hug and a kiss when he got in the car. "I missed you, mo ghra. It's been a long three weeks without you."

"It's been an eternity. I couldn't wait to see you."

"Then take me home."

"With pleasure, Mr. Moore."

We left the airport and got on the freeway. As we drove north, I pointed out several sites along the way. Since it was nighttime, darkness bathed the picturesque view of the coastline. I'd have to give Shane a tour in the daylight.

"What's that facility on our left?" Shane pointed to a large grandstand next to the freeway.

"That's the Del Mar racetrack. It's for horse racing."

"Niall would love that. I'll have to tell him you live by a racetrack."

"See? That's another benefit to living here. I'm sure there's no racetrack within minutes of your home."

"Maybe not, but I have a lot of other venues close by."

"We do too, and I'm betting I have you in love with Southern California by the time you leave."

"You think so, huh? We'll have to wait and see, won't we?"

I peeked over my shoulder at Shane and smiled. He'd issued a challenge when we were in Ireland, and I was ready to take it. I turned my attention back to the road. My off-ramp was next. After exiting the freeway, we headed east. Turning left at a side street, I drove several blocks uphill through a residential area. When we reached the top, I turned into a court. My house was on the corner, with its backyard facing the ocean. I drove down a long driveway, parking in the garage at the back corner of the house.

"That's a nice truck." Shane eyed the Chevrolet Silverado parked against the wall of the three-car garage.

"It was Alex's. I kept it."

"It looks heavy-duty. I like the color."

"I do too. It's called Northsky Blue." I smiled, remembering the day Alex and I had bought the truck. Alex had had his heart set on a red one. It took a lot of effort, but I'd talked him into getting this blue one instead. The truck, like the motorcycle, had been a loved possession of Alex's that I couldn't bear selling.

We got out of the car, and I started to walk around to his side to get Maggie.

"It's okay. I'll get Maggie." Shane stepped to the car door and opened it.

"I better do it. Maggie might not let you unhook her from the seat belt."

"Too late. Maggie let me unclip her, and she's licking my hand. Come on, girl. Let's get you out of the car."

Maggie immediately obeyed, jumping down from the seat and sitting next to him.

"Well, that's interesting. Maggie must like you. Are you a dog whisperer or something? She doesn't normally like strangers to touch her."

"No. I love dogs. I had a border collie when I was a kid named Quinn. He worked our farm, herding the sheep, and I used to get in trouble for sneaking him into my bedroom at night. I always wanted another dog but never seemed to have the time for one."

Shane grabbed his luggage, and we walked through the garage door into the kitchen. Maggie came trotting in with us as I turned on the light. The family room extended beyond the breakfast bar with built-in cabinetry, a large television, and a fireplace facing us from the far wall. Windows and a sliding door to the backyard were off to the right. Maggie ran toward the sliding door and dashed through the doggie door cut into the wall.

"Now I can greet you properly," Shane said, placing his luggage next to the pantry and pulling me toward him. His lips were on mine, his touch intoxicating as his hands slid down my back to my rear. He lifted me, and I wrapped my legs around his waist. "Which way to your bedroom?"

"Make a right off the main hallway and go down the short corridor. You'll run into it."

Shane carried me into my room. Moonlight streamed through the row of small square-shaped windows on the wall above my king-size bed. He laid me down and then joined me, kissing me as his hands deftly unbuttoned my blouse. After unclipping the front of my bra, he took my nipple in his mouth.

I moaned, my body instantly becoming aroused. "Now that you started, you better not stop."

"I don't intend to. I missed you." Shane got up and

removed his clothes, tossing them on the chaise lounge next to the nightstand.

I sat up and removed my garments, throwing them onto the bench at the end of the bed. Then I lay back down as Shane rejoined me.

"Do I need a condom?" he whispered, kissing my neck.

"No. I went to my doctor, and she put me on birth control pills."

Shane rolled on top of me, easing himself between my legs. A groan escaped him when he slid inside. "You feel so good, mo ghra. God, how I've missed you." His moves were slow and deliberate as he gently pushed himself deeper.

I grabbed his hips and pulled him toward me, needing him to fill me. The sound of his moans in my ear made me even more aroused. I brought my knees toward my chest and tilted my pelvis, my breathing becoming labored as my muscles tightened.

Shane grabbed my legs, his rhythm growing intense. "Oh, Jesus. You're going to make me come already."

"Not yet. I'm not ready." I put my legs down. "I want the top. Flip us over."

Shane rolled us over, repositioning himself inside me as I sat on him.

I rode him at a frantic pace, my body on fire, the pressure building as I rubbed myself against his abdomen. I climbed toward the peak, little by little. Then I toppled over the edge. A long guttural moan escaped me as a series of contractions overtook me in quick succession.

Shane flipped us over again. With his body raised on one arm and his other hand under my buttocks, he plunged with frenzied strokes until a groan burst from deep in his throat. Finished, he lay on top of me, his breathing ragged in my ear.

We stayed that way for a long time. I didn't want to move, relishing his warmth, touch, and smell. My world was complete when Shane was with me. Maggie broke our moment of intimacy when she trotted into the bedroom and sat next to the bed.

"I guess we have company." Shane raised his head. "What's she doing?"

"Maggie's probably trying to figure out why you're in my bed since she's never seen anyone in here except me."

"She's likely being protective too." Shane rolled off me and sat on the edge of the bed. He turned on the light on the bedside table. "I suppose we should get up."

"I'm going to jump in the shower." I sat up in bed and looked for Maggie, spotting her lying at Shane's feet. "Just inside the bathroom doorway is a walk-in closet. You can put your luggage in there. There are plenty of hangers and a cabinet full of empty drawers, so you can unpack if you want. The bathroom counter to the right of the doorway is also empty. I have water, juice, beer, and wine in the refrigerator if you're thirsty." I got up and went into the bathroom, stepping into the shower a minute later. When I returned to the bedroom, Shane was watching a movie on the television above the fireplace. A bottle of water was on the nightstand, and Maggie had curled up next to his shoes.

"This is a big house. I hope you don't mind, but I

took a peek around. I can tell you like house plants and neutral colors."

"I do. Earth tones and plants make the house look warm and comfortable. I've never really liked bright or flashy colors or decorating in a way that makes a home look sterile. One of my favorite places is the side patio off the main hallway that connects to the driveway. It's quiet and relaxing and filled with plants. I like to sit out there and read."

"I'll have to check out the patio tomorrow." Shane turned, suddenly looking amused as he gazed toward the fireplace. "I like that cute little teddy bear you have on the mantel. Is there any significance to it? You have a necklace wrapped around its neck."

I focused on the ten-inch-tall caramel-colored stuffed teddy bear sitting on the mantel, its legs dangling over the edge. "His name is Henry, and he's special. My mom gave him to me when I was five or six and sick with chickenpox. The necklace was hers. It's a crescent moon with a star attached to it. The center of the star is a diamond. She gave it to me when she was dying. It was right after my twelfth birthday. She said the moon and the star represented the heavens, and she wanted me to remember that she was up there and always looking down on me. I think of her as my diamond in the sky."

"That's an extraordinary memory. Your mother's death must have been hard on you." Shane got up from the bed and came to my side. There was a softness in his face as he studied mine. "She loved you very much, I'm sure." He kissed me, his arms comforting as they wrapped around me.

I laid my head on his chest, absorbing his warmth. "I miss her. Those were some excruciatingly painful years in my life. Mel and her parents were my initial wall of support. But it was Alex, more than anybody, that helped fill the void in my heart and help me deal with her loss. I met him two years after she died, when my life was going in the wrong direction. He got me back on track." I sniffled, brushing my cheek with my hand. "Okay. Enough of that." I walked over to the bed and fluffed up the pillows. Then I slid under the covers. "I grew up in this house. Alex and I did a little remodeling in some of the rooms and had a swimming pool built in the backyard."

"It certainly looks comfortable." Shane glanced over his shoulder toward the bathroom doorway. "Well, I suppose it's my turn to shower."

"I left you a towel. I hung it on the hook next to the shower. Let me know if you need anything."

Shane nodded and disappeared through the doorway.

"GOOD MORNING." SHANE walked into the kitchen wearing hunter-green pajama pants and slippers. He slid onto one of the barstools at the breakfast bar. "I slept like a rock. I didn't even hear you get up."

"You were sleeping so soundly, I didn't want to wake you. I made some hot tea. I'll get you a cup." I pulled a coffee cup from the cupboard, placing it in front of Shane, along with the teapot, a small carton of milk, and some sugar. "How about some breakfast? I can make you eggs, bacon, and toast."

"I'm starving. That sounds wonderful." Shane fixed himself a cup of tea and then scanned the kitchen and family room. "Where's Maggie?"

"She's in the backyard."

Shane took a few sips of his tea and then walked to the sliding door. "I can't believe your view. You can see the ocean from here." He slid open the door and went outside, greeting Maggie as she bounded up to him.

My cell phone started ringing inside my purse, the sound coming from the counter by the pantry. I pulled it from the front pocket and answered it. "Hello?"

"Hey, Liz. It's Nicole."

"Hi. Give me a second. I'm cooking breakfast and need to put you on speaker." I hit the speaker button and set my phone down next to the cooktop. "Okay. You're on speaker. What's up."

"I was calling for two reasons. First, I was curious how your trip to Ireland went. I haven't talked to you since you've been back."

"It was great. Mel and I had so much fun. We went to a bunch of places and met some wonderful people. We'll have to get together so I can give you the details." I put several slices of bacon in a skillet and some pieces of bread in the toaster oven while I talked.

"That's the other reason I'm calling. I was hoping to see you. We're out here in Borrego. I told you about our trip a while back, remember? Anyway, I wanted to know if you're coming out here? Jesse is asking about you."

I couldn't believe Nicole was still trying to push Jesse on me. What part of I wasn't interested did she fail to understand? Her refusal to listen irritated me. "No. I'm not coming out there. I told you I wouldn't go when you mentioned the trip. Besides, I'm busy this weekend." I cracked open several eggs, depositing them in another skillet.

"I still can't get over your view. It's incredible," Shane said as he came back into the house and joined me in the kitchen.

"Who is that? Liz, I can hear some guy talking to you."

Shane sat on the barstool and peered at me, arching his brow.

"That's my fiancé, Shane." I grinned when I answered, knowing my response would shock her.

"You can't be serious. Just like that, you're getting married. You weren't even seeing anyone. Wait a minute. You didn't bring the guy back from Ireland, did you?"

Shane almost spat out his tea at Nicole's comment. He grabbed a napkin and held it against his mouth as he coughed.

"Hang on a minute. I need to grab my breakfast from the stove." I took the bacon and eggs from the skillets and put them on two plates I had pulled from the cupboard. Then I buttered the toast, setting the slices on the plates next to the eggs. I set Shane's plate on the counter in front of him. After joining him at the breakfast bar, I laid my phone down on the counter between us.

"Hello? Liz? Are you going to say something? You can't leave me in the dark like this."

"Nicole, say hello to Shane." I looked at Shane. "This

is Nicole. She's Alex's sister."

"Hi, Shane. Sorry about that. I forgot you could hear me."

"No problem. I'm sure Liz's revelation was a bit of a surprise."

"Jesus, Liz. He has an accent. You did bring him back with you."

Shane busted out laughing. Finally controlling himself, he cleared his throat. "I can assure you, Liz didn't bring me back with her. We met in Turks and Caicos, and I proposed to her while we were in Ireland together."

There was silence on the phone for a moment. Then Nicole spoke, her words measured. "Is this the guy that saved you from that fish?"

"Yes, Shane's the guy. Why don't we get together next weekend and talk rather than go back and forth on the phone?" I took a bite of my breakfast while I waited for Nicole to answer.

"I suppose that will work. I'll call you Saturday morning, and we can decide where to meet. Before I let you go, Kurt wanted me to ask about the bike again."

"I've already given you and Kurt my answer, and it isn't going to change. I'm not getting rid of the motorcycle. Shane and I are taking it out for a ride tomorrow."

"You're taking the Knucklehead for a ride? Why?" Nicole's voice rose, and she sounded upset.

"Because we want to," Shane said, his voice sounding stern. His jaw was tight, and he looked irritated. "From here on out, I'll be riding the bike, and it's no one's business what Liz does with it. Is it?"

"Umm, Liz, I think I should let you go. I'll get ahold

of you next weekend."

"I'll talk to you then. Bye." I hung up my phone and then looked at Shane. "See? I told you. Every time I talk to her, she asks about the motorcycle. Her husband wants the bike."

"Well, I'll put a stop to that real quick."

"You just did. As soon as Nicole hung up the phone, I would bet she ran to Kurt and told him about you and the fact you ride. Of course, that tidbit of information will piss him off. We'll have to wait and see what happens."

Shane finished his breakfast and put his plate in the sink. "I'll be back. I need to shave and dress. I want to check out the motorcycle and see if she needs anything. If Alex was still riding it, she might only need fuel, oil, and a battery." He disappeared down the hallway to the bedroom.

I turned on some music and started cleaning up the kitchen. I had just finished when Shane returned, clean-shaven and dressed in jeans and a short-sleeved shirt. I could smell his cologne when he kissed me.

"Is there an auto parts store nearby?"

"There's one in the shopping center at the bottom of the hill. It's at the intersection where we turned. You can drive the truck if you want. It's been sitting for a while. I've got every tool you might need too. There are a couple of rolling toolboxes against the back wall of the garage, underneath the workbench."

"That's perfect. I'll go down to the store after I look at the bike." Shane went out the kitchen door to the garage.

I went into the bedroom and dressed. I found Shane crouching in front of the motorcycle when I went out to the garage to join him.

"The Knucklehead is a beauty and in great shape. Alex did a phenomenal job restoring her. The black paint and chrome trim look sharp, and the only change he seems to have made was to put that seat pad on the back for you." Shane stood and took a walk around the motorcycle. "Even the saddlebags are in perfect condition. You weren't kidding when you said this was Alex's pride and joy. I can see why Kurt wants it." Shane walked over to me and gently squeezed my waist. "You want to go to the store with me? I'll drive."

"Sure. I'll go. Let me get my purse and the truck keys."

Shane drove the truck to the auto parts store. He bought several containers of oil, a filter, and a new battery. Before heading home, he stopped at the gas station on the corner and put gas in the container he'd placed in the back of the truck. When we got home, I left him to work on the motorcycle while I did the laundry. Finished, I sat on the patio in the backyard and browsed through my email and text messages on my phone.

There was a text message from Mel. She wanted to go to dinner at a restaurant on San Diego's bayfront and asked if she could pick us up at six o'clock. I replied, letting her know I'd confirm with Shane.

The sliding door opened behind me, and Shane poked his head out the opening. "I'm going to take the bike for a quick ride around the block to see how she runs. Is that okay?"

"Of course. You can use Alex's helmet. It's on the shelf in the garage. Before you go, are you okay with going to dinner with Mel tonight? She wants to pick us up at six o'clock."

"It sounds like fun. I'm up for it."

"Great. I'll text Mel back in a little bit and let her know she can pick us up." I got up and followed Shane out to the garage. The sectional steel garage door was open, and the motorcycle rolled out to the driveway.

I couldn't help thinking about Alex when Shane walked over to the motorcycle to start it. He placed his foot on the kick-starter as he stood next to the bike, bringing his weight down on the lever under his boot. Shane repeated the motion, his actions priming the engine with gas. Then he turned on the ignition and looked at me with his fingers crossed. With his boot back on the kick-starter, he brought the weight of his body down on it once more, giving the bike a good solid kick. The engine started up on the first try.

I stood there, completely transfixed by the scene in front of me. Shane had done everything I'd seen Alex do countless times before. I leaned against my car, Shane's actions and the rumbling sound of the motor overwhelming me with memories.

"You're pale. Mo ghra, are you all right?" Shane rushed to my side and hovered over me.

"I'm fine. It's just...I haven't heard the bike since Alex rode it a week before his accident."

"If you don't want me to take it out for a ride, I won't."

"You're the only person I trust to touch the bike. I'll be fine, I promise."

"Are you sure?"

"Yes, I'm positive. Please take it. I want you to enjoy it."

"Okay. I'll take it. I'll be back in a while." Shane retrieved the helmet from the shelf on the back wall of the garage and slipped it on. He sat on the motorcycle, bringing the kickstand up with his foot and putting it in gear. Then he took off down the driveway.

The sight of Shane riding the motorcycle struck me with a sense of longing. He looked breathtakingly sexy on it, just like Alex always had. Feeling the urge to watch him, I sat on the bench by the front door and waited for him to return. He was gone for quite a while, and I suspected he was having fun. I had gotten up to go back inside the house when I heard the motorcycle rumbling up the hill. The same rush of excitement I had always felt when I heard Alex coming home swept over me. Shane turned the corner, and my heart felt like it skipped a beat.

Shane's face broke into a boyish grin when he saw me walking toward the garage. He took off the helmet and placed it on the seat.

"Well, how was the ride?"

"It was sweet. The motorcycle is in excellent condition. It looks like we'll be taking it for a ride tomorrow."

"Perfect. We can take a ride up to the mountains. That way I can show off our backcountry. Where else can you go from beach to mountains within an hour's drive?"

"It sounds like a date, and I can't wait." Shane folded me in his arms and kissed me.

Nothing else mattered to me at that moment but him.

"So, how do you like San Diego so far?" Mel pushed her empty dessert plate off to the side and looked across the table at Shane. She had driven us to an upscale seafood restaurant on the waterfront.

"What? You aren't going to ask me about Conor again. He's all you've talked about since we've been here." Shane laughed when Mel scowled at him. "Sorry. I couldn't resist teasing you. San Diego. Hmm. So far, it's great, although I haven't seen a lot of it yet. The restaurant is nice, and our view is fantastic."

The restaurant's host had seated us in a booth with a view of San Diego Bay. Coronado Island was across from us, which housed the naval air station. A ship was at one of the docks. We had a stunning panorama of the downtown skyline to our left, a conglomeration of skyscrapers reaching toward the heavens. In the distance, the Coronado Bay Bridge was visible, its majestic span of steel and concrete linking the peninsula to the mainland. The sun was setting on the horizon, a beautiful orange-and-yellow kaleidoscope casting its glow on the land-scape as small wind-generated swells rippled across the water.

"So, what do the two of you have in store for me next?" Shane said.

"Liz and I are taking you downtown to the Gaslamp Quarter for some drinking and dancing. You can't come here without going to the Gaslamp. Besides, I have to help Liz sell you on San Diego. I can't have her moving away from me, now can I?" Mel cocked her head at Shane, the corner of her mouth turning upward into a devious smile.

"Wow. You two are tag-teaming me. Liz, remember that when you come to Washington, D.C. I'll have Dylan and Margaret in my corner, and they're relentless." Shane motioned to our waiter when he walked by our table. "Could I get the check, please?"

"Yes, sir, right away." Our waiter, Raymond, hurried off, returning a few minutes later.

Shane quickly scanned the bill and placed his credit card in the check holder. Raymond took it as he swung past our table again.

"I'll be right back." Shane got up from the table and headed toward the facilities.

Mel and I were chatting when I caught someone standing next to me out of the corner of my eye. I turned my head as Mel gasped. It was her ex-husband, Mark. He seemed to come out of nowhere, his presence taking us both by surprise. Mel's face instantly registered a mix of emotions. One thing was clear. She didn't look happy to see him.

"Hello, Liz. I haven't seen you in a few years. How's it going?" Mark stared at Mel, although talking to me.

"It's been a long time. I'm well. Thanks." I looked Mark up and down. He'd changed. He still had that smug look that I'd always hated, but his dark hair was shorter, and there was now a splash of gray around his temples. He'd also put on a few pounds. I looked closer. He had an abundance of wrinkles on his face that weren't there before. Good. It served him right. I hoped his life had been miserable over the last few years after the hell he'd put Mel through.

"You look terrific, Mel. I hear you're doing well. Could we talk privately for a moment?" Mark was dripping in arrogance as he stood there waiting for Mel's answer. He appeared confident she'd agree.

"Hello, Mark. I couldn't be better. Whatever you have to say to me, you can say in front of Liz. I see no reason for us to talk privately." Mel's voice was shaky. She reached over, taking hold of my hand underneath the table.

"Fine. If speaking in front of Liz is the only way you'll talk, then so be it. I wanted to tell you that I missed you and hoped we could get together for dinner or a drink one of these nights." Mark paused and stared at me, his body tense and a frown on his face. He appeared irritated at having to speak in front of me. "Mel. I made a mistake, and I know it. I'd like to see if we could restart our relationship."

"Hmm. You want us to get back together." Mel pursed her lips. It looked like she was considering his offer. Then her jaw hardened, and a sneer appeared on her face. "I'd have to be delirious and on my deathbed before I allowed you to come near me again. Frankly, you don't deserve me. I'm happy and have a wonderful man who loves me. Go away, Mark. Buzz off like the little mosquito that you are."

Mark appeared shocked by Mel's outburst and stood there with his mouth gaping open.

Shane came back to the table. He stared at Mel, quietly studying her face. Then he took a step toward Mark. "Mel, are you okay? Do you need help with anything?"

Mel gave Shane what looked like a forced smile. "I'm fine. Thank you. The little mosquito was leaving." She turned toward Mark. "Goodbye, Mark."

Mark seemed to come to his senses. He gave Shane and me a cursory nod, and then he glared at Mel. He swung around and retreated from our table.

"Who the hell was that?" Shane said, looking confused.

"That was Mel's ex-husband, Mark. I can't even begin to express how much of an asshole he is. He treated Mel horribly." I looked at Mel, noticing her strange expression. "Are you okay?"

"I am now." A smile began to transform her face. "I swear. Telling that asshole off felt so damn good. I can't believe the powerful feeling it gave me."

"Good for you, Mel. It sounds like he's a jerk and deserved it," Shane said, taking his seat.

"Here's your receipt, sir. Thank you, and have a nice evening." Raymond placed the check folder on the table.

"Thanks. You have a good one too." Shane added a tip to the bill and slipped his credit card back into his wallet. Finished, he grinned at Mel. "I think we need to celebrate your prowess at taking your ex-husband down a few feet."

"I agree with that." Mel jumped up from the table.

"The three of us have some drinking and dancing to do." She led the way out of the restaurant, a visible lightness in her step.

CHAPTER 14

AN AFTERNOON SKIRMISH

SHANE AND I were riding the motorcycle up to the mountains this morning so he could get a glimpse of our backcountry. I sensed Shane was excited about the trip. I was a little nauseous. I hadn't been on a bike since the weekend of Alex's accident and was already anticipating a host of memories to come flooding back to me. Although I'd never ridden with Shane, I wasn't concerned about that part. I trusted him and knew he'd keep me safe. My mission this weekend was to sway Shane towards moving to San Diego, and I hoped today's ride would help.

"Are you ready to go?" Shane had pushed the motorcycle out to the driveway and waited for me to join him. He looked rough and mysterious besides dashingly handsome as he stood there in his leather jacket, boots, and sunglasses.

"I'm ready." I hit the button to close the garage door and dashed through the opening as it started to come down.

"Hmm. You're looking a bit sexy in those knee-high boots and tight jeans. I'm not going to have to chase the men away from you, am I?"

"Not at all. It's in the attitude, and mine says, 'I'm attached. Leave me alone.' So there's no need to be concerned. Besides, you're the one that's a problem. You look a little too hot in your leather and boots. It's hard enough keeping my hands to myself. Now I'll have to warn the women away too."

"Very funny, mo ghra. As I've said before, you need glasses."

"Hardly. I have perfect eyesight." I gave Shane a mischievous smile as I put on my leather jacket and slipped my helmet on my head. My hair pulled into a braided ponytail underneath it.

Shane shook his head at me and smiled. "Okay, back to the ride. I know we went over the directions to Julian earlier, but is there anything I should know about the roads up there before we head out?" Shane slipped Alex's helmet on his head and put on the leather gloves he'd brought with him.

I stared at the ground as I shifted my weight from foot to foot, a knot forming in my stomach.

"What's the matter? You look uncomfortable."

"The road gets extremely curvy in some places between Ramona and Santa Ysabel, and we'll be riding past the spot where Alex died. We'll go pretty far out of our way if we go around it, so I think we should take the direct route. I just don't know how I'll react when I see it. I haven't been there since the accident."

"Are you sure you're up to it?"

"No. But I'll give it a shot."

"I'm sorry to ask, but could you show me where the accident happened?"

I took my cell phone from the small cross-body purse I was wearing and brought up a map of the area, zooming in on the spot. Then I handed Shane my phone.

He removed his right glove and zoomed in and out of the map, handing my phone back afterward. "Thank you. I thought I should be aware of where it was. If you start feeling uncomfortable, I want you to let me know. Okay?" Shane slipped his hand back in his glove, his eyes on me until I answered.

"I will."

Shane started the bike and got on it, pulling it upright and pushing the kickstand up with his heel. After zipping up my jacket and slipping on my gloves, I climbed on the seat pad on the back of the motorcycle. I leaned against Shane's shoulder and let him know I was ready to go. Then he put the bike in gear and drove out the driveway. We were on the freeway in a matter of minutes.

I leaned close to Shane's ear when we reached the outskirts of the small community of Ramona. "Don't go over the speed limit until you get out of town. Law enforcement here is notorious for writing speeding tickets."

"Got it." Shane obeyed the speed limit as he rode through the town's center, passing small shopping centers, mom-and-pop storefronts, restaurants, and bars. He shook his head when we passed two bikers on the side of the road with a sheriff's car behind them.

The spot where Alex had his accident was coming up, the remnants of a makeshift memorial visible in the distance. I felt sick to my stomach, anguish and pain like knives in my chest. I laid my head on Shane's back and closed my eyes. I didn't need to see it; the image had been seared into my memory like a brand three and a half years ago. Shane must have sensed I was struggling because his left hand was suddenly on my leg. He held my hand when I reached out and touched his glove.

We reached Santa Ysabel and began the seven-mile ride up the mountain into Julian.

Nearing the four-way intersection at the town's Main Street, I leaned toward Shane's ear. "Take a left here. There's a place to eat at the next corner with parking available behind the building."

Shane nodded and rode to the next block, pulling into the paved parking lot behind the restaurant and brewery. I climbed off the back of the motorcycle and removed my helmet, hanging it on the handlebar.

"Come here." Shane got off the bike and reached for my hand, pulling me against his chest. "Are you all right? I swear I could feel your body tense up when we got near Alex's memorial. You were shaking when we rode past it."

"It was harder than I thought it would be. I don't want to ride past the spot again. If you don't mind, we'll take a different route home. It'll take longer, but I know I can't go back the way we came."

"It's all right. I understand. Let's get some lunch so you can sit and try to relax."

"Okay." I held Shane's hand as we walked to the front of the building and entered the restaurant.

We waited in line to order our food at the counter.

When it was our turn, we ordered barbeque pork sandwiches and two amber ales. Shane paid for our meal and retrieved the beers the employee had placed on the counter. He led us to a table underneath a tree on the patio and handed me my glass.

"This town reminds me of a movie set for an old western. It's pretty cool, although crowded. I didn't expect it to be so packed," Shane said before taking a drink of his beer.

"Julian is a lovely place to come for a ride, although like you said, it gets crowded. There's a bar northwest of here that gets even busier when the weather is nice. We'll stop there on the way home since it's on the alternate route we'll be taking. You'll see motorcycles lined up and down the highway when we get there."

"It sounds like an interesting place. Taking the motorcycle out for a ride was a great idea, even though you had an ulterior motive. And before you get your hopes up, I should mention you still haven't swayed me to move to the West Coast."

"I will in time. I'm not done yet."

"I'm sure you aren't. So, any idea what you'd like to do this evening since it's my last night here?"

"I hope you don't mind, but I took some steaks out of the freezer this morning. I'd like to barbeque and sit on the patio with a bottle of wine while we watch the sunset."

"I'd like that."

An employee called the number on Shane's receipt, indicating our order was ready.

"I'll get our food." Shane got up and went into the

restaurant. He returned a few minutes later with a tray in each hand and set them down on the table.

We chatted about Julian and the surrounding area while we ate, with Shane confessing he liked San Diego better than he'd thought he would. Finished with lunch, we left the motorcycle in the parking lot and took a stroll along Main Street, checking out a quaint-looking antique store and several shops.

Shane stood behind me while I browsed a jewelry window display. "Are you ready to head out? If we plan to stop at the other place you mentioned, we need to get going."

"I'm ready. We've seen everything here." I held Shane's hand as we strolled back to the motorcycle. After slipping my helmet on my head, I stepped to the back of the bike. "When you get to Santa Ysabel at the bottom of the mountain, make a right instead of going straight. There will be a turnoff on your left to another highway a couple of miles up the road. Take the turn off. The bar and restaurant will be on that highway. You can't miss it."

"Sounds good." Shane put on his helmet and gloves and started the motorcycle. He took off as soon as I got situated on the back.

When we reached the roadside bar, Shane looked for a place to park, finding a spot between two motorcycles in front of the outside beer garden. He made a U-turn in the street and pulled up parallel to the space, waiting for me to climb off the back. Then he maneuvered the bike backward, pushing it with his feet until the rear tire was a few feet from the fence.

I was standing next to the bike, removing my helmet, when someone called my name. Startled, I scanned the beer garden. "Oh, shit. That's not good." I spotted Nicole waving at me from a picnic table full of my old motorcycle friends.

"Who is that?" Shane was still sitting on the motorcycle and had turned to look behind him when he heard my name.

"It's Nicole. She's the one you talked to on the phone yesterday while we had breakfast. The big guy next to her with the dark hair and beard is her husband, Kurt."

"I guess we're about to find out if there are any hard feelings about my riding the motorcycle." Shane got off the bike and removed his helmet. He had a frown on his face as he hung it on the handlebar.

"It looks like Nicole and some of the others are coming over here. I'm so sorry. They must have stopped here on the way back from their weekend get-together in Borrego." I hung my helmet on the other handlebar and turned to face the group of people walking toward us.

"Liz, you didn't tell me you were coming out here." Nicole leaned over the four-foot-tall wood-and-chicken-wire fence and hugged me.

"It was a last-minute decision." I took a half step backward.

Kurt leaned over the fence and gave me an unenthusiastic hug as he eyed the motorcycle. "I'm surprised to see that bike out of your garage." The sarcasm in his voice was unmistakable.

Britney was standing slightly behind Kurt. Tall and

slender, she looked cute with her blond hair in braided pigtails. She grinned as she stepped forward and hugged me. "Girl, it's about time we got to see you. Where have you been?" She looked me up and down and then glanced at Shane.

"I've been working and staying busy. Nothing exciting beyond that." I turned my attention to Britney's husband, Glen, standing next to her. Also tall and blond, Glen wore his shoulder-length hair in a short ponytail. "Glen, it's good to see you. I've missed the two of you." I gave him a big hug.

"We've missed you too, Liz." Glen glanced at the bike. "I'm glad to see her back on the road."

"I am too." I turned to Shane, waiting patiently at my side. "Shane, these are some old friends of mine. This is Nicole. She's Alex's sister and the person you talked to yesterday." I pointed to the man next to her. "This is her husband, Kurt, and the two people next to him are Britney and Glen."

"It's nice to meet you all," Shane said, addressing the group.

Britney raised an eyebrow when Shane spoke. "I like your accent. Where are you from?"

"I was born and raised in Ireland. These days, I call Washington, D.C., my home."

"Nice." Britney grinned at me.

"How did the bike ride?" Kurt said, still eyeing the motorcycle. He had a bitter expression, his arms folded across his chest.

"Good." Shane's short response sounded guarded, and his jawline had hardened.

"Liz, the guys can stay here and talk about the bike. You need to get over here and fill me in on what's been going on with you," Britney said.

"Go ahead. I'll be over there in a few minutes." Shane pulled me toward him and kissed me. Then his mouth was at my ear. "It's okay. I'll come and find you." He pulled away and smiled at me.

I paused a moment and then reluctantly left him, heading toward the bar's front door. I was walking through the building when someone grabbed my arm. Startled, I swung around, finding myself facing Danny. He and Alex had been like brothers, together since they were small boys.

"It's about damn time you decided to show yourself." Danny looked down at me, his eyes gleaming behind a pair of black-framed glasses.

"Danny. Oh, my God, it's good to see you." I leaped into his arms, pulling away after a long, warmhearted embrace. "You chopped your hair off. I don't think I've seen it short since we were kids."

"My boss promoted me at work, and I supervise the day crew now. So I figured it was time to get rid of the ponytail."

"It certainly looks different but nice. So, where's Yvonne?"

"Honey, I'm right behind you," Yvonne said.

I turned around, Yvonne suddenly pulling me into a mini bear hug. "Yvonne. God, I've missed you."

"Aren't you a sight? Damn, we've missed you too. When did you get here?" Yvonne held me at arm's length, her thick black braid draped over her shoulder.

"I got here a few minutes ago. We rode up on the Knucklehead." I was thrilled to run into the two of them. Besides being good friends, I trusted Danny and Yvonne more than anyone except Mel.

"When you say 'we,' I assume you mean you and your fiancé?" Yvonne arched a brow, suggesting she was well aware of Shane. "Honey, don't look so surprised. Nicole has been telling everybody you're engaged. I wish that girl would keep her mouth shut for once. Where is your man, anyway? I want to meet him." Yvonne glanced around the crowded and noisy bar.

"Shane is out by the motorcycle. Nicole spotted us pulling up, and Kurt was questioning him about the bike when I left."

"Was Kurt pissed when he saw the Knucklehead?" Danny said, with a hint of satisfaction in his voice.

"I don't know about being pissed, but he certainly didn't look happy."

"Good. It serves the asshole right." Danny's jaw suddenly tightened. "Kurt's been shooting his mouth off saying that Alex would have wanted him to have the bike, and you should give it to him. So far, his bullshit has been nothing but talk. I'll nail his ass if he tries anything. That bike meant a lot to Alex, and there's no way he'd want Kurt to touch it."

"There you are." Britney was standing a few feet away. "I was waiting outside for you."

"Sorry. These two sidetracked me." I glanced at Danny and Yvonne.

"That's cool. At least you're with two of my favorite people." Britney squeezed between Yvonne and me and put an arm around each of us. "The three amigas are back together. I wondered if I'd ever see that day again."

"Looks like you're having fun." Shane was standing behind Danny. There was a sound of humor in his voice.

"And, there he is—Liz's hot-looking fiancé. Check him out." Britney had lowered her voice so only Yvonne and I could hear her.

"Shush." I nudged Britney with my hip.

"Oh, no shit. Damn, your fiancé is fine." Yvonne uttered her comments under her breath as she raised an eyebrow at me.

"Shane, you already met Britney. These two are Danny and Yvonne. Danny was Alex's best friend, and they grew up together. I've known Danny since I was fourteen." I stepped away from Yvonne and Britney and moved next to Shane.

"Nice to meet you." Shane extended his hand to Danny.

"Same here." Danny shook Shane's hand. "Can I get you and Liz a beer?"

"Sure. I'll take a Budweiser. Liz?" Shane looked at me.

"I'll take one too." I turned, spotting Yvonne walking toward Shane.

"It's nice to meet you, Shane," Yvonne said. "You must be a good guy if Liz likes you. Congratulations on your engagement. She's one hell of a lady, besides a good friend." She gave Shane a welcoming hug.

"Thanks, and, yes, she is." Shane smiled at me when Yvonne stepped back.

Danny got the bartender's attention and held up his

beer bottle and two fingers from his other hand. The bartender nodded and retrieved two beers from the cooler. Danny walked over to him and paid for the beers, handing one to Shane and the other to me when he returned.

Shane and I followed the three of them to a pair of picnic tables outside. Glen was sitting by himself at one of them, so we joined him. Kurt, Nicole, Jesse, and a couple I didn't know were sitting at the table next to us. Nicole introduced Shane and me to the couple, identifying them as Todd and Julie. They were friends of Jesse's. Unable to help myself, I stared at them for a moment, intrigued by their matching bright orange hair and faces full of freckles. They looked like brother and sister rather than boyfriend and girlfriend.

Jesse was sitting at the far end of the other table. He was a tall, strikingly handsome man with a muscular build, shoulder-length dark hair, and blue eyes. Tattoos covered his arms, and he wore a small hoop earring in each ear. Women usually swooned over him, but I pitied anyone unfortunate enough to enter into a relationship with him. I'd seen firsthand how cruel and disrespectful he could be. Jesse had had his eye on me when Alex was alive. After he'd died, Jesse had thought he could swoop in and take me, getting frustrated when I refused to fall for his charms.

Nervous, I glanced over my shoulder at Shane. I needed to introduce him to Jesse. It wouldn't look good if I didn't. I waited for a break in the conversation and turned toward Jesse, becoming startled at the coldness in his eyes as he stared at me. I forced a smile. "Jesse, this is

Shane." I turned toward Shane. "This is Jesse. I've known him for a long time."

"Nice to meet you," Shane said. He nodded pleasantly at Jesse, but there was a tenseness in his body.

Jesse nodded but said nothing in return.

"Shane, how long have you been riding?" Danny said, his inquiry easing the tension in the air.

"I rode my first motorbike when I was six. I competed in motocross for ten years when I was a kid and rode in two Irish road races when I turned eighteen. I sold my Harley about five years ago." Shane put his hand on my thigh and took a swig of his beer, his demeanor looking more relaxed.

"Irish road racing? I've heard of that." Glen looked down the table at Danny. "That's some crazy-ass shit. It's a sanctioned motorcycle race, but it's on a public road instead of a track. I've seen videos where bikes fly over the tops of hills, crash into walls on sharp turns, dodge livestock, and maneuver around potholes while the spectators are only a few feet away."

Danny cocked an eye at Glen and then looked across the table at Shane. "How bad is he exaggerating?"

"He isn't. It's that crazy and dangerous." Shane grinned. "That's why I only did it twice."

The guys got into an animated conversation about Harleys and racing, with Danny and Glen appearing impressed with Shane. I figured this was an opportune time to visit the facilities.

I touched Shane's hand. "I'll be right back. I need to run to the restroom."

"I'll go with you," Yvonne said, getting up from the table.

We walked to the bathrooms housed in a separate structure behind the main building. Only one of the stalls inside the women's restroom was available, so Yvonne told me to go first. I took care of my business, washed my hands, and exited the building, intending to wait for Yvonne outside. As soon as I walked out the door, someone grabbed me from behind and dragged me around the corner, shoving me against the wall.

"Let go of me," I shrieked, trying to push Jesse away from me.

"Who do you think you are? I've made it pretty fucking clear I want you, and all you've done is blow me off. Then you tell Kurt you'll ride out to Borrego with me, only to be a no-show, and now you end up here with this asshole. You're a fucking tease. You're my bitch, not his." Jesse's face was inches from mine as he snarled at me.

"You ass. I never said I'd join you in Borrego, and I've never misled you. Now let go of me." My voice was shrill as I fought to get out of Jesse's grasp, his forearm across my chest as he pinned me against the wall.

"Let go of her," Yvonne shouted, grabbing Jesse's arm and trying to pull him off me.

Jesse shoved Yvonne aside, and then someone ripped him away from me and threw him against the hill behind us.

"Keep your hands off her," Shane growled. He stood there with his fists clenched, glaring at Jesse.

"You piece of shit." Jesse got up and rushed Shane, trying to grab him.

Shane maneuvered out of his grasp and punched

him, sending Jesse reeling backward several steps.

Jesse shook his head to clear it. "You're going to pay for that." He charged Shane, his feet and body in a boxing stance, hands in the air in front of him. Jesse threw a punch, and Shane dodged it.

"Come on. Is that all you got?" Shane said, taunting Jesse.

"I'm going to fuck you up." Jesse lunged, taking another swing at Shane.

Shane pivoted out of the way, responding with a jab from his left hand, followed by a devastating right hook. A crunching sound hung in the air.

Jesse toppled to the ground. He was out cold.

Several people rushed to Jesse's side, trying to revive him. Danny and Glen pushed their way through the crowd of onlookers to see what had happened.

"Are you hurt? Did he hit you?" Shane was at my side, checking to see if I was all right.

"He pinned me against the wall." Shaken, I launched myself into Shane's arms.

"What the hell happened?" Danny was standing in front of us, his gaze swinging from Shane to Jesse, who was still out cold in the dirt.

I turned in Shane's arms. "Jesse grabbed me. He wouldn't let me go."

"That's true." Yvonne nodded her head. "I could hear what was happening when I was in the bathroom. Jesse had Liz pinned against the wall when I came out. I tried to get him off her, and he pushed me away. That's when Shane pulled him off Liz."

"Liz, what did he say to you?" Danny's gaze was

intense as he stared at me.

"He said I was supposed to go to Borrego with him...Kurt told him I would go." I paused, trying to catch my breath. "But that was a lie. I told Nicole I wasn't going."

"Care to explain?" Danny glared at Nicole. She had walked up behind us and was standing next to Britney.

"I'm so sorry, Liz. I told Kurt what you said, but that's not what he told Jesse. Kurt made him think you'd ride out to Borrego with him and then told me I had to get you to change your mind. Jesse looked pissed yesterday when he found out you weren't coming. I didn't know it would blow up like this. I'm sorry." Nicole gave me a pleading look.

Danny marched over to Kurt. He was standing with Jesse, who was now on his feet and leaning against the building. An argument broke out between the three of them, and then Glen rushed over to back up Danny. It ended quickly, with Kurt holding his hands in the air and backing away. He and Jesse disappeared around the corner of the building, and Nicole hurried off to join them.

"They're leaving." Danny looked at Shane and shook his head. "You throw one hell of a punch. No one's knocked Jesse out before. I need to buy you a beer."

We walked back to the picnic tables, and Danny ordered a round of beers from one of the servers. The conversation quickly turned back to the subject of motorcycles.

After we'd been there for a while, Shane put his hand on my thigh. "We should head back, mo ghrá. It's getting late, and we still want to barbeque those steaks when we get home."

"You're right. We should go. We have a bottle of wine to share and a sunset to view." I leaned against Shane as he kissed the top of my head.

We got up from the table and said our goodbyes to the group. After a round of hugs and handshakes, Yvonne came up behind me.

"That name your man calls you is driving me crazy. What does mo ghra mean?" Yvonne said.

"It's an Irish endearment." I smiled at her. "It means my love."

"That's sweet. You've found yourself one hell of a guy."

"I did, and he's one of a kind. Honestly, I didn't think I'd ever be this happy again."

"Honey, after everything you went through, you deserve it. Now, get out of here before you mess up your plans. I'll call you next weekend."

"Sounds good. I'll talk to you then." I hugged Yvonne a second time, and then Shane and I walked back to the motorcycle. A few minutes later, we were heading home.

"THE STEAKS ARE done." Shane placed the platter containing the grilled steaks on the counter. He'd seared the outsides perfectly, their aroma filling the kitchen.

I retrieved macaroni salad and a bottle of wine from the refrigerator, setting them on the counter next to the dinnerware, empty wineglasses, and a pot of baked beans I had pulled from the stovetop. Shane opened the bottle and poured us each some wine.

"Here. Try the steak." Shane cut a piece from one of the steaks and held his fork out so I could bite it.

"It's perfect. Barbequing is one thing I've never done well. From now on, it's your job." I laughed at Shane's raised eyebrow.

We made our dinner plates, taking our food and wine to the table on the covered patio. The view of the coastline was gorgeous, with the sun beginning to set on the horizon. The air was fresh with a salty smell, and a light breeze blew across the yard.

"I had a nice weekend," Shane said, setting his wine-glass down on the table. "Well, except for the fight with that asshole. I'm glad Danny and Glen backed me up."

"Danny, Glen, and the ladies are good people. As I mentioned earlier, Danny was Alex's best friend, and I've known him since I was a teenager. Kurt isn't my favorite person, and Jesse is something else. I've never liked or trusted him."

"I can see why. Jesse seems underhanded and sneaky. He's the kind of guy you never want to turn your back on, so you need to be careful. I got the impression something is cooking between him and Kurt."

"I thought so too."

We finished our dinner. Shane took our plates into the kitchen while I refilled our glasses with the last of the wine. When he returned, we moved to the lounge chairs next to the swimming pool to relax and enjoy the view.

Shane leaned back in his chair and stared at the sky,

the last of its orange streaks fading into darkness. "I have to admit, I've got nothing as gorgeous as this sunset at home."

"Does that mean I get points for this evening?"

"If we were keeping track, sure. But don't forget, you still haven't seen what you're up against, and the East Coast has a lot to offer."

I was about to say something when Maggie walked up between our chairs.

"Well, hello, Maggie." Shane smiled when she laid her head on his chair.

"That's strange. Maggie's never done that before. I swear it looks like she wants to climb in your lap." I shook my head in wonder.

Shane scooted over and patted the space next to him. He started laughing when Maggie jumped on the chair and lay down. "Maggie, you better be careful. You're going to make mom jealous, and then we'll both be in trouble." Shane glanced at me. "You better watch out, mo ghra. Maggie likes me better than you." He reached down and petted Maggie, causing her to roll over on her back and nudge him for a belly rub.

"I don't believe this. Maggie, you're a traitor."

Shane chuckled as he rubbed Maggie's belly.

I couldn't help but smile. Dogs were a good judge of a person's character, and Maggie acted like she adored Shane. She would miss him when he left in the morning, and so would I. One thing was clear. I didn't like living apart from Shane, and one of us had to move.

CHAPTER 15

MAGGIE

I KICKED MY shoes off and sat on my bed. After fluffing up the pillows, I leaned against my headboard and opened my laptop to video call Shane. I hated calling him this late at night, but he had insisted I let him know when I made it home from the multiday conference. While away from home, I had time to analyze our pending situation with an objective mind. Having come to a decision, I wanted to tell Shane I would be moving to the East Coast.

"You made it home from Anaheim. How was the drive?" Shane leaned back against a stack of bed pillows and yawned. It was midnight on the East Coast, and he looked exhausted.

"Horrible. It's typically an hour-and-a-half drive, and it took me almost four hours. It seemed like I would never get here, and then I had to pick up Maggie at the vet along the way." I shifted on my bed and adjusted the screen on my laptop so that Shane could see me better during the call.

"I figured you got stuck in traffic. So, how was the conference?"

"Good, like usual. My San Francisco broker was

disappointed when I told her I was leaving a day early since none of tomorrow's topics pertain to my job." I paused, glancing toward the odd sound coming from the hallway. "Oh, no. Hang on a minute. Maggie sounds like she's going to throw up." I set my laptop on the bed and rushed into the short corridor outside my bedroom door. "Outside. Come on, girl. You have to go out." I shooed Maggie out the sliding door in the family room and slipped the panel into the doggie door to block it. After turning off the lamp by the couch, I went back to my bedroom, shutting my door behind me. I resumed my video call with Shane. "I'm back. I had to put Maggie outside."

"What's wrong with her?"

"She has an upset stomach from the food the vet gave her. I normally leave a bag of her food with the vet, but I forgot this time."

"I hope it isn't serious."

"It's nothing major. Maggie should be fine by tomorrow." I hesitated, debating whether it was a suitable time to broach the topic of moving. Shane looked so tired. I wasn't sure if I should wait. I decided to briefly touch on the subject and see if he cared to discuss it. "When I was in Anaheim, I had quiet time in the evenings to think about our ongoing issue of where we're going to live. I hoped to discuss the subject tonight, but it's pretty late, and you look exhausted. Would you prefer to talk about it tomorrow when we have more time?"

Crash!

I jumped at the noise, the sound carrying through the quiet of the house. It sounded like a loud metallic thud with something shattering. I cocked my head, trying to pinpoint its location. It had to be the plant stand by the sliding door to the side patio. The realization of what that meant hit me. "Oh God," I whispered, staring at my bedroom door.

"What's happening? Why do you have such a terrified look on your face?"

"Someone is in the house." My voice was barely a whisper, my body beginning to tremble. "It sounded like the plant stand in the hallway got knocked over."

"Listen to me carefully. I want you to go over to the sliding door in your bedroom and let Maggie in the house. Do it right now." There was an unmistakable urgency in Shane's tone, making me even more scared.

I put my laptop on the bed and got up. I jumped, eliciting a gasp as my bedroom door swung open. I took a step backward. "What do you want?" My voice shook when I forced the words from my throat.

"Shit. She's not supposed to be here." Todd looked wide-eyed at Jesse as he stood next to him in my doorway. "You said she'd be out of town at some conference."

"Shut up, you idiot." Jesse looked me up and down. He had a sneer on his lips, his eyes ice cold. "Hello, Liz."

"Come on, man. Let's go." Todd appeared upset, his cheeks as orange as his scraggly head of hair. He grabbed Jesse's arm. "She wasn't supposed to be here. We need to leave."

"No. The bitch already saw us. If we leave now, it won't change anything, so I might as well have some fun with her. I'll call it my payback for teasing me and leading me on the way she did."

"Bullshit. We weren't supposed to hurt anyone. I'm not going to be a part of this."

Terrified at the look on Jesse's face, I wanted to run, but there was nowhere to go. God help me. My only chance to escape him was to let Maggie in the house. Jesse was scared of dogs, and Maggie would give me an advantage. I glanced at the sliding door across my bedroom. It was too far away. I'd have to make it around the end of my bed and dash to the door before Jesse caught me. I might stand a chance if I ran for it while they distracted each other with their arguing. Either way, I had to try. I closed my eyes, trying to steel myself, my knees trembling. Then I bolted for the door.

"Fuck." Jesse scrambled after me.

My fingers grasped the handle on the unlocked glass panel, and I desperately tried to hold on to it as Jesse struggled to yank me away. I cried out as my hand slipped, and he tossed me like a rag doll onto the bed. I snapped my head toward the door when the sound of snarling ripped through the air.

Maggie was able to get her nose and most of her head through the gap I created in the doorway when Jesse pulled me away. She wriggled her body, growling and snarling at Jesse and Todd as she pushed through the opening.

"Fuck. The dog's coming in. Go, go, go." Jesse rushed toward the open bedroom door, pushing Todd out of his way as he bolted through it.

"Dammit. Wait for me." Todd ran out the door behind Jesse, the thump of their boots on the tile floor echoing through the hallway as they raced to the front door.

Maggie charged after them, and then there were screams, shouting, and snarling coming from the front of the house. The screaming suddenly stopped, and the front door slammed shut. Then Maggie started barking. I scrambled from the bed and ran from my room, stopping when I rounded the corner and looked down the hallway. Maggie was jumping at the door, trying to get out, and Todd's blue plaid flannel shirt was lying on the tile. He must have used it to subdue Maggie so they could get away. The sound of an engine starting carried through the air as I stood there.

Relieved, I glanced around the hallway. The sliding door to the side patio was partially open, and the wrought-iron plant stand was lying on the floor next to it. The ceramic pot had broken into several pieces, and the plant and a bunch of soil were in a messy pile. I rushed to the tall rectangular window next to the front door and peeked through the shutters. I needed to call the police, and they'd want verification Jesse and Todd had gone. While I scanned the street, a police cruiser came speeding around the corner, stopping in front of my house. Two officers bolted from the car and came running up my driveway.

"Maggie, stay." I threw my front door open and stood inside the threshold, calling out to the officers. "Two men broke into my house. They just took off."

"Ma'am, another police unit stopped a black Dodge Ram a block away as the driver sped down the hill. Can you describe the men, so we can verify if it's them?"

"One of the men is Jesse Hawkins. He's about six feet tall, with shoulder-length dark hair and blue eyes. He has tattoos covering both arms." The words came out of my mouth in a rush, and I could hear the trembling in my voice. I swallowed several times in an attempt to calm down. "Jesse drives a black Dodge Ram, so that has to be them. The other man is Todd. He's medium height with orange hair and freckles."

"I'll call it in." The shorter, bald officer stayed on my porch as he got on his radio.

I pointed to the flannel shirt on the floor when the taller officer came inside. "I found the shirt lying like this on the floor. Todd was wearing it, and he must have used it to subdue my dog so they could get way." I led the officer to the sliding door. "They broke in through here. I heard them knock the plant stand over. That's how I knew someone was in the house. I was on a video call with my fiancé at the time. Oh my God. Shane." I ran into my bedroom with Maggie and the officer running after me.

"Ma'am, wait. I don't want you to touch anything."

I stopped a few feet inside my doorway and stared at the floor. My laptop was open and lying on its side with the screen cracked. My video call with Shane must have gotten disconnected when that happened, and he would have been the one who called the police.

"You mentioned that you were on a video call when the men broke in. Is the laptop on the floor the one you were using?"

"Yes. I must have knocked it onto the floor when Jesse threw me on the bed."

"Are you saying one of the men assaulted you? Are you hurt?"

"Jesse did. But I don't think he hurt me anywhere."

"Can you give me a description of what happened?"

"After I heard the crash, I got up from my bed to let my dog in the house. My bedroom door flew open before I could move, and the two men were standing there. I ran to my patio door, and that's when Jesse grabbed me from behind and threw me onto the bed."

"What else happened?"

"I managed to open the sliding door several inches before Jesse pulled me away, and my dog squeezed through the opening. She chased after the two of them, and I could hear a horrible commotion by the front door. I think one of them used Todd's shirt to subdue her because whoever was screaming stopped, and then my front door slammed shut." I glanced at the laptop on the floor. "Can I please call my fiancé? He was on the call with me when this all happened, and he must be worried sick."

"I believe he's the one who called us. Since he's a witness, I'll need to get his statement before you talk to him. Can I get his name and phone number?" The officer took a pen and a small pad from his shirt pocket and wrote down the information as I gave it to him. "Ma'am. I'll need you to take a seat in the other room." The officer escorted me to the family room.

I sat on the couch and threw the lap blanket lying across its back over my shoulders. Maggie lay across my feet. Protective of me, she was sticking to my side like glue. Two more officers came into the house and joined the first two. They talked amongst themselves, and then the tall officer I'd spoken to earlier walked away. I assumed he was going to call Shane.

"Ma'am, do you have a motorcycle?" One of the officers that had just arrived stood in front of me.

"Yes, why?"

"One of the men we arrested confessed to breaking into your house. He pointed his finger at the other man and blamed him for everything. According to his story, the intent was to steal your motorcycle and burglarize your house, so it didn't appear that the bike was the target. He said they didn't know you were home, and when they discovered you were here, he tried to talk the other man into leaving."

"It must have been the redhead, Todd, who confessed. He did try to get Jesse to leave and told him not to hurt me. I think my sister-in-law and her husband might have had something to do with this too."

"Pete, you and Walt can take off. Lou and I have it covered." The tall officer came back into the room and stood next to the couch.

"No problem, Carl. The lady told me she thinks her sister-in-law and the woman's husband had something to do with this. You'll need to get more information." The officer walked away, rejoining his partner.

"Why do you think they had something to do with the break-in?" The tall officer, who I now knew was Carl, looked down at me from where he stood.

"Because my sister-in-law is the only person besides my coworkers and fiancé that I told I was going to a conference out of town. What I didn't tell her was that I was coming back early. She and her husband are friends with the two guys that broke into my house, so it makes sense that they thought I was gone."

"What are their names, and do you have an address for them?"

"Their names are Nicole and Kurt Thompson. They live out in Lakehurst at four twenty-one Carlotta Street."

"All right. We'll check it out. Do you know if the men were anywhere else in the house besides where they broke in and your bedroom?"

"Only the hallway by the front door, as far as I know."

"Okay. We'll need to see if either one of the men left fingerprints."

"They were both wearing leather gloves, so there won't be any fingerprints. I noticed the gloves on their hands when they stood in my bedroom doorway. Did you get a chance to talk to my fiancé? I'd like to call him."

"I did. Your fiancé gave me his statement. You can call him." Carl walked over to his partner, who was inspecting the sliding door to the patio.

I retrieved my cell phone from the kitchen counter and went over to the two officers. "I'm going to talk to my fiancé in the first bedroom down the hallway. Is that okay?"

"That's fine. We'll let you know when we've finished," Carl said.

I went into the guest bedroom and shut the door, with Maggie by my side. I sat on the bed and called Shane. He answered on the first ring.

"Thank God you called. I've been so worried. I talked to Officer Chastain earlier, and he said you were okay. He told me Maggie went after Jesse and Todd and chased them off. So, is what the officer said true and you're all right? I heard you cry out, and then our video call disconnected."

"I'm fine physically, but I'm still pretty shaken. I can't begin to describe how scared I was when Jesse and Todd burst into my room. The look on Jesse's face was terrifying. He grabbed me as I reached the sliding door and threw me on the bed, and I have no doubt he would have hurt me if Maggie hadn't stopped him. Now that the police arrested them and it's over with, I feel a little better. I'm pretty sure Nicole and Kurt had something to do with this, though. Jesse knew I was going out of town to a conference, and Nicole is the only person other than you and my coworkers that I told about it. I let the police know I thought they were involved. One of the officers told me Todd confessed and said the intent was to steal the motorcycle."

"I'm coming out there."

"No. You don't need to do that. I swear I'll be okay, and you don't have any leave time left. We have a few things to work out anyway."

"What do you mean?"

"I decided something when I was at the conference in Anaheim. That's what I wanted to talk to you about earlier. I'm moving to Washington, D.C."

"You're moving here? To live with me, I hope."

"Of course, and what happened tonight didn't have anything to do with my decision. I've thought and thought about it, and there are several reasons why it makes more sense for me to move than it does for you."

"Such as?"

"For one thing, it's easier for me to switch jobs than it would be for you. And like you said, you'd have to go through the added step of taking the California bar exam to practice in this state. Plus, you'd give up a lot more than me if you left your agency, and I'm pretty sure I could find something comparable to my current job, if not better, on the East Coast. I have to say, the hardest part of my decision was giving up my home. At first, I didn't think I could do it since I'd spent most of my life here. But when I stepped back and looked at the bigger picture, it dawned on me. This place is just a house. I'll still have my memories. Moving to the East Coast won't make them disappear. That realization led to my other reason for moving."

"Which is?"

"This one is a little harder to explain and has to do with Alex. My life with him is gone, and I'm starting over with you. Everywhere I look around here, I see Alex. Like how he used to stand at the sliding door in my bedroom and watch the sunrise. And the way he used to listen to music and sing to himself as he worked on the motorcycles. It's time for that to stop. I don't mean my memories need to stop, or I want to forget about Alex and our life together. I am the person I've become because of him. But now it's time for me to build a life, a home, and a future for you and me. I want to leave here, start with a clean slate, just the two of us with Maggie."

"I don't know what to say. I'm ecstatic but shocked.

That's a big decision and one I honestly didn't expect you to make."

"Well, I did make it, and it will be a huge undertaking. I should start by looking for a job out there. When I find one, I'll put my house on the market and move in with you while it goes through escrow. After it closes, we can take the proceeds and buy a house with a yard in the suburbs—something with plenty of room for a houseful of kids and Maggie. So, are you okay with my decision and ready to help me plan it all out?"

"Of course I'm ready. We're in this together."

"Thank you. After all the drama tonight, I'm exhausted, so I'm going to get off the phone if you don't mind. I'll call you tomorrow. We need to discuss this further, plus I want to come out there for a visit and will need to know what time frame works best for you. I thought you could drive me around some of the suburbs so we could check out the residential areas."

"That sounds like a plan. I'm glad you're safe, mo ghra. Now, get some rest. I love you."

"I love you too. Bye." I hung up my cell phone and leaned against the pillows, reflecting on everything that happened tonight. The most concerning thing of all was the way Nicole had burned me. I had a tough time wrapping my mind around the fact that she had done it. Setting me up was like doing it to her brother, and all for a motorcycle. It was both disgusting and unconscionable. Tired, I could feel my eyes start to close.

A sudden knocking on the bedroom door jolted me awake.

"Hello, ma'am?"

The police officers were still there, and one of them was knocking. I hurried to the door, opening it to find Carl standing in the hallway.

"Ma'am, we've wrapped everything up, and we're leaving. The lock on the sliding door is undamaged, so you'll be able to secure it. I suggest you install an extra lock on the track to keep someone from breaking in again."

"I'll do that. Thank you." I accompanied the two officers to the front door, noticing Todd's flannel shirt was no longer on the floor. I assumed they had bagged it as a piece of evidence. After showing them out, I turned the deadbolt on the door and made sure to lock the sliding door to the patio. Then I went to my room, picked up my damaged laptop from the floor, and lay down on my bed. Exhausted, I closed my eyes.

SHANE DROVE US down Yorktown Boulevard in Arlington in his BMW. We were going to the fortieth birthday celebration for one of his coworkers, Franklin Davenport, who he jokingly referred to as his work spouse. The two of them had become close friends soon after the agency hired Shane. I'd flown to Washington, D.C., three days ago to visit Shane and check out the surrounding suburbs, my timing conveniently allowing me to attend the party.

"Are you sure I look okay?" I smoothed an imaginary wrinkle from my dress.

"You look gorgeous. Stop worrying." Shane reached

across the console and took my hand, giving it a little squeeze. "Everyone I work with is nice. You'll like them. I guess I should correct that. Everybody except one person, Bryce Matthews. He's an arrogant ass and the one who tried to dig up unsavory information about you when we were in Turks and Caicos."

"I certainly remember that episode. He's Anna's brother. Is that how you met her, through Bryce? She won't be there with him, will she?"

"Yes, I met Anna through Bryce. It was at an agency function. I don't see why she'd be at the party tonight since I'd expect Bryce to bring his girlfriend, Crista." Shane slowed down and made a right turn at the intersection. "The venue where Franklin and Claudette are having the party is up ahead on our left. They host a lot of parties, with Halloween their biggest one of the year. Normally, they have them at their house in McLean. But they're doing some remodeling right now, so they had to rent a hall instead."

Shane drove up a private lane to a large estate. After parking the car in a paved lot, he escorted me into the building. A sign directed us to a ballroom at the back of the converted mansion. We walked through an open doorway to a room decorated with balloons and banners. There were tables set up in the center, and a bar was against the wall across from us. The other end of the room had a row of French doors that opened to a patio. A dance floor and stage were near the doors, and people had already filled the room and outdoor space.

"Hey. You made it. This must be Liz." A man of medium height with honey-brown eyes and black hair in a short curly afro walked up to us. He was nice looking, dressed in tan slacks, a collared shirt, and a brown sports jacket.

"Liz, this is the birthday boy, Franklin Davenport."

"It's a pleasure to meet you." I extended my hand to Franklin.

"Ah, hell, no. I get a hug." Franklin took a step forward and hugged me. Then he stepped backward and grinned. "I've wanted to meet the woman who got this guy to settle down. You must be pretty special since I've never known him to be in a committed relationship before. I have to say, your picture doesn't do you justice."

"What picture?" I glanced at Shane.

"The picture Shane has on his desk at work of you. I guess it's from your Turks and Caicos trip." Franklin laughed, shaking his head at Shane. "When he showed me the picture, he said you were his future wife."

"Really? When was this?" I raised a brow at Shane. My lip turned upward in amusement.

"It was after I called you, and we reconciled," Shane said, looking a little embarrassed. "The picture Franklin is talking about is the group shot of us in the restaurant at our hotel in Providenciales. I had Caitlin send it to me, and I printed it. It's in a frame on my desk."

A gorgeous-looking woman in a plum-and-dark-blue sleeveless jumpsuit joined us. Her black hair was in shoulder-length tousled curls, and she had high cheekbones and green eyes.

"Girl. It's about time Shane brought you around so we could meet you."

"Liz, this is Franklin's wife, Claudette."

"It's nice to meet you." I extended my hand, and just like Franklin, she hugged me instead.

Claudette took a step back and smiled at me. "It's my pleasure. I can't wait until we have more time to chat. Right now, Franklin and I need to meet and greet, so please, help yourselves. We have a cash bar and a variety of appetizers. We'll be serving dinner in about a half-hour, and the band should start playing right after that." Claudette took Franklin's arm, and they walked over to the door to greet a group of people that had just arrived.

Shane took me around the room, introducing me to his coworkers. It wasn't long before I had a challenging time remembering names. Just like he'd said, everyone, except one person, was pleasant. Anna's brother, Bryce, seemed rude and looked down his nose at me when Shane introduced us. Bryce's appearance had been nothing close to what I'd expected. Anna was tall, blond, and slim. Her brother was short in stature, a tad overweight, and dark-haired. It made me wonder if they were stepsiblings. Thankfully, our conversation was short, with Shane quickly whisking me away.

"Do you want anything to drink? I'm going to get a glass of wine." Shane stood next to me in front of the wall of French doors leading to the patio.

"I'll have one too. Thank you."

Shane walked over to the bar and ordered our drinks. Before returning, one of the guests standing nearby drew him into a boisterous conversation. I was about to join him when a voice came from the doorway behind me.

"What are you doing here?"

I pivoted in place, finding myself staring at Anna. "I'd say the same thing about you."

"I'm a guest of my brother's. Not that it's any of your business. Frankly, I'm surprised to see you here since I expected Shane to dump you by now. You're not his type of woman. He doesn't stay attracted to homely little plain Janes for very long. He'll come back my way. You wait and see."

"Really? If you think looks are the only thing that sustains a man's attraction, you're a bigger horse's ass than I thought. But then again, I'm not surprised based on how shallow you are. Besides, if Shane wanted you, I wouldn't be here. Would I?"

Anna looked as smug and obnoxious as I remembered. She had dressed in a low-cut solid white jumpsuit with her blond hair pulled to the side in a fancy knot.

"Liz. There you are." Claudette hooked her arm in mine and glared at Anna. "We're going to start serving dinner. I want you and Shane to sit at our table." She walked me toward a table in front of the dance floor, a group of people already sitting there. "Honey, that woman is such a bitch. Don't waste your time with her."

"I already let her get to me and responded in a way I shouldn't have. I know better than that."

"I'm sure she deserved whatever you said. Here, you'll sit at this table with us. Let me introduce you to my family. These are Franklin's parents, Raymond and Tammy. Next to them is my brother James, and his wife, Maxine. Everyone, this is Liz. She's Shane's fiancée."

"It's nice to meet you." I pulled out my chair and sat as everyone greeted me.

Claudette scanned the faces at our table. "We're opening up the buffet. You should get in line while I round everyone up and let them know they can get a plate." She hurried away, her family getting up from the table.

"I saw you with Anna. I'm sorry. I didn't think she'd be here." Shane looked upset as he took a seat next to me. "Franklin told me Bryce and his girlfriend are having some issues, so he brought Anna to the party instead. What did she say to you?"

"It doesn't matter what she said. It wasn't nice. What I said back to her wasn't either."

"Don't let her get to you. She's doing it to get you all riled up, so try to ignore her. That'll bother her more than anything else." Shane stood and eyed the line forming at the buffet table. "We might as well get in line before it doubles in size."

After a short wait, we returned to the table with our plates full. Shane filled up our water glasses from the pitcher in front of him and passed me a basket of rolls.

"So, Liz, Shane tells me the City of Arlington offered you a job as their investment manager. Congratulations. That must mean you'll be moving out here soon." Franklin took the basket of rolls from me as he spoke.

"I'm waiting for their human resources department to finish the background check on me. Once they officially offer me the job, I'll put my house on the market and move here. We've already started looking at prospective neighborhoods in the surrounding suburbs, and so far, I like McLean."

"Great choice. You'll be closer to us, and I'll be able

to bug Shane more often." Franklin glanced over his shoulder at Claudette. "Should we have the band start playing?"

"They're already getting ready to start." Claudette eyed the band as the musicians picked up their instruments, and one of them went to the microphone with a guitar in his hand.

"Hello, everyone. I'm Dave, and we are Midnight Sky. We'll be playing for you this evening. Before we start, I'd like everyone to sing happy birthday to Franklin. We'll do it on the count of three. Are you ready? Here we go. One... two... three." Dave and the band began playing their instruments and singing, with Dave pointing at us to join in. The song finished, and Dave addressed the guests again. "All right. It was a little off-key, but not bad. Let's give a round of applause to Franklin. Happy fortieth, man."

The room instantly filled with rapturous applause. Then the band started playing again.

"Dance with me, Liz." Shane pushed his chair backward and extended his hand.

"I'd love to." I stood and let him lead me out to the dance floor.

Shane pulled me close as we moved to the music. Then he twirled me and pulled me into his arms once again. "I love dancing with you, mo ghra. You always feel so good in my arms."

I laid my head on his shoulder, catching sight of Anna watching us from a table across the room. I kissed Shane's neck and snuggled against him as his arms tightened around me. "I love dancing with you too."

Curious if she was still watching, I lifted my head to peek.

Anna glared at me and jumped up from her chair. She said something to her brother, and then the two of them quickly exited the ballroom.

I turned my attention back to Shane, nestling against him as we danced. Pleased by Anna's hasty departure, I fervently hoped it was permanent.

CHAPTER 16

A HALLOWEEN TO REMEMBER

F RANKLIN AND CLAUDETTE Davenport's annual Halloween party was tonight. There'd been so much hype about the event over the last month that I couldn't wait to go, especially after Shane had informed me some of the costumes would be highly elaborate.

Brimming with anticipation and excitement, I turned from side to side, checking my costume in the full-length mirror in my walk-in closet. The saloon girl outfit was a bit risqué with the way the dress pushed my chest upward and squeezed my breasts, giving them a dramatic effect. The low-cut, snug-fitting bodice was a pink corset with tiny black polka dots and lacy shoulder straps. The adjoining skirt was a hi-lo style, with the front coming to my midthigh. It was black with a row of pink tulle lace six inches above the hemline, and I had topped the outfit off with fishnet stockings and a black lace choker around my neck. Smiling, I had to admit—I liked it.

Claudette was the one who'd picked out the dress and insisted I try it on. She had gone shopping with me for costumes, the two of us becoming close friends after my move to the East Coast three months ago.

"Christ, Liz. That's some costume."

I turned, finding Shane leaning against the door frame as he eyed me up and down, his expression full of hungry appreciation.

"Is it too much?" I gave Shane a mischievous smile as I spun in a circle so he'd have a complete view of my dress. "I have an old witch costume from a few years ago I can wear if you think this is too revealing."

"Oh, I like you the way you are. The problem is I'm not sure if I'll get through the night without putting my hands all over you. You look sexy as hell."

"I'm glad you like it. Your saloon bartender costume is perfect. You make a dashing protector and escort."

"Why, thank you, ma'am." Shane turned to show off his costume. He wore a solid white long-sleeved cotton shirt with a black ribbon as his necktie and a black garter on each arm. A brown pinstriped vest was over it, and there was a white linen apron over his brown trousers. He topped off the outfit with a black derby hat.

I checked my dress in the mirror one last time. "We're late. We should have been out the door forty-five minutes ago. I'll be ready as soon as I grab the cape I bought to go over my dress."

"I'd rather pick you up and carry you off to our bed than go to the party right now." Shane sauntered over to me and slid his arms around my waist. He gave me a long, sensual kiss and then pulled away. "Unfortunately, Franklin and Claudette would never forgive us if we missed it. So, we better go."

I retrieved my pink velvet cape from a drawer and slipped it over my shoulders. Then we left for the party. Having moved two weeks ago from Shane's townhome in Washington, D.C., to a large house with a good-sized yard in McLean, Virginia, we were there within ten minutes.

Shane and I strolled arm in arm toward the front door, Franklin and Claudette's creative array of Halloween decorations notably impressive. They had installed jack-o'-lantern stake lights along the walkway and decorated the yard to resemble a haunted cemetery. It was full of grave markers, cobwebs, and several ghosts, and there was a skeleton climbing out of a casket.

"They must like to decorate. The yard is incredible," I said, becoming even more amazed when I spotted two skeletons playing cards at a bistro set on the porch.

"Wait until we go inside." Shane opened the front door, and we walked into the foyer.

I jumped, eliciting a small shriek as a six-foot-tall Frankenstein got up from a chair. He had a white face full of stitches and black circles around his eyes. He'd even attached fake bolts to the side of his neck.

"Franklin and Claudette have a Frankenstein doorman?" Stunned, I shook my head. "Their decorations are crazy. Do they do this every year?"

"They do. Franklin has a blast with all the decorating."

"Could I have your names, please?" Frankenstein said, his voice a deep monotone.

Shane turned toward the door attendant. "Shane Moore and Liz Whalen."

Frankenstein picked up a clipboard from the table next to his chair and scanned the attached list, making a checkmark on the paper. "Thank you. You may join the party." He placed the clipboard on the table and sat down, his body stiff, eyes staring into space.

Shane and I turned as a five-foot-tall Raggedy Ann approached us.

"Welcome to Castle Davenport. May I take your cloak?"

Shane laughed at my wide-eyed stare. He slipped my cape from my shoulders, handing it to the costumed woman.

"Thank you," Raggedy Ann said before scurrying down the hallway.

Shane escorted me across the foyer toward the living room, the entryway now partially obscured by a wall of fake cobwebs and plastic spiders. Skirting through the opening, we found ourselves in the company of a menagerie of costumed guests.

"Liz. Shane. You're here. You two look fantastic." A tuxedoed Count Dracula greeted us. He wore a red-lined cape with an upright collar, full makeup, and pointed teeth.

"Franklin, you don't look bad yourself." Shane laughed as he reached out and patted Franklin's shoulder.

"Oh, my. I wasn't sure it was you. You look great." I eyed Franklin's costume. "If you're Count Dracula, what's Claudette's costume? She wouldn't tell me what she planned to be when we went shopping."

"You'll have to wait and see." Franklin gave me a fang-laden smile and pointed his black walking stick toward the open sliding door to the backyard. "We have several tents set up outside with tables and a buffet.

There's a staffed bar in the pavilion and a DJ on the patio. Get yourselves something to eat and drink and enjoy the party."

"Thanks. We'll do that." Shane looked amused as he led me toward the sliding door.

We strolled across the patio as the DJ started to play a song, continuing down a concrete walkway lined with more jack-o'-lantern stake lights toward the pavilion. Cobwebs and spiders decorated the bar, with pumpkin string lights stretched across the ceiling. Shane ordered us each a glass of chardonnay, and then we stood off to the side listening to the music.

I was scanning the makeshift dance floor when a couple dressed in mismatched angel and devil costumes caught my attention. The woman's angel costume was boldly revealing, looking like something a Victoria's Secret model would wear on the runway during a fashion show. I couldn't help snicker, thinking how cold she must be in the chilly evening air. I was about to look away when the woman turned, giving me a clear view of her face. I caught my breath. God, no. Why was Anna here? Irritated, I clenched my fists. I couldn't seem to get rid of her.

"What's going on? Liz, you look upset."

"I can't believe it. Anna's here. She's on the dance floor in a skimpy angel costume. Why can't she go away? You know she's after you, don't you?"

"What are you talking about?"

"She told me at Franklin's party that it wouldn't be long before you dumped me and returned to her."

"That's insane. First, you are the woman I love and

plan to marry. Second, nothing on earth could drag me back to her. Please don't let her get to you. There is absolutely nothing for you to worry about." Shane reached for me and pulled me toward him. "Let's just ignore her and have fun tonight."

"You're right. I'm acting silly and letting Anna get to me. We're here to have an enjoyable evening, and that's what we're going to do." I leaned against him as he held me.

A couple dressed as a gangster and a flapper walked up behind Shane. The woman touched his shoulder to get his attention.

Shane let go of me and spun around. He grinned at the couple. "Loren. Randy. You two look great." He reached out and shook both their hands. "Liz, do you remember my boss, Loren, and her husband, Randy? You met them at Franklin's birthday party."

"I do. It's nice to see you again." I shook their hands. "Your costumes look wonderful and very authentic."

"Thanks. I thought the bright red fringe dress might be too much, but I'm getting some nice compliments." Loren adjusted her feathered headband and string of pearls. She smiled as she surveyed our costumes. "I love yours. You two look fantastic."

Someone called Shane's name from one of the tents on the patio. We both turned, spotting several people motioning for Shane to join them.

"It looks like my presence is requested." Shane slipped his arm around my waist. "You'll have to excuse us."

"No problem. We'll catch up with you later," Loren said.

Shane escorted me to the tent. His name called out a second time when we stepped underneath the canopy. He waved at a boisterous group near the buffet tables.

"Let's sit with Tricia, her husband, Bill, and Conrad and Lily." Shane pointed to a table in the corner in the opposite direction.

After several hugs, handshakes, and compliments on our costumes, Shane pulled out a chair for me, and we joined the group.

"Everyone looks marvelous." I giggled as I looked around the table. "Conrad, you and Lily make impressive pirates." I pointed to his shoulder. "By the way, I love your stuffed parrot."

"I told you the bird was cute." Lily laughed as she nudged Conrad with her elbow.

I shook my head, an enormous grin on my face as I looked at Tricia and Bill. "Tricia, your Mad Hatter and Queen of Hearts costumes take the cake. I don't think I've seen anything better, especially Bill's costume."

"Thanks. It took a bit of work to talk Bill into it," Tricia said.

"A bit of work? Hell. She threatened me." Bill laughed as Tricia slapped his arm.

I studied their costumes, amazed at what they'd put together. Tricia's Mad Hatter costume consisted of a purple velvet suit and top hat. She'd added a white shirt with lacy cuffs, an oversized purple-and-black plaid bow tie, and an orange wig. Bill's Queen of Hearts costume was hilarious, and I was trying my best to keep from busting out in a fit of laughter as he sat in the seat next to me. He wore a long red-and-white dress with a hooped skirt and tall standing collar. Red hearts adorned the white part of the dress, and white hearts adorned the red. The dress was low-cut, exposing Bill's chest, and the costume included elbow-length red gloves, a white wig with a crown, and a heart-topped scepter. The hooped skirt beneath the dress appeared problematic since it barely fit under the table.

"Are you hungry? I'm going to get a plate from the buffet." Shane slid his chair backward, placing his hand on my thigh.

"I am a little. I'll go with you." I followed Shane to the buffet tables. There was a staffed taco bar at one table. A variety of finger foods, salads, fresh fruit, and desserts were at the other. "I'm impressed. Franklin and Claudette went all out on this party."

"They always do."

Shane and I filled our plates and returned to our table, the six of us chatting while we ate. Jokes flew back and forth, and Conrad suggested we all go to dinner the following weekend.

"Would you like to dance?" Shane pushed his chair back and stood.

"Yes, I'd love to." I took his hand and followed him to the dance floor, laying my head on his shoulder as we moved to the music. The song stopped, and I stepped away from Shane, catching sight of Claudette as she walked toward the patio.

She had dressed as a vampire in a Victorian bustle dress. The long black skirt was tiered, and the button-down top was red with an overlay of black lace. A black lace cravat was at her neck, adorned with a gold brooch, and she had accessorized her costume with a red Victorian top hat and gloves. For an added touch, she had a set of fangs and, with the help of makeup, a mouth dripping with blood.

Claudette stopped in the center of the patio and addressed her guests. "All right. Listen up. I have the results of the costume contest." A silence fell over the costumed audience. "First, I want to say all the costumes are fabulous. You've outdone yourselves. But we did have a few that stood out for one reason or another. So, I'm going to start with our third-place winner, who happens to be visiting us tonight from Egypt. Will Mark Anthony and Cleopatra please come up here? I have a gift card for you."

Everybody clapped as one of Claudette's coworkers and her husband came to the patio. After receiving hugs and an envelope from Claudette, they returned to their chairs.

"Okay. Everyone quiet. For second place, we go from classic movie scripts and history to a well-known and loved television show. Before I tell you who it is, I just want to say, girl, I want your dress. Will the mysterious Morticia and Gomez Addams please join me up here? I have a gift card for you too."

The patio erupted with laughter and applause. Claudette circled the woman as she fawned over her low-cut, body-hugging long black dress. The couple returned to their table after receiving their prize and a hug.

"Quiet. Everyone hush. This year's first-place winner is unique. We've gone from movies to television, with this couple giving us a fun version of a favorite children's tale. This year's prize winner is the couple we all know and love to hate, the Mad Hatter and Queen of Hearts."

Tricia and Bill got up from their chairs, the backyard exploding with clapping, whistling, and catcalling. They joined Claudette on the patio. After hugs from Claudette and receipt of their gift card, Bill turned toward the tents and took a bow, eliciting another round of applause.

"The Queen isn't supposed to have chest hair," a man yelled out from the pavilion, followed by raucous laughter.

Conrad stood at the back of the tent and yelled to Bill. "Hey, Bill. You should have dyed the hair on your chest white to match your wig."

"It's already white, you blind fool," Bill said, yelling at Conrad as Tricia dragged him away.

Finished with her presentations, Claudette joined Shane and me at the edge of the patio. "There you are. I was looking for the two of you earlier. You look fabulous, Liz. I knew that dress was perfect on you."

"Thanks. I like yours. It's stunning."

"I have to agree with you both," Shane said. He leaned over and kissed my cheek. "I see Franklin at the bar. I'm going to join him. Do either of you want anything?"

"No, I'm good," Claudette said, shaking her head.

"I'll join you in a few minutes. I want to talk to Claudette first."

"All right. I'll see you at the bar." Shane walked down the concrete path to the pavilion.

"Anna's here," I said, waiting for Claudette's reaction. The last time we had spoken, she'd told me Bryce had split up with his girlfriend and was coming to the Halloween party by himself.

"I know. I saw Anna with Bryce earlier in that shameless angel costume of hers. She has half our guests staring at her. I don't know why Bryce keeps bringing her around. It's like those two are up to something. Has she said anything else to you?"

"Nothing since Franklin's party, when she informed me she thought Shane would break it off with me and come back to her."

"Well, we all know that'll never happen. Where is Anna anyway?" Claudette scanned the patio and then the pavilion. "Oh, no."

"What?" I followed her gaze across the yard.

Shane was standing on the left side of the pavilion, next to the stone fireplace. He and Franklin faced each other with Shane's back toward us. A potted shrub partially hid them from the guests at the bar, and Anna was beelining it toward Shane.

"If your eyes were daggers, that woman would be dead."

I frowned, my eyes glued on Anna as she walked up behind Shane. "I guess it's obvious I'm not a fan."

"It is, and I don't blame you. I was hoping Bryce wouldn't come tonight since Franklin doesn't care for him. It would have been easier if I could have excluded him, but it wouldn't look right at the office if I did, especially since he and Franklin work together."

"Oh my God. Anna is fondling the back of Shane's thigh. The bitch is touching him." Mortified, I stared at her. Then I came to my senses and stormed across the lawn toward the two of them. Livid, I wished my eyes actually were daggers as I witnessed Anna's hands knead Shane's rear and move upward as she pressed against him.

Franklin had to be unaware of Anna's actions. I was positive he'd say something if he knew. His face suddenly contorted, taking on a horrified look as Shane reached backward, putting his arms around Anna and squeezing her rear.

"No," I croaked, my feet freezing in place several yards away. How could Shane not know I wasn't the one behind him? With Anna's skimpy costume and exposed body, it had to be obvious, especially with the way his fingers massaged her ass. My stomach lurched as Anna's hand moved back to Shane's thigh.

Standing there wide-eyed, Franklin informed Shane that it was Anna behind him.

Shane jumped away from her as if electrocuted, his hands in the air in front of him, a look of horror on his face. "How dare you touch me," he yelled. "Only my wife touches me like that." Shane's eyes were bulging as he glared at Anna, his voice full of fury.

Several people standing at the bar, including Loren, heard him and turned around to see what was happening.

"You didn't mind me touching you when we dated, and besides, last time I checked, you weren't married." Anna folded her arms across her chest, a smirk on her face.

Shane took a step forward, and Franklin placed a hand on his shoulder. "I may not be married yet, but I consider Liz my wife." Shane glanced past Anna, wincing when he saw me standing in the grass.

"I don't know what you're all worked up about," Bryce said, joining his sister by the fireplace. "Liz isn't the goody two-shoes and perfect woman you think she is. She's using you. Did she tell you she associates with bikers, and the district attorney's office has her listed in a criminal complaint with some of her friends? It had something to do with breaking into a woman's house, assaulting her, and trying to steal a motorcycle. Shane, wake up. You screwed up when you broke it off with my sister and let your little biker babe draw you into her web."

Shane lunged at Bryce, and Franklin grabbed him to hold him back. They wrestled as Shane tried to break away, and then Randy jumped in to help Franklin restrain him.

"Oh, honey. Are you all right?" Claudette came up behind me and placed a hand on my shoulder. "You're shaking like a leaf."

I couldn't do anything but stand there. It was as if someone had stabbed me in the chest. I took small gulps of air as I tried to breathe.

"She's using you, Shane. I'm telling you. Liz is a disreputable woman and hangs out with lowlifes," Bryce said, sneering at me from the pavilion.

Shane lunged a second time, and Franklin and Randy tightened their hold on him. "You son of a bitch. Yes, the criminal complaint lists Liz, but she was the victim. The so-called 'friends' you mention broke into Liz's house, and she was the one assaulted. How dare you twist it around. Liz is a far better woman than your sister could ever hope to be. Say another word about her, and I'll shut your mouth."

"Shane, calm down. Bryce is talking out his ass like usual. He needs to leave." Franklin glared at Bryce as he held Shane back. "Get your sister and leave my house. You are no longer welcome here."

"Hang on a minute." Loren walked up to Bryce, cocking her head as she studied him. "It sounds like you took it upon yourself to investigate a coworker's fiancée with no cause or authority. I'd venture to guess you used agency resources to do it too. We'll be investigating the matter come Monday morning."

"Whatever. I didn't do anything wrong. Go on. Try to prove it." Bryce grabbed Anna's arm. "Let's get out of here. The party's a bust anyway."

Bryce and Anna took off toward the house, and Franklin and Randy let go of Shane. Claudette stepped away from me to join Franklin.

Shane looked devastated as he slowly walked toward me. "I'm so sorry, mo ghra. I thought it was you that had come up behind me. I swear. I didn't know it was Anna. Can you please forgive me?" He reached for me, anguish filling his eyes when he saw me flinch.

"Please take me home," I whispered, my heart and mind defiled by what I had seen.

"Yes, we'll go right now." Shane turned to Franklin. "I'm sorry. We need to go."

"We understand. Claudette and I will walk you out."

"No, it's okay. We'll be fine. I'll catch you Monday morning." Shane walked me back to the house and collected my cape from Raggedy Ann. He drove us home in painful silence.

After pulling into the garage, I stepped from the car without uttering a word and hurried upstairs to our bedroom. My mind was numb, and I couldn't seem to formulate a sentence. All I wanted to do was go to bed and wish the night away. The disgusting scene of Shane and Anna fondling each other was a sight I desperately wanted to unsee. I went into my walk-in closet and removed my costume, leaving my garments in a heap on the floor. Naked, I sank onto the bench in the middle of the room and placed my head in my hands. I felt nauseous and violated. It was like having our relationship, which I held sacred, disrespected, and stomped on. More so because of the fact that it was Anna. Besides having an intimate history with Shane, she'd already thrown it in my face that she expected him to run back to her. Sensing Shane standing in front of me, I lifted my head, instantly struck by the pain and anguish on his face.

"I love you, mo ghra, more than anything in this world. I would never intentionally hurt you. Please tell me you understand that."

"I do," I said quietly, my voice raw with emotion.

"I know I can't take back what happened, so please tell me how to make it better. What can I do?"

"I don't know." I expelled a deep breath, trying to make sense of my fragmented thoughts. After a long pause, I looked into Shane's eyes. "As angry and devastated as I feel right now, I know it would be wrong to blame you since Anna is the one at fault. Although I can't get the thought out of my head that you should have known it wasn't me." I closed my eyes, wishing my mind were a chalkboard, and I could erase what I had seen. I sighed and looked back at Shane. "Anna's malicious efforts split us up once already. Regardless of how I feel, I refuse to let her do it a second time." I was trying so hard to think rationally. The last time Anna had played her vicious game, using Shane as a pawn and spreading her disinformation, I'd let my emotions control me and lost Shane because of it. I wasn't going to let that happen again. I loved and trusted him and knew he'd never intentionally hurt me. As horribly painful as this was, we'd get through it. Anna was not going to win.

Shane stepped forward and tipped my chin up. "Thank you for believing me. I know what happened had to be horrible to witness. I understand that, and I'm so very sorry. One thing's for certain. I've learned a lesson tonight. Anna is far more calculating and devious than I thought she could be and has few limits to her unscrupulous behavior. I need to be wary of her for both our sakes."

"We both do."

Shane leaned down and kissed me, his arms around me as he pulled me to my feet.

Relaxing against his body, I parted my lips as his kiss continued. I couldn't help it. I needed his comforting touch and for him to hold me.

Shane scooped me in his arms and carried me to our bed. He laid me down and then stepped back, his eyes on me as he undressed. Lying beside me, he propped his head on his arm and gazed down at me, caressing my cheek. "The pain I saw on your face completely tore my insides apart. I never want to see anything like that again." He kissed me, and then his mouth was at my ear. "I love you so much. I don't know what I'd do if I lost you."

I put my arms around his neck and kissed him as he slid on top of me. I spread my legs, welcoming him as we joined together, my body needing his touch, my heart needing his comfort.

Shane left kisses on my face and chest, taking his time as he made love to me. He was sweet and tender, whispering loving words in my ear and telling me how much he needed me.

Spent, we stayed in each other's arms, neither of us speaking. I didn't want to disrupt our moment of peace and contentment. There would be plenty of time tomorrow to talk more about what had happened.

CHAPTER 17

THE WEDDING DAY

I GAZED LOVINGLY into Shane's eyes as we stood facing each other. Nervous, excited, happy, I was so many different things.

"Do you have the ring?" The officiant's voice carried through the air.

Shane took the ring when Dylan handed it to him. "I have the ring."

"You may recite the vow you've written for Liz and place the ring on her finger."

Shane held my hand in his palm, his Celtic cross tattoo peeking out from under his shirtsleeve. "Liz. Today and all our days to come, I give myself to you. You are the fire in my veins and the passion in my heart, changing my life for the better the day you tripped into me and stepped on my toes. From this day forward, I promise to be your bridge over raging rivers, your light in the darkness, and your pillar of support and encouragement. With this ring, I seal my commitment to you." Shane slipped the ring on my finger, his face glowing, a tinge of watery redness forming in his eyes.

"Liz. Do you have the ring?" The officiant's voice was soft and comforting as it drifted to my ears.

I took the ring from Mel and passed her my bouquet, turning back to face Shane. "Yes, I have it."

"Then please recite the vow you've written for Shane and place the ring on his finger."

I held Shane's hand in my palm. "Shane. Today, tomorrow, and always, I give myself to you. You are my lover, husband, and friend, and I bind my life to yours. I promise to be the ears that listen to you, the shoulders you can lay your head upon, the arms to hold and support you, and the heart to always love you. With this ring, I pledge my everlasting love and commitment to you." I slipped the ring on Shane's finger, a tear threatening to spill as we held each other's hands.

"Before I declare you married, I need to ask you each a question. Liz, I need to know. Are you happy?"

I turned toward the voice, facing Alex as he stood in front of me. Filled with joy, I smiled into his blue eyes. "Yes, very much so. I love Shane, and he is everything to me."

Alex's face softened, taking on a look of relief. He turned to Shane. "Do you promise to take care of Liz for me? To love her, keep her safe from harm, and never abandon her?"

"Yes, I promise." Shane squeezed my hand, a look of love in his eyes.

"Then I'm honored to declare you married. Shane, you may kiss your bride."

We kissed, and a profound feeling of contentment enfolded me.

Alex spoke when we parted. "I'd like to offer an Irish blessing." He smiled, an aura surrounding him.

"May you always walk in sunshine.

May you never want for more.

May Irish angels rest their wings.

Right beside your door."

Alex slowly backed away, a bright light shining behind him.

Suddenly confused, I sensed he was telling me goodbye. "Wait. You can't go." Tears streamed down my cheeks. "Please, Alex. Don't leave me."

"Liz, I may be gone, but I'll always be with you. I give you and Shane my blessing. Love him as you loved me." Alex backed away, disappearing into the light.

I cried as Shane held me underneath the tent; the rose garden stretched out before us. But I wasn't sad. I was strangely happy.

"Wake up. You're having a nightmare. Mo ghra, wake up." Shane gathered me in his arms.

"The dream. I had it again." I choked back a sob, tears wetting Shane's chest. "But I saw it all this time."

"It's okay, mo ghra. Shh…it's over. Everything is fine."

"No, you don't understand. I saw the whole thing. It was Alex. He's the officiant in my dream. It was him all along. He needed to know that I was happy and that you'd always love me and take care of me in his place. Alex gave us his blessing, and he told me to love you the way I loved him. He said he'd always be with me even though he's gone." I curled up against Shane's chest. It was like Alex had lifted a burden from me, filling me with an overwhelming sense of relief. At that moment, everything became clear, and I wasn't scared anymore.

My deep-seated fear that the people I loved would always leave me felt gone. Alex was right. Although he, my mother, father, and grandparents had died, they were still with me. I had loving memories of them all.

Shane pushed a strand of hair from my cheek and kissed my forehead. "Alex told you what you needed to hear and gave you closure."

"He did, and the sense of relief I'm feeling is almost palpable. I can't describe it any other way."

"I can't help but feel the significance of what you saw, heard, and felt went beyond that. As strange as this is going to sound, I think Alex was affected too. Your dream was like a mechanism for him to communicate with you. I believe there are forces in life we cannot explain, and I'd venture to say the bond you shared with Alex was one of them. He must have loved you so completely, you were a piece of both his heart and soul. He needed to know you were happy and taken care of before he could properly move on. Now that you've seen the missing pieces of the dream, it sounds like that time has come."

"In my heart, I know you're right. Alex gave me his acceptance and approval to close one chapter of my life and open the next." I kissed Shane's chest and snuggled into the crook of his neck, his body warm and comforting. "I can't believe how my life has changed since I met you. A year and a half ago, I was sure I'd never fall in love again. I didn't think a person could experience that all-consuming emotion twice in a lifetime, but you proved me wrong. And I have to say, all the torment we went through, although horrible, taught me to keep my emotions in check when dealing with my problems. The outcomes are certainly better that way."

"We've both come a long way, mo ghra. Until you came along, I'd never really been in love or completely trusted my partner. Because of past experiences, I'd learned to hold back and keep information like my finances secret. You taught me how to share and that with the right person; it didn't and shouldn't need to be this way. I love you." Shane kissed me and then peeked at the clock on the nightstand. "We can talk about this more later. It's three o'clock in the morning, and we need to get a few more hours of sleep before everyone in the house wakes up. It's going to be a long day and longer night with the hustle and bustle and craziness of the wedding this afternoon."

"I don't know if I can sleep, but I'll try." I kissed Shane's chest as he pulled the bedcovers over my shoulder. Everything was going to be all right.

"TELL ME WHAT you think." Ginger handed me a mirror to look at my hair and makeup.

"Oh, my. Are you sure that's me? I have to say, it looks stunning." I turned my head from side to side to check her handiwork.

"Of course it's you. The makeup only enhances what you already have, and sweeping your hair back in a curly chignon was a perfect choice. The silver comb with the pearls and crystals gave it an elegant touch. You, my dear, are lovely. Your groom is going to melt when he sees you."

Ginger was a beauty professional, and I'd hired her and her assistant, Heather, for the wedding. Since there were six of us, we'd already been at it for five hours, with me being the last one done. Mel and Neasa, as the maid of honor and surrogate mother of the groom, finished before me. My three bridesmaids, Caitlin, Yvonne, and Britney, had gone first. The group of us cloistered in my guest suite at the castle, garment bags, shoes, makeup, and accessories spread around the room. Shane and all the guys were in Dylan's room. Dylan was Shane's best man.

"Liz, do you want another mimosa?" Mel held up a filled glass.

"I do. Those are good." I caught the clicking sound of my photographer's camera as she snapped several photos of Mel handing me the glass and the two of us toasting each other. "Well, are you going to tell everyone, or can I?" I raised an eyebrow at Mel.

"Shush. We agreed not to say anything. It's your special day, and I don't want to take anything away from it. So be quiet."

"Nonsense. Your news is too exciting to keep to yourself, and it's not going to bother me in the least if you share it."

"Girls. What's up? What doesn't Mel want us to know?" Britney came over to join us. "I overheard part of it, so now you have to tell us."

Mel beamed as he stuck out her hand. "Conor proposed to me last night."

"Oh my God. Ladies, Mel is engaged. The big guy proposed to her." Britney hugged Mel while everyone came rushing over to congratulate her.

Mel appeared to glow with the attention.

"All right, ladies." Neasa clapped her hands to get everyone's attention. "Off with the robes. We need to get all of you dressed. We're already running a little bit behind." She unzipped the garment bag lying across my bed and took out my dress. "Liz, Mel and I will help you with yours."

After removing my robe, I started to step into my dress while Neasa held it for me and then stopped. "My garter. I forgot to put it on. It'll be easier to do it now than after I've put on the dress. Yvonne, can you grab it out of the bag on the bed?"

"Sure." Yvonne dug through the bag, pulling out the garter. "Oh, honey. This garter is adorable. It's got little horseshoes and shamrocks sewn into it."

"I was trying to follow Irish tradition. The bride is supposed to have a horseshoe on her for good luck." I took the baby-blue garter from Yvonne and slipped it on my leg, making sure to have the ends of the horseshoes facing upward. I stepped into the dress, and Mel secured the hooks and eyes and laced up the back.

"You are breathtaking. I can't wait to see Shane's reaction." Caitlin turned to my photographer, Sandra. "You'll have to take lots of photos of Shane when Liz walks down the aisle and joins him."

"Oh, I'll have plenty of photos. Right now, I want some of Liz by herself, and then I'll take more group shots when you're all lined up for the processional."

Sandra took photos of me while the ladies finished getting ready. Their dresses were sleeveless and empire-waisted with a V-neck and crossed bodice. Since Mel was short and the others tall, I had chosen them to be knee-length. The beautiful plum color went well with their silver shoes and hair adornments in silver and pearl.

There was a knock on my door. Yvonne opened it, letting Danny into the room. In the absence of a father, I had asked him to give me away at the wedding. From the time they were boys, he and Alex had been best friends, and I'd met him in my teens while hanging out at Nicole and Alex's house. I loved and trusted Danny, and it seemed fitting that he fulfilled that particular role of handing me off to Shane.

"You are absolutely stunning." Danny kissed me on the cheek. He had dressed the same as the groomsmen in a light gray tuxedo, white dress shirt, and a plum necktie to match the ladies' dresses. He reached out and took my hands in his. "I'm honored you asked me to give you away. I've known you for so many years; we're like family. Alex would like Shane, and I know he'd approve of your marriage."

"I know he would too." I smiled at Danny, remembering what Alex had said to me in the dream.

The hotel's wedding specialist, Rowena, hurried into the room and came over to Neasa and me. "The best man and groomsmen are waiting downstairs by the lobby entrance, and Shane is on the terrace with the officiant. We need the ladies to wrap it up, so we can start the wedding." Rowena smiled as she took a step back and studied me. "You are exquisite." She turned toward the others. "Ladies, I need your attention. After Neasa takes her seat, the officiant and Shane will enter the garden from the south staircase off the terrace and go to the altar. Then we'll start the processional. You'll all enter from the north staircase by the hotel lobby one couple at a time. The maid of honor and best man will precede Liz. Now, is everyone ready?"

Neasa looked around the room. "I believe they are."

"Well, let's go, then. We don't want our beautiful bride to keep her dashing groom waiting. And don't forget your bouquets." Rowena hustled everyone out of the room and led us downstairs. "Ladies, I want you to wait with the gentlemen outside by the lobby entrance. My assistant Deirdre will line you up in preparation for the processional. I'll be right there as soon as I get Liz situated." She shooed the ladies toward the front entrance and then opened the door to a small office near the elevator. "Liz, I want you and Danny to stay here so no one sees you yet. You can peek out the window, but don't make it obvious you're in here. I'll come back for you after I get the processional going." She hurried out, shutting the door behind her.

Danny and I peeked out the window. We were too far away to see details but close enough to see what was happening. The garden was full of beautiful red roses, and the wedding tent was beside it. Even though I was aware of the guest count, I was momentarily surprised to see so many people.

"Neasa is walking down the aisle to take her seat. Danny, look. Shane and the officiant are heading down the staircase toward the garden." I brought my hand to my face, struck by how handsome Shane looked when he turned toward us to converse with the officiant. His tuxedo was the same as the groomsmen's but in a darker shade of gray.

"Rowena should be coming for us any minute. How are you doing?" Danny looked down at me, his eyes searching my face.

"I'm a nervous wreck. I can feel my knees shaking under my dress. God, Danny. Wouldn't that be horrible if I stumbled while you walked me down the aisle and laid on the ground with my legs in the air, flashing everyone my lingerie and stockings?"

"I wouldn't say horrible. But it sure would be a wedding to remember and an image I'd never forget. We'd have to tell everyone I tripped you, and then Yvonne would kick my ass."

"I don't know which would be worse. Yvonne mad or me being completely embarrassed." I started laughing, and Danny joined me. The humor seemed to help ease my nervousness.

"The processional is starting. It's time for your grand entrance." Rowena had burst into the room, startling the two of us. She held the door open. "Your groom is going to melt when he sees you. Let's not keep him waiting."

We went outside and waited near the staircase that led down to the garden. Deirdre had just sent Yvonne and Niall down the stairs, and Mel and Dylan were next. Caitlin and Patrick would have gone first, followed by Britney and Conor. I listened to the sounds of the wedding march as the processional continued.

"You look gorgeous, Liz. I can't wait to see Shane's face." Dylan ran over to me and gave me a quick kiss on the cheek. Then he hurried back to Mel so Deirdre could send them off.

Rowena waved Danny and me over to the railing that overlooked the garden. As soon as Mel and Dylan reached the altar, the music stopped, and the bagpiper standing a short distance from the groomsmen began to play his bagpipe.

"Are you ready?" Danny looked at me and held out his arm. "No tripping either. I still can't get that mental picture out of my head."

I couldn't help grinning at Danny as I took his arm. "I'll try to stay on my feet."

We started our walk down the stairs, and the guests stood. In my nervousness, it seemed like our processional down the gravel path to the wedding tent and subsequent walk up the aisle took forever. When we neared the altar, I looked at Shane. He seemed overcome with emotion, his hand on his face as he wiped his eyes. I smiled at him when our eyes locked, and he came over to take me from Danny. He and Danny shook hands. Then Danny kissed my cheek and took my hand, placing it on Shane's arm. Shane led me to the altar.

"You took my breath away when I saw you, mo ghra. You are my heart and my soul." Shane leaned over and kissed me.

"Hold on, no jumping the gun, young man. You're supposed to kiss your bride after I declare you wed, not before." The short gray-haired officiant chuckled, his words and humorous tone audible to the guests since his microphone was on.

The guests and wedding party erupted in laughter.

"Sorry." Shane grinned at the officiant.

I hung my head, trying desperately not to laugh.

Turning my attention back to Shane, I kept my eyes on him as the ceremony continued. It was a blur as the officiant gave his opening remarks and welcomed the guests. He talked about the significance of marriage and then a bit about Shane and me. I only half-listened. All I could think about was how happy I was and how much I looked forward to spending our lives together and raising a family.

"Now, Shane and Liz will recite their vows and exchange rings." The officiant looked at Shane. "Do you have the ring?"

Shane took it from Dylan. "I have it." He held my hand in his palm and began to recite his vows. "Liz. Today and all our days to come, I give myself to you. You are the fire in my veins and the passion in my heart, changing my life for the better the day you tripped into me...."

I stared at Shane in disbelief. His words were the same as he had recited in my dream. But how could that be? We'd never discussed that part. Stunned, I had to wonder. Did the mirroring of Shane's vows give solid validation to it all being real? Was our life together somehow predestined from beginning to end? Trying to put aside my thoughts, I looked down at my hand as Shane slipped the ring on my finger. Our eyes locked as he lifted my hand to his lips and kissed it, a feeling of warmth and love radiating between us.

"Liz, do you have the ring?" The officiant turned his attention to me next.

I took the ring from Mel and handed her my bouquet. "I have it."

"You may recite your vows to Shane and put the ring on his finger."

I looked lovingly at Shane as I held his hand in my palm. I began to recite my vows. Having practiced so many times, I knew them by heart. Finished, I nervously slid the ring on Shane's finger, peering up at him when done. A rush of emotion washed over me when I saw the tears in his eyes.

"Shane. Liz. It is with immense pleasure that I now pronounce you married." The officiant looked directly at Shane. "Now, young man, you may kiss your bride."

Shane leaned forward and kissed me, his arms sliding around my waist as he held me.

There was a burst of clapping and cheers from the guests.

"We did it. I hope you're as ecstatic as I am, Mrs. Moore." Shane leaned his forehead against mine.

"Completely. I've never been so happy."

"Shane. Liz. Check out the sky." Dylan took several steps backward, so he was out from underneath the tent. "Man. That looks weird, but it's pretty cool."

Comments and shrieks of excitement erupted from some of the guests.

Shane and I stepped toward Dylan and looked upward. I caught my breath. I'd heard of situations where the clouds formed into strange-looking phenomena, but I'd never seen anything as profound as this. I gazed in awe at the sight. The clouds had developed into a figure of a man with outstretched wings, the sunlight hitting it just right, so it had a beautiful golden glow.

Shane slipped his arm around my shoulder and tenderly pulled me against him. "Alex is saying goodbye, mo ghra."

I had a lump in my throat as I nodded at Shane, the vision making me believe the same thing. Alex was gone, and now it was time to start a new chapter in my life. I wiped tears of happiness and contentment from my cheeks as the bagpiper began to play.

"Are you ready to make our exit?" Shane said, a blissful aura surrounding him as we turned toward our guests. "We have a night of celebrating to do." He led us down the aisle, the next of our many journeys together hovering on the horizon.